The Game
of
Pirate

Ed Wicke

GW00502962

Some other books by Ed Wicke:

Wicked Tales
Wicked Tales Two: Even Wickeder Tales
Wicked Tales Three: The Witch's Library
Wicked Tales Four
Billy Jones, King of the Goblins
Akayzia Adams and the Masterdragon's Secret
Akayzia Adams and the Mirrors Of Darkness
Mattie and the Highwaymen
Bullies
Nicklus
The Muselings
Screeps

For my good and loyal friends, who have kindly put up with me for so many years!

Published by BlacknBlue Press UK
13 Dellands, Overton, Hampshire, England
 blacknbluepress@hotmail.com

This book copyright © Ed Wicke, March 2012
 edddwicke@hotmail.com

Cover illustrations copyright © Tom Warne, March 2012
Internal illustrations copyright © Rob Wicke, March 2012

All rights reserved; no part of this publication may be reproduced or transmitted by any means without the prior permission of the publisher and author. The author's rights have been asserted.

ISBN 978-0-9840718-6-9

At 196 for 220, seek the small harbour on the island of breasted stone.

Follow the eyes a full turn at seven for the first treesure sunken low and springing high.

Follow the Mermaid until you glimpse the Rock. Anchor before you founder and follow the mermaids' silver summons to worship.

Hand high, spy where the finger points. Be black widowed there widdershins and fight the black gulls for their booty.

Follow the plough. What fate and fortune are crafted of, there seek your fourth, sweet fortune beyond the fourth fate.

As the Whale spouts five, look upon the level and take up the crown.

The dog hangs above and the old temple below, a hundred distant.

Take the berg two turns at twenty and climb the steeper path. Seek the maiden beneath the midden, two fathoms deep.

Hail the sun for seven days at full six, then pass on foot beyond the high pass. The lost one bides in the highest window of the highest tower.

1 The King's Prison

The equipment shall be the Spinning Compass, the Wind Dice, the twelve-sided Runes of Destiny and the cards of Fate and Fortune.

It's a gloomy start to a strange adventure. A slender, brown-haired youth of fifteen – myself - follows a fat prison warder through damp, evil-smelling stone corridors lit by oily torches. Outside, the sun hesitates at the horizon; but no daylight ever shines here, in the rocky depths of the King's Dungeons in the city of Magus...

I knew these cold flagstones well. I'd trodden them twice a week for the past year, carrying a basket of food and wine from my aunt, most of which the warder took as a bribe.

We reached a gateway. Keys clanked, hinges groaned, and we began to climb a narrow, spiralling staircase. This was the only entrance to the strongest cell, which was set at the top of a high tower. To escape, a prisoner would need to flee down these stairs, break through the iron gate at the bottom and then creep along dark passageways until he reached another set of gates, beyond which waited half a dozen bad-tempered guards armed with clubs and pistols.

The warder stopped at a dark oaken doorway and put

5

down the lantern he was carrying. He sifted through a handful of heavy keys, puffing noisily. He was a coarse, sullen man with tiny eyes and a dripping nose, which he wiped on his sleeve before pushing open the creaking door and waving me inside.

'Get in, you.'

This was the second of three phrases I heard each time. The first was always 'You again?' and the last would be 'Out you go, boy.'

I hesitated a moment, and the warder hit me on the back of the head with the keys. I stumbled forward into the greyness of a stony cell lit only by the twilight seeping in from high, narrow slits in the thick walls.

The warder entered cautiously, gripping his heavy club - not that he had much to fear, for he weighed more than the two of us together. I was a willowy boy and the prisoner was a man weakened by a year of imprisonment, and – if more advantage was needed - with his legs loosely chained.

The prisoner was seated at a small table in the centre of the room. His long black hair had been pulled back and fastened in a neat pony tail, and he was wearing his best uniform of deep blue silk with gold brocade on the shoulders. He rose as I entered and gestured to the seat opposite him.

'Good evening, Jack,' he said. 'Good to see you again.'

'Good evening, Captain Jones. Aunt Emma wishes to be remembered to you, and sends you this basket.' The same stiff formula at the start of each meeting, with the same polite bows. Behind us, the warder locked the door and settled his bulk onto a broad bench next to it. The bench creaked and the warder began a tuneless mumbling to himself.

'Pray be seated, lad. Sip of wine?'

'Yes, sir. I mean – aye, Captain.'

The small table was set as usual: a star-shaped game board in the middle, its sixteen points matching the points of the compass. To one side, a wooden box held several odd objects and on the opposite side there were two piles of wooden cards – one dark, one light.

'Good lad. We'll have a short game tonight, if you don't mind. We need to finish it, see. Did your aunt tell you?'

'No, Captain.'

'My appeal to the King wasn't successful, Jack. I swing tomorrow, an hour after dawn.'

I couldn't meet the man's eye at first. Then I was ashamed of myself and looked across at the seaman who sat so straight in his chair. The Captain reached to his left and lit a couple of candles against the nightfall. Their light picked out the white strands in his hair and showed the wrinkles at the corner of his eyes. Prison had aged him quickly.

'I'm sorry, sir.'

'Ah, Jack: I always thought it would be so. How many King's Pirates have died in their beds? I'm prepared for it. We won't let it spoil our game, right?'

'Aye aye, sir.'

'I don't want you to feel sorry for me, lad, and let me win out of pity!' He laughed freely and I joined in. I'd won only a handful of matches in twelve months.

The Captain began setting out the pieces on the board. 'We'll play the Typhoon version tonight. Remember how? ... I thought you would. Anti-clockwise winds about a chosen point, and tangled Fate and Fortune: that means you always draw a card from both. Here's to fine booty, fair women and a safe harbour!'

We clinked glasses and drank. The red wine was strong and made my eyes water: that, and the sudden thought that this was the last game of 'Pirate' I would play with Captain Jones.

I rolled the dice and spun the compass. My hand hovered over the board, choosing where to place my ship. You could start from any of the ports set at the compass points, each of which had its own hazards – and its own name.

The Captain nodded his approval. 'The Monkey, hey? I'd

have done the same, given that wind speed and direction. A rascal's move.' He laughed and picked up the dice, weighing them thoughtfully before rolling them and then placing his own ship. West by northwest: the White Whale.

'You've never asked about my crimes, Jack,' he said, passing across the dice.

'It's not my business, sir. And we've always had enough to talk about.' It was true. I'd begun the visits as the go-between for my aunt, but now I came for the fellowship and the fine tales.

The Captain said, 'I'll tell you about it now, for this is my last night and we've become good friends. I've no one else to tell, and I can't go off to the other world without having at least an echo - a shadow - a remembrance of me remaining. I've no family to carry on my name or cherish my memory. Even your aunt - bless her! - even she's unlikely to think of me in a few years' time.'

I was embarrassed at this and pretended to study the board. Aunt Emma's interest in the Captain had faded sharply when he entered prison, and many of her letters had been dashed off at the last minute as I fretted by her elbow. The past few weeks had been different, though. She'd even made a visit herself last week, after a full morning at her mirror. Perhaps she'd known something was about to happen; but she hadn't told me.

The Captain rolled the Runes of Destiny: a beautiful white stone, its twelve faces decorated with curious markings. The face that came to rest on top was like a spear piercing a half-moon: Fortune.

He turned over the first of the light wooden Fortune cards and exclaimed, 'Treasure, lad! But I need to secure it. And since we're playing Typhoon style, let's see what the Fate card brings... ah, I'm to be short-masted for the next move... what to do?'

He moved his ship, heading closer to the wind.

'What think you, Jack?' he asked, turning down the treasure card. I wouldn't be allowed to see it until three moves later and so didn't know the bearings of the treasure. The Captain was smiling broadly now, taunting me. 'Where's the treasure, boy?'

'I think you're bluffing, Captain,' I said. 'The wind blows from the east for you and you're tacking into it, but I guess the treasure's north and west. That is - if there really *is* any treasure worth seeking.'

The Captain laughed. 'Well, you'll find out soon enough! Anyway – my crimes, Jack. It was like this. I was the King's Pirate for thirteen years, and gave good service to the kingdom of Albion - better service that anyone knows, lad, and much of it surprisingly peaceful.'

'Aunt Emma says you're a gentleman pirate.'

The warder on the bench snorted at this in a disbelieving way.

The Captain said, 'That's generous of her. And it's three parts true. I didn't set out to be the King's Pirate, not at first. I was a friend of your father's, Jack. You knew that?'

I shook my head. One of the first lessons I'd learned from Aunt Emma was that my parents, who had died when I was scarcely a year old, were not to be discussed. Their names were mentioned only in whispers between her and her friends, with much shaking of heads and sympathetic looks in my direction.

The Captain raised his eyebrows at my ignorance. 'Like him, I wanted to be a Guardian. But then it became dangerous to be a Guardian, and I hadn't the courage to carry on – oh, I know it's odd, hearing the King's Pirate saying he's a coward, but I didn't have half the courage of your father and mother. So when things became too hot, and the King began to throw the Guardians into the prisons he'd built throughout this fair land, I drifted away. I quietly joined a ship sailing to a far island. Your move, Jack.'

I threw the dice, spun the compass and drew two cards, neither of them helpful to me. I considered asking about the Guardians – of which I knew very little - but thought it best to let the Captain talk on. It was his last night, after all.

He shook his head at some memory. 'We were boarded by the nastiest set of cut-throats I've ever met. I was branded with their mark – you can just see the scar on my hand, Jack – and forced to scrub decks on their best ship. I learned quickly, lad. I soon knew everything about her – the ship's always a woman, you know – and everything about the men sailing her. I was scarcely twenty, but I had this instinct for the sea and an ability to command. Within a few months, that crew was mine and we tossed the captain and his bloodthirsty mate into the ocean and sailed back home laden with treasure, heroes to a man.'

The game continued, with many a stifled oath and some laughter. As always, he had the better of me: he knew what was in my mind before it was clear to myself, whereas his plans always baffled me. Yet he seemed pleased with me, saying I would make a pirate yet.

'King Arinaeus made me a Captain for that, and an Admiral soon after – at twenty-one! And for five years I floated around the seas that surround these troubled islands, excited at first but soon bored with it. I needed a challenge. And when the King's Pirate – Black Ben he was – was found floating in the Largando Sea, nailed to a rudder and his eyes pecked out by seagulls, I went to the King and made my case for taking the evil shilling in his place. No more to be a lofty Admiral pulling strings at court in Magus, wearing starched collars and commanding thousands: instead to be a mere Captain again in charge of a ship – ah, but what a ship!'

He paused, seeing a troubled look on my face. I'd always been quick with figures, and had worked out that his story had come to a time of sorrow for me.

He said gently, 'Yes, Jack: this was just after your parents died. Those strings I pulled at the King's Court – well, they weren't strong enough to save the only true friends I'd ever had. And suddenly nothing mattered, nothing moved me or made me desire to live - not food nor drink, neither work nor frolic. Therefore, why not throw myself into something that would at least occupy me to the full and blank out my sad memories?'

I said nothing to this. I rolled the dice again, half-doubting his easy words.

He continued, 'The King was happy to waste my youthful zeal on a couple of shady dealings he had in hand in the South Barbardies, so he gave me a chance on the *Firebird*, the fastest ship in the world, with a picked crew of vagabonds, rogues and out-of-work actors.'

I smiled at this. He had spoken often of his 'Troupe' of actors – more than he had spoken of his pirate crew. He reminisced about them now. The plays he had written on the tilting desk of his Captain's cabin. The performances they had taken from port to port ('They loved us in Rio, lad!'). The arguments between troupe and crew, and the mutiny when he brought the first woman actor on board. The greasepaint, the backgrounds constructed by the ship's carpenter, the phosphorous lightings, the sorry band of pipers and fiddlers that he moulded into a twelve-piece orchestra.

He was a man for whom nothing could be straightforward; everything had to be twisted a little and then a little more, until you nearly had to stand on your head to look at it. He needed – always – to be finding something different, turning each idea inside out until the result was complicated enough and odd enough for his restless mind. And now that implacable mind was approaching its final resting place, its finale... but without an applauding, whistling audience demanding an encore.

He asked now, 'Why should Piracy not be considered an art, Jack? Why should it not have style, and grace, and depth? And even a morality of sorts?'

He paused as if to ponder this, then said, 'I'll tell you something that no other King's Pirate can claim. For the next thirteen years I did the King's dirty work and did it well: but I kept my own hands clean.'

The prison warder laughed at this – a long, sneering laugh accompanied by a sly wink.

'Oh, but it's true, Jack,' the Captain said gently. 'I killed only when I needed to, and tortured only those I knew had tortured others - for I thought it only right that they should taste what they'd served up, damn them! And though I stole and lied and tricked and cheated, I did so only when on the King's business. I prided myself in this – that I would be honest and true, and not harm so much as one hair of an innocent man's head; but that I would carry out my King's orders without flinching.'

I asked, 'But how can that be right, Captain?'

'You talk like a Guardian,' he said wryly. 'Just like your father himself!'

He added more quietly, 'And Jack, I sometimes heard your father's voice in my head, asking just such a question. Him, I could ignore; but when your mother's voice started up as well, I was cut adrift; nay, shipwrecked. For I'd loved your mother – from a distance, young Jack, so you can take that look from your face! She chose your father, and thereby saved herself much heartache, I'm sure.'

He looked at me steadily for a moment, as if to reassure me of his candour. He continued, 'But to return to our tale: here was I, the King's Pirate, a man that others scarcely dared look in the face, a man for whom royal doors would open in any land, though usually they were the back doors, for most of my work was hidden and devious. And yet a whispered question in a half-forgotten voice could so un-man me that I lost my bearings.'

'And at such a critical time, too, Jack. The Curchan Ruby! Believed lost to the world but within my grasp at last! The King's fortunes had grown immensely, his coffers swelled with my smuggled treasures and his reputation blossoming through my backdoor statesmanship. Albion controlled half the known world – and we didn't much care for the other half anyway. Except for the Ruby.'

I was on the edge of my seat now. He had never spoken

of the Ruby; I'd heard it mentioned only in whispers when Aunt Emma gossiped with other ladies.

'Ah, the Ruby... Power beyond imagining! *Magical* power! Not the weak mutterings of witches and uncertain spells of warlocks, not the enchanters' devious tools that so often wound those who wield them, not the sly genii who serve only for a time and then find a way to cheat and enslave their masters. No! Terrible, world-ruling power to him who holds the stone, power to create and destroy, unsearchable power!'

'The King had heard a rumour – he has spies everywhere – that the Ruby was back within Curchan itself. It's a small, weak country, rich only in mountains and mountain goats. The people are peaceful and clean, and live dull, tidy lives. They are innocent folk, and therefore easily tricked by someone like myself. A bit of clever talk, some flattery, some tales of evil strangers from the East trying to steal their greatest treasure; a promise to assist them; then the evil strangers arrive – being some of my own crew disguised as mysterious Easterners of course; I seem to save the Curchans from these evil folk; we are now great allies; I steal the Ruby and have crossed the mountains before they discover I've left the house they'd given me.'

I didn't like what the Captain was saying and my face must have shown this, for he laughed and said I was as solemn as my own father, and that I should know by now – being all of fifteen years – that this was the way of the world.

He added, 'It's a tangled world, Jack, and those called to rule it must embrace the bad with the good.'

'Then I don't want to be a ruler, sir.'

He looked at me curiously, then said, 'Oddly enough, that's the very thought that was troubling me then. You see, ruling was suddenly a possibility: I had the Ruby. I can feel – now – in this hand – the very contours of that stone.'

He was gazing at the open palm of his right hand, as if seeing something there that still astonished him. He shook his head, sighed and picked up the white Runes of Destiny, weighed it a moment, then rolled it softly across the table. A lightning bolt showed upon its upper face: dangerous weather.

He smiled ruefully at this reminder of his position. 'And Jack, I knew how to use the Ruby. Oh, the King thought he had forestalled all that; he had two men put on the ship just to watch me, each with a key to the double lock of the metal safe built into a solid beam in my cabin. But I know how to pick locks, and can swap a fake for an original under the nose of any number of King's Advisers.'

'So here I was at midnight, stroking this beauty and wondering which name I should take when I became Emperor; I knew the words of command, see. And would you believe it, Jack? That sweet voice whispered once again and I slipped the stone back into its silk bag and hung the bag about my neck, renouncing my chance of immortal power. And then I climbed into my bed and slept like a baby for the first time for twenty years...'

At this the warder called out angrily, 'You lie! You stole the Ruby and wouldn't tell where you hid it! Everyone knows that!'

'*Knows?*' asked the Captain quietly, speaking to me. 'All that is *known* was taken from me by the King's Torturers. I hate such men. Experts at their craft, I give them that; but if I were out of this place tomorrow, my first task would be to ensure that they and their masters discovered how it feels to have your fingernails pulled out and red hot metal laid upon your most sensitive places.... Oh, you can be sure that I told them everything I knew, and quickly. But I knew nothing. It had gone, Jack: wiped from my mind.'

'But how?'

'I don't know. From the morning after I took the Ruby to a month later, all is a blank. Oh, the ship's log recorded our progress and the crew could list the places we visited, telling the Inquisitor they knew not why I took such an odd route – rounding capes that good sailors never went near;

landing upon islands known to be inhabited by savages or dangerous beasts; and at a whim climbing Cursed Rock, a slanting mass of stone that rises from the Boiling Sea and shakes an angry fist at the heavens, said to be the petrified arm of the Devil himself. There was no reason for any of the commands I gave at that time. I have puzzled over them myself, with a Torturer at one elbow and the Inquisitor at the other, calmly writing in a book the screams and babbled confessions of my ignorance.'

I asked, 'Were you trying to find a place to hide the Ruby?'

'I suppose so; and perhaps I did. But I couldn't name the day or place, or say how I laid it to rest. If indeed I did so; for perhaps I merely sent it to the bottom of the sea where it would be safe from faithless men like myself.'

I persisted, 'Why didn't they take you back over the same route? Retracing your course, in case that helped you to remember, Captain?'

'They did that, lad: and a sorry time it was for us all. I stared out to sea, or wandered moodily across sandy wastes with soldiers at my heels and a few of my old crew as witnesses. But it was no good. And Jack, I came to the same conclusion as the King: I took that Ruby, which in the King's way of thinking was *his* Ruby, and dropped it into the deepest sea, never to be found by man.'

He moved his ship one last time and pointed at the board. 'I'm back to port, Jack.'

'I almost caught you, Captain.'

'That you did. But you hesitated, didn't you? Five moves ago.'

'I played safe, sir,' I said. 'I always do.'

He laughed. 'There comes a time to gamble, lad: and you must seize that time with both hands. But I'm pleased you're not a gambling man. When you're sitting at your desk in a week's time, overcome with the boredom of another day's clerking, think of me: for I'm The Gambler personified, and here am I spending my last moments in a prison cell, waiting for the hangman. Or think of your parents – for they gambled more recklessly than I did, and their end came much sooner.'

I remember that I nodded wisely then, thinking how true it was that a dull life was a safe one. I'd started my studies as an articled clerk and within five years would be a junior bookkeeper, and in another five years perhaps a fully qualified accountant; and then there would be a slow, dull climb to senior departmental supervisor, sitting in a quiet office and looking out upon rows of clerks and bookkeepers and accountants, all scribbling, pausing to work their adding machines, comparing, considering, and scribbling some more.

It was what I was good at. It was what I was comfortable with. Safe with.

'I'll remember your advice, sir,' I said.

We had another glass of wine, I recall. And as we sipped it slowly, he brought out a rolled, sealed parchment.

'Our friend opposite,' he said softly, nodding toward the warder, 'has agreed that I can pass this to your aunt. For a price, of course: there's a gold tooth I won't need after tomorrow morning, you see. The paper will guide her to a small investment I've hidden away. She reminded me a few days ago that I'd promised it to you, and therefore to her as your guardian. I give it happily in recognition of the friendship of your parents, and now your own friendship to me, Jack.'

I took the document and tucked it into a pocket of my light woollen cloak. I would have thanked him, if my voice had worked.

'And this is for you alone, lad.' He packed the remaining pieces of the Game of Pirate into its beautiful wooden box and handed the box to me.

He laughed lightly. 'I know your overbearing desire to always keep to the rules, Jack, so it's just as well that I wasted some thoughtless hours on my final, fateful voyage writing them out, on the inside of the lid.' He removed the lid and showed me the delicate writing in good, black ink. I read the first line:

THE RULES OF THE GAME COMMONLY CALLED "PIRATE"

'Thank you, sir,' I said at last. 'I'll think of you as I play this. Always. And – and I hardly know how to say this, sir – Captain - but you've been to me like the father I hardly knew.'

He nodded his head slowly. 'And he would have been proud to hear you say that, Jack. Your hand, lad. We've had some good times in poor conditions, haven't we?'

'Aye, sir.'

And then I was gone, hustled down the corridors by the warder, who was now whistling to himself in an eerily cheerful fashion. He unlocked the final gate, nodded to his fellow guards, and pushed me roughly towards the open doorway that looked out upon the main street.

'Out you go, boy!' he ordered.

I felt him watching me as I walked away, the precious box clutched to my chest, thinking that it was all over now, that everything from now on would be quiet and unadventurous.

But I was wrong.

2 Losses

The players will choose one of the four ships: the brig, the caravel, the schooner and the sloop. To their ship they may earn the right to add one or more of the following during the game: the bell, the rat, the parrot, the monkey, the cannon, the seven-sided charm and the telescope. Each one of these provides an additional 1 knot of speed, except when totally becalmed.

I stood at the top of the steps for a moment, letting my eyes grow accustomed to the dark, dirty street lit by the occasional lantern outside a shop. The housetops of the dusky, sprawling city of Magus before me fell away towards the harbour in the south, from which a soft breeze drifted, salty and cool against the warm night. I heard seagulls calling in the distance.

There were many people hurrying home, and others dawdling about the shop windows. I counted the twenty steps down from the prison as I descended, and considered going home a different way. But I chose the route I always took: direct and simple, heading east. I remember that I laughed to myself, thinking of the shrewd assessment the Captain had made of my character. I was not one for adventure.

I crossed a couple of dark alleys to my left and then slowed as I came to another.

A man was walking just behind me and to my right. He was too close, almost pushing me, so I stepped away and was nearly touching the wall on my left as I came to the alley. I hesitated a moment on the curb, not liking to be so close to the odorous blackness to my left. I began to run across the gap, but it was too late.

The man on my right closed in and put an arm about my shoulders, pushing me around and into the alley. At the same time, another hand seized my left elbow and I found myself being marched into the darkness, too surprised to resist – and too small for my resistance to have any effect anyway.

Just as I was wildly considering some foolish action, my captors pulled me around a second corner to my left and I found myself in the middle of a group of large men whose evil features were exaggerated by the smoking torches held by two of them.

One man – the tallest, with red hair and a freckled face crisscrossed with scars – snatched the box from my hands and pulled off the lid. He tipped the box to the light, swore, and threw it aside. Then he grabbed me by the jacket with one enormous hand and lifted me from the ground. His other hand was balled into a fist the size of a small pumpkin – or so it seemed to me.

'Where is it?' he demanded grimly, and then the fist hit me in the stomach. I suppose it wasn't a hard blow by his standards but it hurt me badly and I hung there, sucking at air that wouldn't come. He didn't insist on an answer and I realised that the question and the punch had been for his amusement rather than information.

He reached into my cloak pocket and took out the rolled parchment, pushing me to one of his men to hold. He snapped open the seal, held the parchment to the light of a sputtering torch, and began reading it slowly with his lips moving and his brow furrowed, as if he found reading difficult.

Meanwhile, I was searched more thoroughly. The few coins I had were taken and snatched from hand to hand.

'Treasure, boys!' one of them joked. 'Five coppers!' I also had a clean handkerchief; one brute blew his nose on it and then stuffed it back into my pocket.

'Is that all?' the tall one asked. I nodded, not trusting my voice.

'He's lying!' one cried out.

'Slit him!' hissed another.

'Shall I?' asked the man holding me, and I was suddenly aware of a cold, hard blade against my throat. The leader paused, thinking.

'No, lads,' he said presently. 'For as you know, I'm a merciful man.' There was laughter at this, and he smiled evilly.

'I'm a fair man, Jack,' he said to me – and I shuddered to discover that he knew my name. His voice was slow and menacing. 'I'm fair but I'm firm. It might happen that we need you, boy: just to ask a few questions, you know? So I'll make you a fair but firm offer, young Jack.'

He brought his face close to mine and I smelled the rum on his breath. 'If you promise to stay at home the next few days, then we'll let you keep those things that are dear to you, such as your eyes and tongue and liver. If we need to speak to you, we'll come see you at Aunty Emma's, right?'

He paused for my response, and I nodded.

He added in a chilling voice, 'But if you should feel the need to wander, and we was to come upon you in the streets, then we might feel we've been betrayed. And betrayal leads to revenge, don't it?'

I nodded again.

'I *said* "Don't it"! Answer me!'

Before that fist could punish me again, I croaked that yes, it was true. Despite this, I could see the fist preparing itself – and was relieved to hear shouting from the street nearby, and see the gang look to one another before slipping away into the darkness.

More torches came around the corner and their bearers paused to stare at me. I must have looked a pitiful sight. I was on my hands and knees, feeling for the pieces of the game with one hand and holding my stomach with the other.

'Are you all right, Jack?' asked someone tall and pretty with long black hair, whom I recognised as one of the women who sometimes visited Aunt Emma. She tried to pull me to my feet.

She asked, 'Where's the par–?' But she stopped herself and asked instead, 'What have you lost?'

'My Pirate game,' I said.

'Oh,' she said, sounding relieved. 'Is that all they took?'

'No,' I said. I continued picking up pieces. The cannon, the monkey, the spinning compass, the seven sided charm, the telescope... The lady was still talking, but I ignored her. I didn't like the way she talked to me. And I didn't like the way that everyone seemed to know about the parchment meant for Aunt Emma.

They helped me home, with miserable pauses for me to retch up my supper. The first lady's name was Minerva and her friend was called Amy. Amy didn't say much but appeared genuinely sorry for me. With them was an elderly gentleman they didn't seem to know; he hurried off as soon as we came in sight of Aunt Emma's gate.

Aunt Emma was a fussy woman who liked things to be neat, tidy, luxurious and fashionable. I now know that most of her money came from the Captain, who after the death of my parents had provided for me and her.

She was my mother's much younger sister and at one time had been the object of the Captain's affections – though he would have rarely seen her, being in port only one month in twelve, and with much business to attend to.

The house was in fact the Captain's, but Aunt Emma and I had lived in it for as long as I could remember. He sometimes visited, when he would stay in the attic room that was filled with his books, maps and formal costumes. I'd rarely had the chance to speak to him; and when he did appear at dinner, I was dumbstruck by a mixture of awe for the man and a fear of letting Aunt Emma down with a badly chosen remark.

The women hurried me along the garden path. The grand front door was opened by the ancient manservant that Aunt Emma referred to simply as "Butler" and I was taken into the drawing room.

What I most wanted was a drink of water, and then something warm to hold against my stomach; but apparently there were more important things to do.

A circle of ladies were seated in the parlour, waiting in some agitation it seemed. A shared gasp escaped from a dozen lips as I was pulled into the room by Minerva's firm hand.

'They took it,' she said grimly.

The gasps were succeeded by groans, hisses and a few swear words not commonly associated with fashionable ladies. But then, these were not common women.

'Bring him here,' said a calm voice.

Madame Helena was seated to my right, facing the one window. She was dressed as I usually saw her: in purple and black, with long sleeves, a high collar and a black veil across the top of her face. Her dark hair was neatly mounded beneath a small black hat. A hand gloved in black velvet took my chin and turned my face to look into the shadowed eyes that smouldered beyond the veil.

'You will tell me everything,' she said quietly. 'Begin at the moment you entered the prison.'

She held my face in this velvet vice as I stumbled through a patchy history of the evening. Her questions were few but piercing, like her eyes.

'Who else might know what he gave you?' she asked at one point.

I tried to think through this logically, which was strangely difficult with Madame Helena's veiled eyes searching mine. Somehow, the veil made me especially uneasy. It was as if she could see my very thoughts, whereas I could see nothing but shadows.

She had always made me nervous. She called herself a

witch, and a high priestess of witches. I didn't believe in witches: I thought they were just silly women playing games. But Madame Helena was different.

She was a woman of medium height and no particular features. You would pass her in the street without noticing her - but then you might stop, unsettled, as if you'd felt a cobweb across your face.

And if you met her face to face, at first you might think she was a sweet, middle-aged woman. At least I did once, though to be truthful anyone over the age of twenty-five was "middle-aged" to me then. But once she turned her eyes upon you, you suddenly weren't sure what age she was, whether she was beautiful or ugly, and whether she intrigued, disturbed or simply frightened you.

I finally came up with an answer. 'He – the Captain – only talked about the Warder knowing. I... I put the parchment straight into my jacket. So I'd guess that no one else knows, unless the Warder decided to tell someone, Madame Helena.'

I know this sounds rather stilted. I was trying to be precise; that's the way adults affected me. Especially scary ones.

Madame Helena nodded. 'And how long did it take you to walk from the prison to the street corner where you were taken by the two men?'

'About a minute. Maybe two, Madame Helena.'

I saw her gaze shift before I answered; she was looking beyond me, at someone else.

'And did you notice any of my girls on the street? Minerva or Amy perhaps?'

'No, Madame Helena.'

'And how long was it from the time you were taken until you were rescued?'

I considered. 'Maybe as much as five minutes.'

'Thank you.' Her eyes behind the veil stared into mine once more. After almost a minute of this silent interrogation, she said quietly to the Sisterhood, 'This boy is honest but cannot be relied on. He has wrong dreams.'

There were worried murmurings at this odd comment, as if she'd said I had the plague. Then she nodded to Aunt Emma, who rose and escorted me from the room.

Aunt Emma hugged me in the corridor – she was genuinely fond of me – and told me to go to "Butler" if I needed something for my stomach. She looked at the box I was still holding and asked what it was.

'Just a game,' I said. 'The one I play with the Captain.' I opened the wooden box and showed her.

She wrinkled her nose at the lovely pieces made of brass and wood. 'If only you could have kept hold of the parchment instead of the box,' she sighed. 'This is such an expensive house to maintain. Ah, well – go to your room and rest there until the Sisters have gone. We'll have a spot of dinner later on.'

Then she hurried back to the parlour, leaving me standing in the hallway, stunned by a sudden realisation: she didn't really care about the Captain; not at all.

She hadn't asked how he was feeling on his final night alive, whether he had sent any final messages, whether there was anything he needed. All she'd been thinking about was his money.

I washed in my room and put on some clean clothes. Normally, I would have stayed there obediently. But something possessed me that night. I was burning with all manner of new feelings and driven by an odd curiosity.

I crept down the stairs and positioned myself near the parlour door. When I found I couldn't make out what was being said, I tried something foolish: I stealthily opened the front door and went outside, creeping behind bushes to the half-open parlour window. The curtains were thick and overlapping, but there was just enough of an angled gap for me to see about half of the room, through the uneven glass of the latticed windows.

The two young women – Minerva and Amy - had just finished giving their accounts of the evening and the room had fallen silent. The tall, pretty girl named Minerva was looking smug; Amy was crying. I couldn't see Madame Helena, but I heard her measured voice.

'Amy, look at me. Thank you. Why did you not see the boy as soon as he left the prison?'

Amy was about my height, with blond hair and a face that was pleasant without being striking. 'I was lookin' at the prison, Madame, really I was, whatever Minerva says. I was lookin' at it in the reflection of the shop window. I thought it'd be better that way. I thought someone might be suspicious if I was watchin' the prison direct.'

The reply was calm but ominous: 'You have not answered my question, Amy.'

Amy began crying again. 'I know, Madame. And I *can't* answer it. I just know that I missed him for a moment. When I turned around, he was already walkin' towards Miss Minerva. So I waved to her, as was the plan. And I hurried off after him, like I said before.'

'Why did Minerva not do anything?'

I saw Amy's face colour. 'I couldn't say, Madame. You'd have to ask her.'

Minerva put her nose up at this and spoke confidently. 'I didn't do anything, because Amy never waved. She was too busy looking at pretty dresses and flashy shoes.'

There was another silence, during which I had to fight the desire to cough. During that silence, Minerva's haughty nose had slowly dropped and her proud eyes had turned shifty.

'Minerva.' The calm, controlling voice again.

Minerva whined a little: 'I did my best, Madame Helena. The mistake I made was to trust Amy. By the time I realised what had happened –'

'Minerva!'

'Yes, Madame Helena?'

Madame Helena laughed drily and said, 'Although we serve the Prince of Lies, you will not lie to me, Minerva. I will have from your lips either the truth or your final, rasping breath.'

Minerva's face went through an odd transformation. At first, she pursed her lips primly and seemed to return Madame Helena's gaze in a confident manner. Then her eyes shifted to one side, but snapped back again, as if she was trying to look away but couldn't. She pulled back her head and angled it to one side, but her eyes remained fixed at where her mistress was sitting.

Then panic rose in her face, and I could see that she was fighting for breath. Her right hand went to her throat and her mouth started opening and closing helplessly, like a fish out of water. Her face turned a dusky blue. Her other hand reached out, palm upward, begging. Her eyes bulged.

'You will tell me now?' asked Madame Helena calmly. Minerva tried to speak but couldn't. She nodded her head desperately.

'Speak, then.'

Minerva's lungs suddenly worked again, and she gasped at the air while tears streamed down her cheeks.

'Speak!'

'I – oh - sorry – Madame Helena, so sorry –'

'I don't wish to hear your pathetic blatherings, Minerva. Tell me what happened.'

Minerva gulped another litre of air. 'I was with Tom. He's – ' She paused a moment, considering a small deception I think, before rushing on. 'He's one of them, Madame. One of Red's crew that took the parchment. I've been seeing him off and on.'

'Without telling me.'

'Yes, Madame. But it wasn't serious, not on my part anyway. He turned up, and I suppose... maybe I was looking at him when Amy signalled. If she did. She never –'

'Minerva!'

'Sorry – I –'

'When did he leave you?'

Minerva considered. 'Amy came along, pointing down

one of those dirty alleyways. I followed her and I think he… yes, he must have gone then. We looked about for help, Amy and I did, and Tom wasn't to be seen. So we asked a middle-aged gentleman to come with us. And – and you know the rest.'

There was a long silence, during which Minerva gloomily studied her very elegant shoes and the ladies studied Minerva, mostly with rather nasty looks on their faces. Amy was looking away, embarrassed I think.

Then Madame Helena spoke again. 'Two things. First: Minerva, you are a very stupid girl and are not fit to be one of the Sisterhood. You have allowed yourself to be used by Red's gang, and have nearly ruined our chance of recovering the treasure we have schemed about for these past twelve months.'

'Yes, Madame.'

'I did not ask you to speak! Second: you are to take steps to repay us for this stupidity. You will find that man Tom and will use him on our behalf. You will employ whatever means you have – by lies, by promises, by witchcraft, by the offer of your fair body. You will enchant and entrance him. And you will make known to him that we have something they need. Do you understand?'

'I think so, Madame. But what do we have?'

'We have the boy; we have certain information they will require; and we have a ship. I purchased it this morning, and am looking for a crew. But you will not tell your man Tom any of this until you have snared him. Understand?'

'Yes, Madame. And how long –'

'We sail in two weeks. You have one week to make this Tom your personal slave, and use him to pry open the mind of his master. In a week's time, I wish to have Red seeking to negotiate a deal with me.'

'Yes, Madame.'

There was another long silence, during which there came upon me a feeling of dread, as if I'd blundered into a spider's web and was waiting, frozen, for the tickle of legs upon some part of my body. Then the spider spoke:

'Emma, please ask your servant to go outside and bring in the boy, whom he will find near that window opposite.'

I prepared to run, but then recalled the Red-haired villain's promise to remove my liver if he found me anywhere in the street. Therefore I walked slowly back to the front door, which opened to receive me.

I stood once again in that crowded parlour. The faces were no longer so welcoming, except for a sympathetic glance from Amy.

'Oh Jack, how *could* you?' my aunt exclaimed, and there was an awful tut-tutting from the other ladies in agreement.

'Come here, boy,' said the voice which now frightened me more than any other.

I stumbled across the room and stood before her. She had removed the veil, and I realised that I'd been wrong to think it was the veil that gave her an advantage. Her unshielded eyes transfixed me like a snake's.

She said in a low voice, 'You have been listening to words not meant for you. We have a penalty for that. Whatever nightmares you ever had, whatever terrors you have imagined in your waking thoughts, they are as nothing compared with the punishments we would apply in normal circumstances.'

I said nothing. My mind was suddenly alive with remembrances of dark dreams.

'It is fortunate for you that these are not normal circumstances,' the woman continued. Her naked eyes were dark and yet burning, as was her quiet voice.

'You will come with us tonight to a place of safety. You will serve us while we recover the parchment and then recover the treasure. Then, and only then, will your crime be paid for and your punishment forgotten. Do I make myself clear?'

I tried to return her steady gaze, but failed. 'Yes, Madame

Helena,' I said in a voice that sounded unlike my own. It was cracked and uneven and very, very frightened.

The next hour was confusing. I was taken to my room by Aunt Emma, scolded, hugged, forgiven and then condemned all over again for the shame brought upon her. Butler appeared with water and toasted crumpets. I was ordered to pack a case, then made to repack it into something smaller, then permitted to wash and change my soiled clothes.

As I pulled on my socks, Aunt Emma summoned me downstairs again. I meekly followed her into the parlour, to find a dozen ladies arguing about dress sizes.

'Stand over here, boy!' commanded one of them, taking some dressmakers' pins from her mouth to do so. Then she began measuring me against a scarlet dress held by another woman.

Despite my protests, I soon found myself wearing the dress, with a broad-brimmed hat to match. I refused to try the high heeled shoes, and they allowed me this small act of defiance.

'But you must wear the dress,' Aunt Emma insisted. 'It's in case anyone is watching us leave.'

We left the house in a tight group, Madame Helena at the front, wearing her veil again and gripping my hand firmly in her own. Behind me were two of the bigger "girls" (as Madame Helena called them – they must have been in their early twenties): Vicky and Sandra, both with short-cropped dark hair, short skirts and clubs in their hands. After them came Aunt Emma carrying my case, followed by ten or so other ladies.

We stepped through the gate of the walled front garden and strolled towards a carriage parked a little ways to the left. I tried to walk like the ladies but couldn't mimic their mincing steps and upright posture. I knew what I looked like: an awkward boy dressed as a girl.

As we drew near the carriage, a shadow left the railings opposite and crossed the road to stand in Madame Helena's way. A low voice spoke.

'Excuse me, ladies, but ain't it a bit late for fine flossies like yourselves to be out walkin' the streets?'

I recognised one of the larger members of the gang - and was sure that he recognised me, too. A grin spread across his broad face as he stepped around Madame Helena and towards me.

Madame Helena spoke quietly: 'Vicky; Sandra.'

Vicky stepped in front of the man, who let out a sharp whistle, for she was a big-bosomed girl in a low cut blouse. But then she swung upwards the long club she carried in her right hand, striking him between the legs.

He groaned, then groaned again as Sandra hit him behind the knees with her own club. He fell upon his face and rolled about on the ground, clutching his private parts.

Madame Helena looked back at him over her shoulder. She said firmly, 'Please inform your leader that I will be in touch once he has learned some manners.'

Half of us climbed into the carriage while the others sauntered away down the road, laughing.

The carriage rolled quickly through the quiet streets and I watched to see where we went. We drove past the road I'd been dragged down, rattled along the cobblestones in front of the prison and continued westwards. As we made our way to a more luxurious part of the city, I listened with one ear to whispered conversations.

'Will they go and try to find the treasure immediately, d'you think?' asked one.

'I never trusted Minerva,' said another.

'That watcher saw the boy, I'm sure he did.'

'We should have known the dressin' up wouldn't work.'

Madame Helena's voice was icy: 'Of course it worked, Becky. It worked exactly as planned.'

'You mean he didn't recognise the boy?'

'He *did* recognise the boy. That was the point of the exercise. Oh, some of you are absurdly dense, aren't you?

Think, Becky: we want them to believe there's something special about the boy, so special that we must try to smuggle him away unseen. The pirates are stupid (like most men), and we have to rub their noses in this fact. So we parade the boy past them, dolled up in a ridiculous disguise. Then we make our intentions and abilities obvious by a little thuggery. Now their leader will spend a sleepless night wondering what we know and what we have. He will invent half a dozen explanations, each more distressing to him than the one before. In a week or so, his mind will have been manipulated into the correct state of fear and exhaustion; then he will be like a weary child, and we will take him by the hand and lead him wherever we wish.'

There was silence in the carriage, while the feet of the horse clapped regularly along the uneven flagstones and I studied the street for landmarks. Then one of the ladies said reverently:

'Oh, Madame Helena! So clever!'

I looked across at the witch priestess and wondered at the depth of her planning. And a question came to me which I didn't share with the others: *Why had she sent Amy and Minerva to keep an eye on me, rather doing it herself with a team of her tougher girls?*

Perhaps she had wanted me to be taken. Perhaps it was her way of entrapping the pirates within her own plans. But as I pondered this, the carriage turned left through a high gateway into a short, curving drive. It halted before a large, square house with big windows and heavy curtains that allowed scarcely a gleam of light escape. From behind us came the sound of a heavy metal gate being shut, and then locked.

3 Choices

The play may start at any port marked on the board, corresponding to the sixteen points of the compass. Once the first player has chosen a port, the second must place his piece at least two compass points distant from the first. Further players must similarly distance their pieces from ships already on the board.

I woke in the middle of the night with a fierce thirst. I rose in the darkness and felt for the door handle to my left, before remembering that I wasn't in my room at Aunt Emma's.

I recall knocking over several items, one of which broke, before finding the door. But then I remembered that I'd been locked inside anyway – "for your own safety", Madame Helena had said.

I returned to my bed and tried to sleep. But I kept imagining Captain Jones in his dark cell, waiting for the dawn and knowing it would be the last dawn he would see. I remembered the many kindnesses he had shown me, and the pleasure of our friendship. And though it was clear that he must have merited his punishment – for he had been tried and convicted in open court - my mind wasn't easy about it. A man like him deserved a second chance.

Then I was troubled by another disturbing thought: for all these years, I hadn't noticed that what my aunt really cared about was the Captain's money.

Oh, she was affectionate enough whenever he came to stay – laughing at his quiet jokes, encouraging him to talk about his journeys, taking his hand and stroking it as they sat before the fire. It was embarrassing sometimes, the way she flirted with him; even more embarrassing because I knew that when he wasn't around, she had a busy social life that included a number of men – all of whom disappeared when Captain Jones came to stay.

He'd known Aunt Emma wasn't sincere: I saw that now. Even before his imprisonment, she was full of transparent excuses for not writing to him, not keeping his rooms aired and his clothes free of moths while he was at sea. He'd accepted her over-fulsome attentions when he was present and her taking him for granted when absent - and her inability to remember what they'd talked about only the day before (for she wasn't actually interested) - with a gentlemanly reserve and a kindly smile, making no comment.

He deserved better. And suddenly I knew what I must do. Perhaps it was the madness of thirst that placed the thought in my head; or perhaps this minor suffering brought me to sanity. But my mind was changed in a moment, and I flung the sheets to the floor and began searching for my clothes.

Shortly afterwards I was balanced on a narrow window ledge four metres above the ground, snatching at the branches of an oak as they swung past me in the wind. When finally I caught one, I stood a long moment doubting the wisdom of this idea. Then a sudden gust swept the branch and myself into space.

I limped towards the front gate, leaning on the broken branch I held in my hand. Somewhere a dog was barking and too late I recalled that Madame Helena had referred to some creature she called "Wolf". I did however discover that I could scale a wall quite quickly if a snarling beast was biting at my legs.

As I hobbled eastwards along dark roads for the next hour, I tried to form a sensible plan; but it was no use. All I was clear about was that I would find some water and then go to the prison, where I would beg to be allowed one last visit to the Captain. Then I would set him free somehow.

After drinking deeply at a pump by a horse's water trough, my mind cleared and I knew I was on a fool's errand. But I pressed on, telling myself that the Captain would perhaps be grateful for some company in his final hours: and having come so far, I could at least give him that.

I arrived at the prison as the stars were fading and the eastern horizon before me was threatening to burst into flame. I paused and studied the high, black northern hills to my left with their cascade of rounded downlands rolling towards the city; then I looked south, beyond the falling rooftops to the flat, dark sea. Somewhere a bird chirruped and I cocked an ear, listening. More birds began their sleepy welcome to the dawn and I stood there a while, oddly at peace. Then I shook the sleep from my head and climbed the last of the twenty steps to the prison.

The guard inside the door was half asleep. He hailed me as I tried to pass, and I walked back to him cautiously.

He gestured towards the inner gate with a thumb. 'You just missed him,' he said. 'The boss went up a few minutes ago. Come on.'

He led me through the guardroom, where another soldier nodded at me and then put his head back on the table. Another lay on a mat in the corner, snoring; others stirred in a small room off.

He unlocked the gate and waved me away down the dark corridor. Clearly he thought I was visiting by prior arrangement.

I walked as quietly as I could along the corridor and then through the second gate at the bottom of the stone steps. The warder had left this unlocked as usual. I climbed the steps and paused outside the closed door to listen.

The sounds from inside the room confused me – gargling and groaning and the occasional thump, then the warder's deep voice, uttering a swear word.

I eased the door open a crack.

'That's one!' the warder crowed.

Another gargle.

'Yeah. I know *one* was all we agreed. But you're nobody now, see? *Less* than nobody.'

A thud, and a muffled groan.

'They tortured you, did they? Not enough, by my book! I got friends, see? And my friends say you ain't suffered enough, not by a long chalk, 'cause you didn't treat 'em fair. That Ruby would've meant a prize of twenty golden Guineas for each man, and you stole that from them. You're givin' me one gold tooth, hey? Well, that's payment for the parchment, I s'pose. Not that the ladies got it, mind! My friends has that.'

A groan.

'Yeah, you should've known, right enough. You think you're so clever.... Givin' yourself airs, like you was better'n me... Well, you don't look so clever now! We got the parchment, and now I'm gonna have those other teeth, the real teeth. One by one... '

I pushed the door open a little further. The fat warder was standing in front of the Captain, whose arms and chest were tied to his chair and whose mouth was forced open by a tight gag fastened about his head.

'Think I'll have some of them fingernails, too...' the warder gloated. His back was to me. He was holding a pair of bloodied pliers in one hand and peering at something in the other – the gold tooth, I assumed. He took a step towards the Captain, chuckling to himself.

I went all hot then and grabbed the nearest weapon I could find: the warder's heavy club, which was leaning against the wall. Raising this above my head with both hands, I ran forward and hit the warder with all my strength.

He heard me coming and turned slowly, without concern. The blow caught him on the side of his head and cannoned off his shoulder. He stared at me, his pig eyes bulging with surprise.

I waited for him to fall. But he simply laughed and came at me with the pliers. When I next swung at him, he twisted the club from my hands and threw me across the room. Then he went over to the door, shut it, and locked it from the inside. He turned and looked at me.

'Playin' the hero, boy?' he asked softly. Oh, and I'm so glad you've come, 'cause now you're gonna get some punishment and no one's gonna hear you cry out ...'

He began chasing me about the prison cell, me running and him following slowly with the club, waiting his chance. I'd completed two harrowing tours of the room when I saw the Captain making signals at me, jerking his head and rolling his eyes. I didn't know what he wanted but changed course to pass close in front of him, thinking to circle around him and try to untie his arms.

The warder must have guessed my intentions, for he broke into a run and pursued me past the Captain's chair, one long arm stretching for me and a crazed, triumphant look in his eyes.

Then suddenly his legs went flying up behind him, caught in the chained legs that the Captain had flung up as the warder passed. The Captain had thrown himself backwards too, and he and chair and chains and warder spiralled through the air in a balletic arc, before everything crashed to the hard floor and rolled over once.

I halted, frozen, until the warder's club clattered across the floor and rapped me about the ankles. Then I instinctively snatched it up and ran to stand over the tangle of bodies.

The warder was lying still as if stunned, and I knew I should be pounding him with the club until I was sure he couldn't recover. Yet I couldn't bring myself to hit a helpless man.

I saw the Captain trying to free himself, so I dropped the club and pulled at the ropes securing his wrists to the chair arms. They must have been worked loose by his fall because the loops came away in a few seconds; then he threw himself forward, snatched the club from the floor and shuffled forward (still tied to the chair about his chest) and raised the club high, preparing to smash the warder's skull.

Then he stopped. And I saw what I should have noticed immediately – that the warder's head was lying at a very odd angle to his body.

Captain Jones set down the club and felt about the warder's belt until he found the short knife the warder carried there in a sheath. He cut away the ropes that held him to the chair, then ran to the door and overturned the bench against it. Only then did he cut through his gag.

He coughed and spat blood on the floor; tried to speak but couldn't. He picked up a pitcher from a table and rinsed out his mouth. He turned to look at me.

'Well, young Jack,' he rasped hoarsely, with a curious smile. 'So you took a gamble after all?'

'I suppose I did, Captain.'

He kneeled by the warder and turned him over, then cut the keys free from the dead man's belt.

He looked at them carefully, then chose one and tried it on the manacles that secured the chain to his ankles. It worked first time.

He glanced at me as he headed across the room. 'Talk to me while I'm getting things ready, Jack. Tell me what's been happening.'

So while he rushed about – listening at the door, snatching things from drawers, searching the warder's pockets – I told him all that had occurred, and all that I'd heard from Red, Aunt Emma and the Sisterhood. He listened grimly, though he did laugh when I told him about being chased over the wall by a dog.

'You've done well, Jack,' he said finally. 'And now we must be making sure we don't spoil all your efforts. Tell me how many of the guard there are downstairs, where each one was when you came in, and what he was doing.'

I had to think hard. 'There were five – no, six – no –'

'Belay that! One guard at a time. Think now: when you come up the stairs from the street, the main door's before you. Anyone standing at the door itself?'

'No, sir.'

'You pass through the door. There's a wall to your left, with a low table along it. A short, broad corridor with a small room off to the right. Anyone there, just inside the door?'

He took me through each corner of an entrance area and guardroom that he had passed through only once, a full year ago, but could recall as if it was there before his eyes. I struggled to remember who was in each part, the weapons they carried, and whether they were awake. Finally he was satisfied.

'Well done, Jack. Next time you'll do better, but that's good enough. Five men, three of them pretty much asleep, all with pistols and clubs; probably knives, too. Let's see: we need to get past them, and we need them to think you're innocent, else you'll be up here next week in my place. So here's what we do...'

A few minutes later he unlocked the door and took one last look around the room that had been his home and prison for a year.

'Ah! There it is!' He bent and picked up the gold tooth that the warder had pulled out. 'I expect I'll be needing that, Jack. Ready?'

I nodded.

He turned to go, then hesitated. 'Two last things, Jack. First, I don't expect to see you after this, not for a year or so at least. I've things to do; and it'll be no favour to you any-way if there's even a hint of a connection between us.'

'Aye, Captain,' I said, wondering why I suddenly felt dis-appointed at this promise of greater safety.

'And second: thank you. I'll never forget this.' He saluted me gravely.

Then he followed me out the door, locked it, bent the key

until it broke in the lock, and hurried quietly down the stairs behind me.

We crept along the passageway as silently as we could, pulling most of the torches from the walls as we went and stubbing them out. As we approached the gate, he went ahead and eased past it, going far enough up the corridor to extinguish the first torch there before tiptoeing back and hiding himself the best he could, just beyond the gate itself.

I saw him pull out the bunch of keys and find the one he thought would unlock the gate – though this was, we hoped, unnecessary. He raised a hand and dropped it twice: our signal.

I retreated back along my corridor as far as the second gate, which I slammed shut with a mighty clanging. Then I started shouting as I ran towards the main gate, stomping my feet on the echoing stones and trying to sound like someone running in fear for his life.

Two of the guard were waiting at the main gate as I came along the corridor. I began pointing behind me as I raved:

'They're fighting! He knocked the warder down! Didn't you hear them? There's blood *everywhere* – you've got to come – he's –'

And then I broke into incoherent cries and groans, for I was aware that my words didn't sound at all convincing.

I must have done enough, for the other guards had been woken by now and were crowding forward as the gate was thrown open.

'Where are they?' one was shouting, and to my horror seemed about to turn left, towards the hidden Captain Jones.

'Up the stairs!' I screamed, pointing behind me, along the corridor to the prison cell. 'Oh God, *quickly!*'

The swearing and screaming seemed to work better than anything else, and four of the guard charged off, leaving one standing with me at the gate.

Out of the corner of my eye, I saw the Captain creeping

towards us, weighing the club in his hand and frowning because he had wanted a clear run through. I had a sudden inspiration.

'I'm going to be sick!' I shouted, lurching forward towards the guard as if about to puke all over his legs. He stepped back; I followed, retching; he grabbed me and dragged me to one side, turning his back on the gate for a moment.

There was a soft sound, as of someone slipping past in stocking feet. I groaned and retched and grabbed at the guard's legs, falling to the ground in a pretended swoon.

I lay on the floor for a minute, hearing the muffled, distant sounds of a heavy oak door being attacked with an axe. I reflected that I hadn't noticed the axe when passing through the guardroom; perhaps it had been under the guard commander's desk.

It would take them some time to hew their way through the locked door and find the warder inside, hidden in the small washroom. Then they would rush down the steps again and start checking the other passages. Finally they would start questioning me. But I could invent a good story, I was sure; and the bruises I'd received from being thrown across the room would be my best witness.

I sat up. 'I'm feeling better now,' I said.

The guard didn't answer. He was looking across the guardroom towards the far end of the entrance hall, and frowning at the open door he could see there.

4 Chances

Each player will roll the two six-sided wind dice at the beginning of their turn. The wind direction and speed is set individually for each player and normally remains constant unless changed by either the rolling of a seven, a double one or double two. However, where a player enters a sector occupied by another player, that second player acquires the new wind speed and direction.

The next week passed quickly, even though I spent all of it in Madame Helena's house or gardens. The many "Sisters" bossed me mercilessly: sending me on errands to far corners of the house, calling me to hold a curtain they were hemming, making me slice vegetables in the kitchen or chop wood in the garden, demanding that I turn the music sheets while they played the piano, or that I write for them some letter they were too lazy to write for themselves.

I didn't mind this, for I was simply happy to be alive, and happy to think that Captain Jones was alive too. And if the ladies took pleasure in reversing the normal order of the day, where men bossed the women about – well, I could understand that, for I too had turned the world upon its head and found it looked better that way up.

On the seventh day, the man we always referred to simply as "Red" came to see Madame Helena – exactly as she had predicted. I was fetched from the side garden, where I'd been standing with skeins of wool wound about my hands so that one of the Sisters could puzzle out whether she had enough broad Navy to knit a jumper.

Red was leaning against a window ledge in the main parlour (there were three of them in that rambling, ramshackle house). He looked grim and tired, and not at all the lively and bloodthirsty seaman who had threatened to remove more organs than I could spare.

'This is the boy,' said Madame Helena from a low chair. She was wearing her veil and had her favourite black staff across her knees, the one with a heavy brass knob at the top and a sharpened brass tip at the other end.

'I know that!' said Red irritably. He glared at me, as if I was the cause of all his troubles.

She said, 'He spent two evenings a week with the Captain and you will need his assistance as much as you need mine.' She turned her head towards me and I caught the warning glance from behind the veil: but she had already rehearsed me for this visit and I knew that I was to say as little as possible.

Red studied me with clear dislike, then waved a roll of parchment in my face. 'Your cheatin', lyin' friend was a lover of riddles, wasn't he?' he asked slowly.

'Yes, sir.' I took him to be referring to the Captain, and to what the Captain had written in the instructions he'd prepared for Aunt Emma, which Red was now crushing in a meaty hand.

Red swore, and shook the parchment at me again. 'God, I'd like to have him here now. I'd squeeze some answers out of him!'

He unrolled the parchment a little and traced along the lines with a dirty finger. 'What's a black widow?' he asked suddenly.

I looked to Madame Helena, who nodded.

'It's a poisonous female spider that eats its mate,' I said. 'And it's what Captain Jones called a certain type of woman: one who marries with the purpose of seeing a rich husband die.'

Red snarled and readied one large fist, so I added hurriedly: 'Also, it's a move in a game we used to play. You position your ship so that it ends up next to an opponent's ship, with a reef to the lee side beyond them. That counts as a shipwrecking. In real life, you would sail alongside them, following the land, forcing them downwind towards the reef. At the last moment you veer windward; but it's too late for the other ship.'

Red looked down at the parchment and read the passage again, nodding to himself.

He looked back at Madame Helena. He spoke softly but his words were edged with violence. 'You've got me against a lee shore, I'll grant you that,' he said to the woman dressed in purple and black. 'But if I hit the rocks, I'm takin' you with me. Understand?'

'You should look at the positives, Captain,' she said briskly. 'I have a ship nearly fitted out: the fastest ship outside the King's own navy, Jones' old ship, the *Firebird*. It wants only a captain who's man enough to command it, and a crew to work it. I have money and I have a boy who is near enough to being Jones' own mind.'

Red nodded, eyeing me with what might have been a glimmer of respect.

She continued, 'And I have a hunger equal to your own, Captain, with a mind and spirit you'll not find on any ship or in any harbour.'

'My men won't accept women on board.'

She laughed. 'Your men will accept what you tell them to accept! And what we *pay* them to accept. Is it not so?'

Red opened his mouth to argue; but he gave a sigh, rubbed his reddened, sleepless eyes and nodded once more.

She asked, 'You accept my terms, then?'

'Yes, damn you!'

And thus began a series of meetings between myself, Madame Helena and the moody, vicious Red. Each day – sometimes twice a day – we would work upon some part of Captain Jones' instructions and try to decide what he was going on about. Some of the time I could explain what he meant; often I had to shake my head, mystified - when Red would curse and slap me about the face until Madame Helena chose to stop him.

After this first meeting, Madame Helena waved me away and I crept back to my room, where I managed to read a chapter of my book before someone shouted, 'Jack! Where are you? *Jack!*'

I rose gladly this time, for it was 3 o'clock and time for me to go to Amy.

This was an arrangement that had been made on the day I arrived back from the prison with a guard's rough hand clenching my shoulder. Amy was responsible for the ship's accounts, and I was to be the slave who copied out invoices and added up columns.

That was meant to be my punishment, but I loved every moment of it. I delighted in its precision: in the solid reassurance of numbers carefully entered, totalled, extracted and balanced one against the other.

At first, Amy treated me with some coolness; but once she discovered that I could add a column of figures in my head faster than she could enter them on the adding machine, she became almost friendly.

I was soon carrying out most of the basic tasks, leaving her free to catch up with all the work that Madame Helena piled upon her. She produced summaries and forecasts and lists of what she called "variances". She drew graphs and charts. She made lists that the fierce Madame scanned and asked questions about, but more respectfully now. Madame Helena smiled upon her once, and then three times in one day; and Amy smiled also upon me.

I went now to the small study we used for our accounting and took up my quill pen. Soon we were immersed in quiet scribbling, broken by the occasional mild oath as a pen nib broke or the list of numbers didn't tally.

I took up a bill received from a minor ship's stockist, a "chandler" named Omar Vlstg. I wondered for a moment at the name and then entered the details in the book of the cost ledger before turning to a separate book to record the amount we owed him.

'A fifth of a penny?' I asked Amy. 'Is there such a thing?'

She shrugged. I entered the amount, then paused, suspicious.

'He's provided the ship with a thousand candle ends,' I said, reading the bill. 'Who in their right mind would want to buy the scummy ends of candles?'

'Mice,' she suggested, her eyes fixed on a line of figures.

I drew a mouse on the bill, a shifty looking creature with half a dozen candle ends clasped to his furry breast. I passed the bill across to her, and she laughed delightfully.

She took a fresh piece of paper and drew another mouse, an Accounting Mouse this time, chained to his desk, eyes sad, little paws scribbling away. The bill read:

"For the provision of Triple Entry Accounting Services... one-third of a farthing (errors and omissions excepted).... Payment within one year... signed with a sigh... Omar Vlstg"

She passed the new bill to me, and I saw how much better an artist she was than I. I also saw that the first bill was a total fake, created by herself.

Over the next few days we expanded the account of the astonishing Omar Vlstg. He billed us for Small Dreams, the Tips of Albatross Wings, and Illustrated Copies of the works of the mouse philosopher Bunstropple; he bought from us the Worn Linings of Sea Boots and several buckets of Ocean Froth - all in units that defied monetary expression, such as fifteenths of a shilling or cubed farthings. His account balance was never more than a few pence in total and he never asked for, or offered, payment.

Every bill and every sale was recorded on an elaborately designed document. There would always be a drawing of Omar himself, sometimes with attendants: pirates, dragons, dwarves, rats dressed as kings, rabbits in shabby waistcoats and fish wondering why they were so far out of the water.

The fourth day after Red's visit, we were working quietly when Madame Helena entered with a bill from the sail maker. She and Miss Amy had a long discussion about what had been ordered, and Amy began fishing through some papers on her desk.

'What's that?' asked Madame Helena suddenly, pointing.

I saw Amy redden, and guessed what Madame Helena was looking at.

'It's just a bill, Madame.'

'May I see it? ... Thank you.'

The bill was studied in silence while Amy and I tried not to look at each other.

'Who is this man who claims to have removed all the knots from the ship's rigging?' asked Madame Helena. 'I don't recall seeing anyone do that.'

I could see that Amy was terrified about being found out, so I said the first thing that came into my head:

'You might not have noticed him, Madame Helena. He's quite... umm... *small.*'

Amy stifled a nervous giggle.

I saw the danger in what I'd just said and added, 'Not that I've seen him myself, of course. Miss Amy told me that he's small. And he always goes about in grey, and avoids sunlight.'

Madame looked at the ceiling, thinking. 'Short hair?' she asked.

'Very short,' I said. 'More like fur than hair, really. And his ears stick up. Or - or so I'm told.'

Amy had covered her face with her hands now, and her shoulders were quivering.

'Yes,' said Madame Helena. 'I think I remember him. Why has he charged us so little for a day's work? A third of a farthing?!'

'He's not very good at it, Madame Helena,' I said gravely.

Amy rose suddenly and dashed from the room, holding a handkerchief to her face and making odd sounds.

'What's wrong with that girl?' demanded Madame Helena, glaring at me accusingly. 'Have you been upsetting her?'

'It's Omar,' I said, again clutching at the first thought that came to me. 'She – she *feels* for him. He's not very strong, you see, and I think she pities him.'

Madame's doubtful eyes were boring into me, and I became reckless in my invention: 'And.. and she likes him. A lot. You know... the way women sometime do... because she thinks he's handsome, and timid, and because he draws so beautifully. All the bills he sends us are like that one.'

Madame Helena looked down at the invoice for knot removal, decorated with a picture of a mouse hopelessly entangled in knitting yarn, being forced to walk the plank by an angry, piratical rat armed with a sword.

'I do *not* believe in charity,' she said with distaste, as if she were being asked to kiss the feet of a beggar. 'Even a third of a farthing is too much for work done badly. Don't pay him for it.'

'I will make a note of that, Madame,' I said, taking up my pen and scribbling on a piece of scrap paper.

Amy returned then, wiping her eyes. 'I apologise, Madame,' she said. 'I was overcome sudden-like.'

Madame Helena looked down at her coldly, saying, 'This Omar, whom you no doubt imagine yourself in love with –'

Amy gasped with astonishment.

'– I know what you girls are like, Amy! This Omar deserves neither your sympathy nor our finances. I have instructed that he will not be paid for this - this *incompetence*.'

She waved the bill at Amy, then added, 'However, he draws well, and if he were to provide some small sketches of our ship, I might be interested in purchasing them. See to it.'

'Yes, Madame,' Amy said in an unsteady voice, then hid

her face in the handkerchief again.

'I'm disappointed with you, Amy!' Madame Helena exclaimed sharply as she left the room, shutting the door harder than she needed to. As her footsteps died away, Amy looked up from her handkerchief and we both melted into uncontrollable, guilty laughter.

The time for departure was coming soon, but it was undecided whether I should go with the ship. Madame Helena was still squeezing concessions from Red: the size of cabin she and her ladies should have, the firearms permitted, how much fresh water, how much white wine in comparison with rum; and of course, the shares to be had of the treasure.

She was planning to sit down with Red and myself as soon as agreement had been reached. We would go through Captain Jones' directions line by line, and I would tell them what the Captain had meant by the remaining odd phrases that he had cunningly worked into the document (to such an extent that Red now despaired of finding the treasure without my guidance).

Once they had the answers they needed, I could be left behind. I must admit that I liked this idea. I felt sick even in rowboats; and for this journey, I knew I had much more to fear than simply being seasick for a couple of months...

Yet I wasn't happy about staying here, either. I tried to work this out when I woke in the night, telling myself that these feelings meant nothing – that I didn't desire adventure, nor pirate gold, nor even the chance to stand next to the lovely Amy, both of us leaning upon the railing and gazing upon a sea dappled in moonlight.

Perhaps I would be waking at night still, if something had not happened which changed my mind.

I was in the middle of recording another bill from Omar Vlstg, this time for the Polishing of the Taffrail Log.

'What's one of those?' I asked Amy.

'It's a piece of wood on a line, which they throw out from the back of the boat. They use it for calculatin' the boat's speed.'

Amy had read up about boats and knew more than most sailors, I think. I was looking at the latest drawing of Omar – holding an oddly shaped piece of wood between his little paws – when the Sister called Sandra pushed open the study door, tweaked my hair from behind, and told me there was a man come to see me.

She added, 'Madame says if you don't say exactly as she's taught you, then you can be sure he'll have your balls pulled out through your nostrils. And that's nothing compared with what *she'll* do to you!'

I rose slowly, trying to recall my many lessons with Madame Helena. Amy came over to me and squeezed my hand kindly.

'You'll be all right,' she said. 'Really you will.'

I tried to believe her as I followed Sandra to the front parlour. I had a suspicion as to who was waiting for me.

I passed between two large men at the door armed with knives, swords, pistols and pungent body odour. One of them was tall, broad and black; the other was pale skinned but otherwise no different in shape or intent.

Madame Helena was in her usual chair, veiled and with her cane across her knees. She was talking quietly to a tall, thin man seated to her left; he turned his head as I entered and studied me like a butcher sizing up a piece of meat.

He was an old man, but upright and elegant and conscious of his exalted position. He was feared by every person in the nation apart from the King himself, and knew it.

He waited until I was standing before him, then turned to his left and received a large book from a boy standing at his elbow. He opened it to a blank page and took up a pen that the boy held out for him.

'Thank you, William,' he said.

The boy William – who was perhaps a year or two older

than I – was dressed in gold and green, with lace cuffs and curled blond hair. He sneered at me and then looked away, yawning with pretended boredom.

'Mr Jack... Hampton?' the tall man asked. 'You do not take your father's name?' His voice was soothing and melodious, but softly accusing; it was beautiful and cold, like a dagger carved from ice.

'I was brought up by my aunt,' I said. 'It was her choice.'

'But from the tone of your answer, you do not agree with her choice?' he asked smoothly.

I clenched my fists and said nothing.

'I see.' The man wrote something in his book. 'And do you know who I am, Mr Hampton?' He looked at me steadily.

'You are the King's High Inquisitor,' I said, returning his gaze.

He seemed to be waiting for me to say more. When I did nothing but look back at him, he said, 'That is merely my calling, Mr Hampton: it is the role I perform for my King. My title is Lord Pinces, and my family has been ennobled within the Royal Court for generations. One of my forebears wrote the charter that united the four kingdoms. I was the King's High Sherriff when we overcame the Picts, Celts, Moors and Blacks. We stood with the King against the Guardians and completely destroyed them. We are the King's men: brave and loyal.'

I nodded, aware that I had no similar claims to make about me or my family: and knowing that this was exactly what he wanted me to feel.

He continued, 'And do you know why I am here?'

I fought the desire to say something rude. I said nothing instead.

He shook his head at my silence. 'I believe you have spent many evenings recently with Mr Jones, formerly the King's Pirate.'

'Yes, sir. *Captain* Jones was very kind to my aunt and myself.'

'Oh – Mr Hampton – there is no need to justify your visits to me. Mr Jones' kindness or otherwise is no concern of mine.'

I smiled at this; he had put me in the wrong so effortlessly. 'If you say so, sir,' I said.

'I believe you were there when Mr Jones escaped from the prison.'

'Yes, I think so,' I said, trying to look as if I was seriously uncertain about it.

'You *think* so? Did you not witness his escape? I believe that is what you told the guards.'

I glanced at Madame Helena. Her eyes were watching me from beyond the veil.

'It was a confusing time,' I said. 'When I arrived, there was a fight between the Captain and the warder. I was thrown across the room by the warder, and then ran down to warn the guard. I don't know what happened to the Captain, and I didn't see him escape.'

This was the way I'd been coached to tell it. Unfortunately, I am a bad liar and I think the Inquisitor sensed this.

He flicked back through his book and ran his finger down a page. It was as if he was drawing an icy finger down my spine.

He said, 'It was a confusing time as you say, Mr Hampton. You gave two slightly different stories that morning, and I believe you have now given a third.'

I shrugged and looked away to my right, back towards the door – but found myself looking into the face of the Inquisitor's assistant, who was smirking broadly, thinking no doubt that his master had caught out another common little liar and would soon burn the truth out of him.

The Inquisitor continued in his calm, crushing voice: 'Perhaps there is something more, Mr Hampton - something you are keeping from us because you wish to protect your friend? That is noble of you, but foolish. The truth will come out; why resist it?'

He looked at me steadily and I found my eyes were now

fixed upon his, much against my will. He said quietly, in a voice that chilled me to my core: 'I could have you delivered to my rooms tomorrow, Mr Hampton. I know that I would have the truth from you within minutes: painful minutes that for you would seem to last for hours.'

He paused to let that sink in. Then he said, almost kindly, 'Tell me what truly happened, and I give my word that you will not suffer for it. Mr Hampton - Jack - tell me now and I will not bother you with it again: what was your part in this escape?'

I lost my good sense and asked angrily, 'What are you suggesting? That I broke into the prison, beat up a warder four times my size, and carried the Captain out in my pocket?'

Madame Helena was shaking her head at me, but it was too late. I couldn't stop now.

'He was too good for you, wasn't he?' I raved. 'You can't bear it when a man plays the game all the way to the end and wins it on the final throw of the dice, leaving all of you looking like fools. I'm glad he's escaped. I would have helped him escape, if I could. But I tell you this - and it's the most truthful thing you'll hear tonight - when I walked up the steps into the prison that morning, my only thought was to be with him during his final hours before he was hanged.'

There was silence now, with everyone looking at me; Madame Helena sorrowfully I imagined, the Inquisitor with curiosity and the sneering boy with a triumphant scowl.

The Inquisitor wrote for several minutes in his book while I stood awkwardly before him, regretting that I'd opened my mouth. Finally, the man looked up at me once more and asked whether I trusted "Mr Jones".

'Of course.'

He shook his head at me. 'Jones was one of the most accomplished deceivers of our time, Jack. Had you never thought that perhaps he sometimes deceived *you* a little?'

I bit my lips to stop myself from arguing; I knew I would just make this worse.

He continued: 'Jones robbed and cheated his way across the world, lying effortlessly and with enormous skill. He twisted men's minds and tied them into knots, Jack. He was the best King's Pirate ever known. And why? Because he made people trust him and then betrayed them, time and again. He even betrayed your parents; surely you know that?'

I couldn't stop the words this time. 'That's a lie!' I shouted. 'He loved them! He wouldn't – he *couldn't!*'

There was a snigger to my right. The pampered fool of a boy was looking at me with a fine mixture of condescending pity and scorn.

The boy said archly, 'It's a fact of science, that when you deny something so strongly, it's proof that you believe it.'

I went cold with anger all of a sudden, cold and sick to my stomach, feeling - alongside all the victims of bullying since the world began – how the powerful can turn all things against you and can destroy all your hope, simply by agreeing amongst themselves that they're right and you're wrong.

But I wasn't about to go down without giving the bully as least one good kicking.

'Is that true?' I asked William the Inquisitor's Boy. 'And is it also true what they say at Court – that you've got a willy so small that the ladies call you Wee Willy behind your back?'

'How dare you!' The boy put up his fists and stepped towards me, but stopped at a sign from his master.

'Ha!' I said. 'What did you just tell me? "*It's a fact of science, that when you deny something so strongly, it's proof that you believe it*"? Looks like it's true this time!'

The Inquisitor waved his boy towards a corner of the room. He said to me, 'William is of noble birth, and you will not insult him. Are you not aware that a commoner can be imprisoned for an outburst such as yours?'

I shrugged.

'I will make allowances for you, because he should not have baited you. I make allowances for him also, for he has good cause to hate you: your father killed his father.'

While I was trying to take this in, he returned to his measured questioning.

'I do not wish to cause you any grief,' he lied. 'Yet I would be doing you a discourtesy if I hid from you the true nature of Mister Jones. Let me suggest, humbly, that you are a trusting child of fifteen who quite rightly respects and even likes this mysterious man who has provided you and your aunt with food, shelter and a position in society. You do not of course truly know this man or fully comprehend the tangled history of his life, in all its good and evil dimensions.'

'I accept that,' I said, not accepting it at all.

'Let me suggest one further thing: that perhaps it was no coincidence that you were at the prison just before dawn. No, no – I do not suggest that you planned this together; that was never Jones' way. But he may have said things the night before, dropped hints, painted in your mind such a picture of the following day that you were bound by honour to turn up just as - and when - he intended you to do.'

I said nothing. I was aware that I was holding my breath and that my mind was racing, turning over all that had happened in that prison cell, wondering, doubting.

Finally, I shook my head. 'He said goodbye as if he never expected to see me again,' I said. But I knew the Inquisitor had planted a ugly seed in my head, which would grow into a weed of doubt.

'He was a fine actor,' replied the Inquisitor.

'*Was*?' I asked. 'You keep talking of him in the past. Is he – did he - ?'

'I was hoping *you* would know the answer to that,' the man answered coolly, his eyes upon mine. When he found no reply forthcoming – for I knew nothing – he said something else, as if it was of little importance but with an odd spacing of the words as if he had come to a matter at the centre of his concern, something beyond the control of both his power and his voice.

'Did he speak to you of… a man named Fat Mathers? Or one called Smithson Black?'

I shook my head.

'They were the Technicians involved in questioning Mr Jones. They were excellent men, Jack. Dedicated. Thorough. Inventive. And kind men, too. Mathers was involved in his local guild; he raised money for children's hospitals. Black had three children and an adoring wife. They were solid citizens who liked a joke, a good song and a few drinks.'

'They were his *torturers*, were they?'

'Call them that if you must. They served their King in the calling that He chose for them, and were true to that calling for twenty-five years. But no longer. Four nights ago, Mathers was killed on a circular rack he had built himself, a brilliant piece of machinery that he thought would save our clients much anguish in the long run. It was so painful, you see, that confession would come quickly. We found him the next morning, stretched around it backwards, with his toes touching the back of his head.'

I shook the image from my mind and tried not to listen to the unyielding voice that now trembled a little:

'Smithson Black was an expert on what the vulgar call water-boarding. A client is secured to a board and nearly drowns for long periods; it is always effective in securing confessions, though sometimes it is *too* effective and the client claims to be responsible for a dozen crimes that he or she cannot have committed. Black died two nights ago, on a board set a fraction too low for survival. It would have been a long, slow, uncertain death.'

He paused, and I closed my eyes against the urgent searching of his own eyes. I tried to imagine the lives of men like him and his "technicians", but couldn't. There was a cold evil in their work: an evil specifically human and yet somehow empty of all we wish to call humanity. I could make no sense of it, as if my thoughts were trying to climb a wall of glass and could find nothing to hold onto.

I opened my eyes again and asked, 'Are you saying the Captain did this?'

The Inquisitor shook his head. 'I do not need to say it; the facts proclaim it for themselves. And yet … yet I wish not to believe it.'

He leaned forward out of his seat towards me, and for the first time I saw that his face was lined, the wrinkles hidden by powder but deepening as he spoke, so that he looked haggard and exhausted. I knew, suddenly, that he was terrified.

'Mr Hampton – Jack – did he speak of me?' His voice was again uneven.

I opened my mouth to deny it; but there came to me a memory of the Captain talking of what he would do if he were out of the prison.

'Yes, sir,' I said softly. I was surprised to hear the pity in my voice. The Inquisitor heard it too; and he turned his head to the floor.

I said, 'I'm sorry, sir. He spoke about you and his torturers on his final night. He –'

The Inquisitor cut me off with the wave of a bony hand. 'There's no need,' he said.

He stood up suddenly, shutting his book with a snap. 'In any case, I have nothing to fear. I have the King's own guards about me day and night. I have done my duty and have earned the right to live in peace. Which I shall do.'

Yet his face gave him away. I never saw a man who so dreaded the coming night.

After seeing the Inquisitor, his sullen boy and the enormous guards out the door, Madame Helena returned to where I stood in the parlour, still staring dully at the floor. She slapped me hard across the face.

'How dare you?' she shouted at me. When I continued to

look at my feet, she slapped me again.

'I gave you clear instructions,' she said more calmly. 'They were crafted for your own safety. Yet you ignored them.'

'But he said –' I began.

'*Of course* he said such things! Did I not warn you? Everything he and the boy said – *everything!* – was devised for the purpose of entrapping you. All you had to do was hold your tongue. And now –'

She removed her veil and fixed me with naked, burning eyes. 'Tomorrow he will open his books and decide whether to send for you. If he does, I will meet his request; and gladly. Do you understand?'

'Yes, Madame Helena,' I said glumly. 'And if he doesn't send for me?'

'Then I must decide what to do with you.'

I nodded. 'Can I go with you?' I asked. 'On the ship?'

'Saving your skin, are you?'

'Yes, Madame.'

She turned and strode to the door, paused, turned back and said with the ghost of a smile:

'You gave that despicable boy a bloody nose. Well done.'

And by such unexpected twists was my fate decided. I was to join the pirate crew, if I was still alive in three days' time.

I spent a wretched night. Even in my dreams I saw that crafty, cruel face considering me: deciding what to do. When I turned from that face and tried to flee, strong hands seized me and two hulking brutes – one dark, one light – took hold of opposite arms and began pulling me apart.

5 Trial by Ordeal

When a seven is rolled, the thrower of the dice will next cast one of the dice for the wind speed (up to Force 6) and spin the wind compass to determine the direction. When a double two is rolled, both dice will be cast, giving a total of up to Hurricane Force 12. The wind compass will also be spun.

I woke to a calm morning. Through my window I heard the chickens clucking happily in their small yard, seeming not to care that I might be dragged off and tortured at any moment.

I considered flight but quickly realised that I was being watched: Madame Helena had no intention of putting her expedition at risk to save me, and had set two of the sterner ladies as my warders.

I spent a day tormented with regrets and hallucinations. I couldn't do my accounting and upset Amy by my gloomy silences. Even the arrival on my desk of a new bill from Omar Vlstg didn't amuse me. I looked at the request for three-sevenths of a penny for Straightening the Mizzenmast, sighed and dropped it on the pile of Things to Do if I Live that Long.

As the day passed, the shadows of fear began to roll back. In the late afternoon I was able to drink a cup of tea and eat a little cake, and was just considering having a second slice when one of the ladies came bustling into the kitchen and whispered something to my minders.

In a movement that brought a sudden memory of my dream, each of them took an arm and pulled me along the twisting corridors to the front room.

He was waiting for me: the enormous black guard. He didn't say anything; he simply nodded to the ladies and to the veiled figure of Madame Helena at the window, then placed a hand upon my shoulder and propelled me firmly out the open front door.

There was a carriage waiting. The driver looked at me and said to the guard with a hard laugh, '*He* won't last long, will he?'

The guard said nothing. He pushed me into the carriage and climbed in beside me. The coach tilted and groaned to his weight, and he elbowed me along the seat so that he could sit in the middle. I was pressed against the far door, sick with the smell of him: the smell of foreign skin and sweat and unknown spices and endless pain.

The carriage lurched drunkenly along the rutted, curving drive. My guard reached across me and pulled open my window flap, so that I might watch the heartless chickens delighting amongst the tomatoes. I also caught sight of a slender arm waving at the house door behind us, before another arm pulled it back.

We travelled in silence for half an hour, along roads lined with larger houses. I was cautiously feeling along the door, working out where the handle was and deciding whether there was a lock I needed to release.

The guard looked at me, and I gave it up. Jumping out would get me only two things: some bruises, and another reason for the Inquisitor to punish me.

'Not going to try it?' the guard asked gruffly. 'Don't want to be free, then?'

'As if you cared!' I retorted.

I saw his face change. He grabbed my shirt front and twisted me round to face him.

He hissed at me: 'You think I like this? I've got a boy at home your age!'

I didn't like his pretending to have a heart. 'That makes it even worse,' I said. 'I suppose you'll say it's just your job, right? And you've got to earn a living somehow?'

He balled one great fist and said fiercely through clenched teeth, 'This – is – *not* – my – job! Get it? I'm a King's Guard. I don't work for His Inquisitorship. I'm supposed to be protecting him from attack, not escorting mouthy boys to his torture chambers. Don't you ever – *ever!* – accuse me of serving that man.'

He threw me back into my corner and unclenched his fist. He looked at me levelly and said in a whisper, 'If a boy was going to get away from me on this journey, he would have to do it as we passed the forest in about a mile from here. At one place the trees on our right come up to the edge of the road. If the coach was to fall over – (here he shifted his weight suddenly to show how this might happen) – if it *was* to fall over, then a bright boy might climb out the window and be away into those trees double-quick.'

I nodded, thinking. It would be a risk, even then. The driver probably had a weapon. The forest was an easy place to become lost in – and yet an easy place to be found in by pursuers, once the bloodhounds were released.

Then I realised something else. My guard too would be risking something. He might never again work as a King's Guard. He might even end up in prison, or worse: for the same Inquisitor who awaited me would doubtless torture the truth out of my companion.

'Why?' I asked. 'I mean, why are you doing this?'

'I've got a boy your age,' he repeated; and this time I believed him. Then he added: 'And – *the Guard stand together.*'

I stared at him. The words meant nothing, but they sent a chill through me. 'What?' I whispered.

'I knew your father,' he said, dropping his voice still lower. 'He was a good man. I've fallen since those days... fallen far. But we still stand together.'

I understood now. It was a password, from long-buried days of valour and glory.

'*The Guard stand together,*' I said slowly, wonderingly. He had been a Guardian, as my father had been – as the Captain had been, before things had become "too hot" for him.

'My father –' I began. But he shook his head at me. Even for him, it was a forbidden topic.

The forest began to close in upon us. I saw the trees thicken and gather. I looked into the welcoming darkness, then back at my huge guard and guardian.

'I'll take my chances with the Inquisitor,' I said. 'I've nothing to hide.'

'He won't care about that,' he said.

'I'll be fine,' I insisted. 'I'm not afraid.'

And for a brief time, that was true.

The Inquisitor's mansion stood half a mile off the road, surrounded by graceful gardens and soaring trees of great age. I noted yews and elms and stout oaks, broad cedars and soaring larches – and then I lost my concentration as we rolled through a grey stone arch and turned towards the house.

It was formed of granite, grim and solid in the late sun. Greys and pinks and flecks of white in glassy stone rose before me, five storeys high. It wasn't quite as broad as it was high: a stylish fortress rather than a castle.

There was a grand covered area in front of the door for the carriage to drive into. The other large guard was waiting there, one hand resting on his sword butt as he watched us dismount.

Inside, we passed along a corridor and I was delivered by my guardian to two smaller, weasel-faced men dressed in green and black uniforms – the Inquisitor's colours, I assumed. They had badges on their black peaked caps: a green hand grasping a parchment upon which was written "Seize the Truth".

One of them took my elbow in a grip that pinched and numbed it, and marched me down some stairs. The air was cold and damp and whispered to me of mouldy dungeons where men hung in chains and rotted at the King's whim...

We passed through lighted corridors panelled in dark wood, with heavy doors off at intervals. I was pulled to the very end, where my new guard knocked quietly at a door and was ordered to enter.

The Inquisitor was at the end of a long room, seated at a table facing me. He looked up from the book he was writing in and beckoned for us to approach him.

The soldier led me forward, still crushing my elbow. When I got to the table, he pushed me into a chair on the near side of it, opposite the Inquisitor.

There were four curious leather straps before me, like dog collars stapled to the table. While I was puzzling at them, he placed my right wrist onto one of the furthest straps, pulled the strap tight, then buckled it.

The buckle bit into my wrist; I shouted and struggled and head-butted my captor in the stomach, but in another moment the left wrist was also secured, followed by both forearms. The soldier stood up from his work and slapped me three times, hard, before the Inquisitor said something quietly, whereupon he bowed and left us.

I heard the door close with a click.

We were alone, and the silence was dreadful.

After many minutes of being studied and then (I assume) written about in the Book, I became aware of another sound. It was a clock, ticking somewhere behind me. I tried to screw myself round to look at it, but the fastenings prevented this.

'Tell me about the Captain.'

The pen was poised above a fresh page and the Inquisitor was looking into my eyes. The desk was narrow enough for him to be able to touch my hands without leaning forward, and he did this now, checking to see if the bonds were secure.

'What do you want to know?' I asked.

'How often did you see him?'

'Twice a week, after he went to prison. Before that, maybe once a year. He would come and stay with us for a week or two. But we didn't talk much then.'

'Did he give you anything when he was in prison?'

I hesitated, not wanting to get my aunt into trouble about the parchment. I tried to divert his curiosity:

'He gave me a game. Have you heard of the Game of Pirate? You roll some dice and choose where to place your ship and....'

The Inquisitor sighed heavily and turned from the desk. From a small table to his right he picked up an oddly shaped metal object which looked a little like the nutcrackers Aunt Emma had: a heavy ring of metal with a fat screw fixed so that when you turned the screw it bore down upon the nut you had fitted into the cracker, until it burst.

He fixed this implement about my right thumb and turned the wings of the screw until the shaft pressed against the base of the thumbnail. Then he gave it another turn.

I gasped and my stomach lurched. I hadn't dreamt there could be such pain.

He settled back in his chair and wrote again in the book, while tears streamed down my face.

'Now, Jack,' he said gently. 'You know what I was asking about. Will you answer me now?'

I nodded.

'And the answer is - ?'

I said, 'There was a parchment. I was to give it to my aunt. But then these men –'

He held up his hand and I stopped dead while he wrote in his book.

'These men, you say?' he asked when he was ready.

I told him about being captured and the parchment being stolen; and then I jumped immediately into the second meeting I had with Red, eager to get this over with and have the thumbscrew removed.

Again he stopped me and forced me to go back and tell

every humiliating detail of the evening at Aunt Emma's. When I was slow to respond to his next question - about my final visit to the prison - he sighed again as if burdened with great sorrow and tweaked the screw once more.

I think I lost consciousness for a moment. But too soon I was looking into those sharp eyes and recounting again the story of my visit to the Captain at dawn. He wrote nothing this time, simply looking at me, daring me to lie. I hesitated once, and his hand moved across the table; then I began babbling at speed, telling him everything, reckless of what harm it might do to myself.

'Good,' he said. 'You are being sensible at last. So you were responsible for Mr Jones' release? I expect you can guess the penalty for that.'

I should have been frightened; but just then all I wanted was to have the thumbscrew eased a fraction. 'I'm sorry,' I said.

'It doesn't matter,' he said. 'Jones has been recaptured and will hang tomorrow.'

I stared at him, speechless. My heart ached and I could do nothing but weep.

'Cheer yourself!' he exclaimed with an odd smile. 'This is good news for you. In the circumstances, I am inclined to be merciful – so long as you continue to co-operate.'

I continued however to cry bitterly instead, and he looked at me with distaste. 'You really are an odd child,' he said.

He turned a page in his book. 'The parchment,' he said. 'Tell me about the parchment. What is written in it?'

I shook my head, feeling stubborn now and telling myself I would protect my aunt. But I'm ashamed to say that another turn of the screw was enough for me to abandon all morality and tell everything I knew - and when he pressed me for details I was ignorant of, I simply made them up.

After half an hour of this humiliating babble, he leaned forward and eased off the screw a little. The relief was intense and I would have fallen upon my knees to thank him, if I could have done.

But he hadn't finished. He went back to the days before the Captain's imprisonment, wanting to know the names of everyone who came to the house, what they said, and if they were friends of the Captain or only of my aunt. He moved onto the Sisters, demanding everything I knew of them. I hesitated several times here, and each time the screw was tweaked and I immediately told what I knew – except that I never named Amy, and for this I suffered greatly.

He knew I was hiding something here; he had some sixth sense, as if for him there was an unnatural perfume given off by a lie or concealment.

He encircled me with questions, trying to find out who did what in the Sisterhood – arranged the meals, carried weapons, did the spying, kept the diaries. He grew annoyed with my evasive answers; but I could see he didn't much care about these facts, for he turned the screw half-heartedly and scarcely scribbled a line in his Book.

'Now, what of the Ruby?' he asked suddenly.

I knew not to hesitate now, and told him all that the Captain had told me. I rushed to the end of my little knowledge and then stopped, feeling relieved: I'd told him all I knew, and now the pain would cease.

But he turned to his table again and picked up another thumbscrew. As he fixed this to my left thumb, he said casually, like a gardener discussing the merits of one variety of tomato above another:

'This one has small dimples in the rounded part, which some find increases the pain considerably. Let me know whether you agree.'

'But – but I've told you everything!' I cried bitterly.

He shook his head.

He paused after fixing the second screw and said, as if seeking to justify himself: 'Some people call these "instruments of torture". That is simply ignorant. We call them "instruments of truth". Without them, this process would take much longer.'

'But I told you –'

'You have told me all that you *think* you know. That is not enough. There are matters you are hiding. Some of them are things honestly forgotten, and others are things you are trying not to recall, for you still have some shreds of loyalty to things and persons that long ago ceased to deserve your respect.'

There followed half an hour of intense pain. At first I babbled on, telling him meaningless details – the books the Captain owned, the few words I'd read of letters passed between him and my aunt, my suspicions that she didn't care about him and was just using him. I jabbered on until he became impatient and forceful.

'Tell me about the Ruby,' he said again. 'The truth this time!'

I went over it once more, reporting every look the Captain gave and every inflexion in his voice that told of his own puzzlement.

The Inquisitor said with some anger: 'And this parchment – did he not give you some hint that it was connected with the Ruby?'

I halted, thinking. This had never occurred to me.

He repeated, 'The parchment. Tell me about it again!'

'But if you want to see the parchment, go and get it!' I exclaimed. 'Stop asking me about things I don't know!'

He sat back in his chair and said with a triumphant smile, 'Perhaps I have already seen the parchment, and have a copy. Perhaps I think it means nothing in itself. Perhaps I think that its true meaning is known only to you.'

I shook my head.

'Come,' he said. 'Let us make a truce, and a new beginning. You and I will go through the parchment line by line and you will tell me what you know. Then I will let you go and ask you no more. But first you need to refute and condemn all traces of your former loyalty.'

'What?'

'You understand me, Jack. You are the friend of one traitor and the son of another. Curse them both, and have done
with them forever.'

I gaped at the man. What had this to do with the information he wanted?

'Enough!' he cried. 'Tell me you curse all traitors to our
King and our land!'

'I – I – of course I do,' I stammered.

'And you curse those whom the King curses.'

'I th-think I do.'

'You *think* you do?'

'I don't know them,' I complained. 'I don't know their
crimes. I – I am not their judge.'

'And you refuse to accept the judgement of your King
and his Advisers?'

'I don't know,' I said. 'But I know that my curse would
mean nothing. It would be empty words – words I say out
of fear and nothing more.'

The Inquisitor rose from his seat and began walking to
and fro before me. He said with some passion in his voice,
'Your father was leader of a sect that calls itself the Guardians. It is an evil faith. He sought to bring what he called
freedom to the peoples, setting free the slaves and raising
servants above their masters. He spoke against our teaching, our science, our way of life. When we pried him from
his hiding place, he refused to confess his crimes and the
planned crimes of his fellows. As a result, this kingdom of
Albion was almost destroyed. King Arinaeus himself was
forced to flee for a time.'

'My – father – refused to talk?' I asked.

The Inquisitor said nothing, but his face was flaming. He
continued to pace to and fro. And as he strode before me in
angry silence, I was consumed by shame that I had confessed so easily, when my father had held out to the end.

'I invite you to curse that man,' the Inquisitor said at last.
'That man - and the movement he belonged to - and the

false beliefs he held.'

I said, 'My father wouldn't have cursed at your command.'

The Inquisitor stopped, unsettled. 'Of course he did,' he said. 'They all do.'

'He didn't,' I said. 'Nor did the Captain.'

I could see that my guess had struck him in a tender place. He immediately reached across and gave each thumbscrew a vicious twist.

For a few minutes I couldn't speak; I could hardly breathe for the pain. But in those minutes something changed inside me, and I knew I could withstand him now.

'Curse him!' the Inquisitor demanded. 'Curse him, and be released!'

'We stand together,' I said in hoarse voice.

'What? *What?!*' he exclaimed.

'The Guard still stand,' I said, 'and we stand together.'

I had the pleasure of seeing the colour drain from his face. His right hand clutched at his chest and his eyes narrowed to slits.

He seemed about to do something dire, when the clock behind me made a sound – as if it was striking the hour with a muffled hammer. A moment later, there was a quiet knocking at the door.

'We will continue this in half an hour,' said the Inquisitor in a strained, gasping voice.

A queer and twisted smile forced itself upon his face. 'My assistant will be arriving soon,' he said. 'You remember William, of course? He begged to be allowed to help me today. He is a fine inquisitor; but you will discover that yourself soon enough.'

My face must have fallen, for his smile grew yet more twisted and triumphant.

'Please can I use the toilet?' I asked, for I'd been aching to go for the past hour.

He ignored me and bent to make one more scribble in his book before walking away. I was about to ask again, but realised that this was all part of the torture: me begging to be allowed to go, being ignored each time, and then the humiliation as I eventually wet myself, or worse.

I heard the door open and close, followed by muffled sounds in the corridor that retreated and died. I put my head on the table and thought about weeping.

But not for long.

I sat up again and tried to look around, to fix on something – anything – except the continuing pain. I *must* have a plan. When that boy William came in I would – what? My hands were fastened to the...

With a hoarse croak of joy I leaned forward and began pulling with my teeth at the strap that fastened my right hand to the table. I just needed to pull the strap back through the buckle and over the metal tongue, and I would be free!

I was congratulating myself as I bit and tugged at the salty leather, tasting the sweat and tears of countless victims. I told myself that I must have upset the Inquisitor so much that he forgot to tie me to the chair back. Just a few more tugs and the strap would come through the first part of the buckle...

I heard a noise behind me – the door opening and heavy footsteps approaching quickly. I bit and pulled frantically, feeling the leather slide, tugging against the metal: only a fraction more now.

But then a heavy hand took my shoulder and eased me back into my chair.

I had been so close...

A deep voice said, 'Well done, boy.' A large black hand reached over and pulled the strap a little more: and my oddly thin and pale hand flopped free.

The large black guard then unfastened both screws and the other straps. I tried to stand but fell immediately, so he pulled me up and held me upright as I walked.

There was a small room off to the right just before the

door and he pushed me into this, saying he would be back in a few minutes.

'You need to be washed and looking fresh when I get back,' he said. I found myself in a tiny bathroom, and not a moment too soon.

When he returned, I was pacing the room slowly, trying to get the blood moving in my legs. He took a small jar from a pocket and smeared some evil-smelling ointment onto my bruised and throbbing thumbs.

'It'll hurt to start with,' he said gruffly. I nodded: it stung like the fires of hell.

'Come.' He led me out the door and back along the corridor.

'But why – what –'

He looked at me sternly and said, 'The Inquisitor has ordered your release. You'll say to anyone who asks, that he questioned you closely and that under torture you told him all he wanted to know. You'll tell them I came and escorted you from the house and sent you home.'

'But –'

'That's all.'

We passed the guards' station, which was empty now. The King's Guard picked up a green and black hat that had somehow been left on the floor and dropped it behind a settee a little further along. My eyes followed the hat and came to rest on a pair of black boots sticking out from behind the settee – boots with motionless legs attached. I looked at my guardian and he shook his head at me.

'Don't ask,' he said.

As we came to the front door, the other large King's Guard ran down the stairs and gave my guard a small, rolled scroll before turning and running back up.

The scroll was passed to me.

'The Inquisitor has signed your release,' said the guard. 'That's all you need to know.'

I unrolled the scroll and read:

By the power vested in me by His August Majesty
~~ Arinaeus the Deathless ~~
I hereby proclaim and instruct all others:
The youth named Jack Hampton is declared a loyal and true sub-
ject of His Majesty and is to be given free passage within the
Kingdom, and may come and go at his pleasure.

Sealed by Johannes Pinces
Grand High Inquisitor to His Majesty the King.

The scroll was dated and sealed with fresh red wax. I ran my finger over the lines of the seal, hardly able to take it in.

'The carriage waits,' said my guard, pushing me towards the open front door, where my carriage was outlined against the early evening sky. We passed through and I turned to thank him; but he wasn't looking at me. He was again the remote King's Guard, handing me over to the waiting driver.

As I prepared to board the carriage, a rather grander craft came bouncing along the drive, pulled by fine white horses. Its driver reined in just behind my own carriage, then jumped down to hand out the noisome youth I had met the night before.

The boy William – the Inquisitor's assistant - was dressed in white silk and had an absurd tasselled white hat upon his head.

He stared at me. 'What's this?' he demanded of the guard. 'Where does he think he's going?'

'He has a release,' said the guard quietly.

The boy strode up to me and snatched the scroll from my hand. He read it to the end, with an expression of utter dismay on his face.

'I do not – this cannot –' and he made as if to tear the precious document in two.

A large hand closed over the boy's right wrist and squeezed it hard, until he released the scroll. The guard passed the document back to me.

He said to the boy William, 'I am asked to say that His Inquisitorship –'

But the boy turned from him with a flounce and tried to push past him up the steps.

The guard moved between him and the door.

'I'm commanded to let no one in tonight,' he said.

'I am *not* "no one",' said the boy with a proud, simpering smile. 'He will see *me*.' And he tried to push the guard to one side.

The guard caught him and lifted him from the ground with one hand; then he threw him down the steps.

The Inquisitor's Assistant rolled in the gravel and gave a howl as he rose from the ground. I thought for a moment that he was hurt; but it was his dress he was concerned about.

'You fool!' he cried. 'Look what you've done to my suit! And I've got horse crap on my hat! Oh, you're for it now. When I tell the Inquisitor what you've done, you'll never work again. You might never walk again either...'

He put on an evil sneer, which didn't have the effect he hoped for, since he had manure on his left cheek.

The guard shrugged his massive shoulders. 'The Inquisitor will be pleased that I've done my duty,' he said. 'You may tell him whatever you wish – but not today. I've been commanded to say that you may wait upon him at this time tomorrow.'

The boy put his nose up at this and walked back to his carriage. 'You're dead!' is all he said before slamming shut the carriage door. His carriage shot off down the drive and disappeared out through the gate before mine had worked up to a gentle trot.

6 On Board

There are two things we truly long for: the assurance that we matter and the assurance that we are right. The rest is only appetite. (From the collected works of Bunstropple, mouse and philosopher)

The journey home was uneventful. The driver asked how I'd fared, and I showed him my thumbs.

'Ah, you're one of the lucky ones,' he said. 'I seen 'em not able to walk afterwards. Or not comin' out at all.' He didn't seem to care about it either way – it was just something that happened to some people.

When we arrived at the house, Amy came running out, with a couple of the other girls behind her. I was fussed over very nicely for the evening; but then woken early the next morning as usual and ordered to light the kitchen fire and sweep the floors.

The day passed happily after that, apart from my aching thumbs. Yet even here I found some comfort, for from time to time I would stop and gaze at my hands and think: *I survived this. Maybe I was weak to start with, but once I knew what was at stake, I could bear the pain, and hold out.*

But when I wondered what would have happened if the Inquisitor had returned to torment me, my pride seemed very empty indeed.

As night fell, I thought of the boy William and his return to the Inquisitor's mansion. I didn't have to wonder long about this, for within an hour there were soldiers banging at the door and demanding to see me.

While one soldier questioned me, his captain read through my Release several times. Then he snapped his fingers to stop his inferior and took over the interrogation.

'When did you last see the Inquisitor?' he asked.

'When he left me to write out my Release,' I said. This was stretching the truth, but I was fighting for my life.

'What happened next?'

'He sent a King's Guard to escort me outside and I was put into a carriage with that Release in my hand,' I said.

He was looking directly at me, and I looked back at him coolly.

'Is that all?' he asked. 'Nothing else? Nothing unusual?'

'Nothing unusual, except –' I paused on purpose, trying to look as if I was thinking hard.

'Yes?'

'That boy – his assistant – he came and argued with the King's Guard as I was getting in the carriage.'

'Oh.' He drummed his fingers on the table we were sitting at, then pushed the Release back to me.

'Has something happened?' I asked as I fingered that wondrous document.

He shook his head and rose from the table. 'Thank you for your time,' he said.

As the last soldier closed the door, Vicky – who with the equally tough and shapely Sandra always accompanied Madame on her trips to town, their dark hair cropped short and both of them dressed in frills and low cut tops like a burlesque bodyguard - turned about and began dancing down the corridor.

'He's gone!' she squealed. 'Gone! Never coming back!'

'Victoria!' exclaimed a deeper voice and we all turned to look at Madame Helena, standing at the other end of the corridor.

'The Inquisitor's gone, Madame!' squealed Vicky again, not in the slightest dismayed by Madame Helena's evil gaze. 'One of the soldiers told me! He wasn't there when that poncey boy went to see him at his house this evening – *no one* was there!'

Madame Helena's face was impassive, but I could see her

eyes glowing. She turned one bright eye upon me then, a knowing eye: for I'd told her all I had seen, including the motionless feet in the boots behind the settee.

By lunch on the following day, most of the city knew that the Inquisitor had disappeared, and with him the two enormous King's Guards; and no one knew where the Inquisitor's own guards were, either. There were a dozen theories but no facts, and I liked it that way.

I applied myself to tidying up the accounts, and then to packing my trunk for the voyage we would take the next day. I hesitated before adding the Game of Pirate to the trunk, thinking that I would lose its pieces or come back with my beloved box waterlogged and broken. But then I tucked it into the lopsided sweater that Aunt Emma had knitted for me in an unusual fever of affection a couple of days earlier.

I slept that night better than I'd done for weeks. The only thing that troubled my dreams was the recollection that the Captain had been recaptured. I knew that the Inquisitor might be lying, but I also knew that there was no particular reason for him to lie. Yet in my dreams the Captain was still alive and riding a great white horse up a beautiful hillside, laughing fit to burst....

The next morning saw me dragging a great sea trunk behind me as I climbed a gangplank to the *Firebird*.

Before now, I had seen the ship as a total of diverse invoices for so much tar, pork and biscuit. Now the ship itself rose above me, an object of such intense beauty that I had to stop every few paces and gaze up at its sleek lines and soaring masts.

It was what they called a caravel redonda. It had three backward-slanting masts which gave it great agility, and the ability to sail close-hauled against the wind. Two of these masts could be moved and set upright, when it became a square rigged galleon that could outpace almost any craft with the wind behind it.

I pulled my trunk over the end of the gangplank and looked around for help. I asked a passing sailor where I should stow it.

'Up yer arse,' I was told. He slapped me about the head and continued about his business.

I pushed my luggage to one side of the deck and went in search of the Sisters. Madame had decided that she would bring only Amy and the two big toughs: Vicky and Sandra.

I ended up sitting in a dark corner, watching the final accounts being settled. Amy had come with a handful of bills neatly ordered in a packet, and now she sat at a desk in Madame Helena's cabin while various tradesmen came, tipped their caps to an unveiled Madame Helena, winked at Red, met with Amy, then retreated scowling.

Amy was common, blunt and firm. She could smell a scam at fifty paces and knew the difference between kiln-dried oak and shoddy yellow pine. A good third of the applicants ended up shouting at her: but it was no good – she would point at what they were charging and ask them to explain it. Then she and Madame Helena would stare them down as they blustered, complained and finally settled for a much smaller figure.

One man stepped forward, making as if to swing at the two, but Red coughed meaningfully and his fist hung in the air. Another was not so lucky. He did swing, and then collapsed in pain. I didn't see what happened but saw Madame Helena's smile and felt the now-familiar twisting in my stomach as I wondered what power she truly wielded.

The man on the floor was groaning over and over again:

'You cheating bitches... I'm an honest man... you cheating bitches... I'm –'

Amy had thrown her hands before her pale face to shield off the blow, but had recovered herself now and was studying her papers again, brushing aside her blond fringe.

'Mr Collins,' she said, 'you were to provide twelve casks of rum. There were twelve, I agree, and they were all full. But only the first cask had full strength rum in it. I tested the others with your own man in attendance, and they were half water. By lip, by float, by flame, by every measure they were half strength.'

'They was rum when I loaded 'em on the ship,' said the man. ''Twas your own evil magic what changed the alcohol to water.'

'Then take them back,' Amy invited. 'Perhaps the magic will reverse itself.'

'You can shove them up your –' the man began, but another spasm shook his body and he gave a cry of pain.

'Half rum, half price,' Amy said briskly. 'After deducting what you owe us for wasting our time, of course. Eleven shillings and a groat we'll pay. The groat is for your abject apology, which we are willing to receive now. No? Eleven shillings flat then. Take it now, or whistle for it from the dockside.'

She held out a small fabric bag. The unfortunate man reached up one shaking hand, claimed the bag, and staggered out of the cabin. I heard him swearing every step across the deck and down the gangway.

'Are we done?' asked Madame Helena, looking to Amy.

Amy checked a list and answered, 'Yes, Madame. Huggs and Co are the only ones who haven't come, but they know we won't pay a penny for their mouldy flour.'

'What about that small man – the one you've formed an attraction for?'

'I don't know what you mean!' Amy said haughtily.

'Oh yes, you do,' said Madame Helena with a wicked laugh. 'Made him a private payment, have you? Settled with him *personally*?'

Amy's cheeks burned as she shook her head. 'If you're speaking of Mr Vlstg, there was no debt to pay, Madame.'

I spoke up from my corner, 'He always bought as much as he sold, Madame,' I said.

'*Bought*? What on earth would someone buy from us?'

'For a start, he owns all the ship's rats,' I said from my corner. 'However, he's not been able to catch them yet...'

The harbour was a broad half circle lying to the south of the city, with dockyards and shambolic warehouses along the western side and better houses to the east, topped by a fair castle. As the sun dropped, the shadows of the warehouses stretched across the quay and climbed the side of the *Firebird*.

Sailors had gathered at the railings to watch the dying sunlight, argue, jest, and stare at our ladies standing further forward on the ship. I loitered somewhere between these two groups, not feeling part of either.

Captain Red – I couldn't think of him as simply "the Captain", for that seemed somehow disloyal to Captain Jones – came and stood beside me, looking surly. He kicked at a belaying pin and shouted to someone to "come pick it up before I poke it through your shiftless eye and pull it out through your fat, lazy backside!".

Or at least that was the meaning of what he said - his language was even fouler than usual.

Then he shouted to the tall Tom, his first mate (and Minerva's suitor), 'Where's Wheezy? Has he done a bunk?'

Tom lumbered across and said quietly so the ladies wouldn't hear, 'Nobody at his lodgings. The lads checked the local bars; no sign of him since noon yesterday.'

Red slapped the railing and cursed long and hard. 'The bitches will give us hell for this,' he concluded, jerking his head towards Madame and the girls. 'No Cook: that's all we need.'

'*They* could do the cooking.'

'Yeah – and pigs can fly, but only if you throw 'em off a cliff. Sourpuss over there won't hear of it. We'll have to bide in port another day, unless we can find a replacement cook tonight.'

As I listened to this, I noticed a lone figure moving across the darkening quay. He was pushing a barrow loaded with a large trunk and (on top of that) something covered with a bit of cloth that flapped slowly in the evening breeze.

As he approached the ship, various of the sailors – the older ones mostly – began a new argument and then I saw coins changing hands. I was accustomed by now to their incessant gambling; they would even bet on which bird of a group perched together would fly away first.

The man began to heave his barrow along the gangplank. He was in his forties or fifties, of middle height, wiry, and with a head so closely shaven as to appear bald. He had a large brassy earring in his left ear and wore a bright red shirt above black seaman's trousers. His seaboots clonked merrily and he was whistling a tune I'd not heard before but was soon to know well. *Storm at Sea*, they called it.

I'd already noticed his rolling way of walking and his somewhat bow-legged stance; now, as he came to the top of the gangway, I saw he had an odd habit of twitching his head to the right from time to time.

He came to the ship's deck and tried to push his barrow onto it, but Captain Red had moved across to bar his way.

'What the hell do you think you're doing?' he demanded.

The man took a red kerchief from a cloth bag hung over his shoulder and wiped his face with it. This done, he saluted briskly and said (with one halt for a twitch of the head): 'I'm told you're lookin' for a ship's cook, Cap'n sir – and here I am.'

His accent was what they called Airish (though Amy insisted that it should be written as Eirish) – light and cheerful, with a musical lilt to it.

Red's brow wrinkled. 'And who told you that?'

'Ah. Well, dere was dis man, you see – met 'im in a pub over in the Leet area. Name of Wilson, I t'ink he said. We had a few drinks, and he said you was a great captain and he was sorry to let you down, but his old mother was ailin', you see...'

Red shot out one massive hand to grab the man by the throat, but he grasped at thin air as the man dodged and put the barrow between them.

Red shouted, 'You're a lying son of a –'

'Captain! *Captain!*' the man said soothingly. 'Dere's ladies present!'

Red shook his huge fist at the man, who wasn't in the least bothered by that.

'Well,' the man said, twitching once more, 'if it's the truth you're wantin', dis Wilson said you was the meanest, stupidest sailor he'd ever served with and for a few florins he'd mitch off to a tavern out west, where his brother was wantin' a rough cook. So - as I've been a ship's cook before and was looking for a berth, I traded him a few florins for some of his cooking gear. And here I am: William O'Hara at your service, sir.'

The ladies had come closer to view this spectacle; the man bowed low to them before mopping his cropped head once more with his red handkerchief.

One of the older crew stepped forward and whispered in Red's ear. Red puzzled a moment, then laughed suddenly.

'Take your shirt off!' he ordered the man O'Hara.

'But Cap'n –'

'Take it off!'

O'Hara unbuttoned his shirt and removed it. Several of the crew crowded forward, and then money started changing hands again.

'Well, well, well,' said Captain Red. 'Billy Halfbones!'

The man said stiffly, 'I don't call meself dat.'

Red laughed at this and turned to me and the ladies, saying, 'Look at this tattoo – on the left side of his chest. See that? A skull and crossbones, but the skull hardly an out-line, and only one of the two bones inked in.'

One of the crew added, 'Bones here was with a sweet lit-tle tattoo artist – in the Key islands, weren't it Billy? – hav-in' a tattoo done. But they got sidetracked part way through, and then the artist's boyfriend came in and caught 'em doin' more'n just tattooing, and Bones had to run for his life.'

"Bones" shrugged his shoulders. 'Dat was long ago. I'm a better man now, I'd like you to know.' He bowed towards the ladies as he said this, but somewhat falsely I thought.

Red laughed again and asked, 'And what's the real rea-son you've come beggin' for a berth? Been caught by an-other boyfriend?'

'Nothin' of the sort!' protested Billy Bones, but with a wink to the crew and a softer comment that the ladies weren't meant to hear: 'Just dat I was livin' with a pretty young lady and her lovely sister, and dey became jealous of each other, as women do – and I thought I'd better make for the open sea afore it came to blows.'

The crew laughed knowingly.

'I thought you was dead, Billy!' shouted a grizzled and scarred sailor with an evil eye.

Bones looked at the old man. 'I know you,' he said. 'Jeb Forrest, am I right? You was one of the hands back den.' He took an old pipe from his cloth bag and poked some tobac-co into it before continuing:

'I t'ought I was dead, meself,' he said.

'Fell off this very ship, didn't you?' Forrest said, looking at Billy Bones oddly.

'Fell? *Pushed*, you mean,' the man replied quietly.

'Thought you was drunk as a dog, and bein' sick over the side when a wave tumbled you. That's what we was told.'

Billy Bones paused from lighting his pipe. 'Wasn't so drunk I couldn't hold onto a rail,' he said. 'And I sobered up pretty quick when I hit dat cold water in the darkness and saw the ship sailin' off without me - quick enough to work out who'd pushed me over the side.'

The crew were all quiet now, watching the man intently. Billy Bones put the unlit pipe to his mouth, then took it out and said, 'Cap'n Jones. Must have been him. Heard his footsteps I did, and swear I saw his fancy boots as I tumbled.'

There were murmurings at this, and I heard the one called Forrest exclaim, 'I *knew* it! The bastard!'

Bones continued, 'Makes sense, don't it? He knew I was one of Jaggy's men, one of the plotters. Can't say I blame him. Anyway, mustn't speak ill of the dead.'

'Dead?' Several voices spoke – my own included, I think.

Bones nodded. 'So they say. Took 'im the other day and stretched him this morning - dat was the local gab. But no one's seen a body, so I don't say it's for sure.'

Forrest's voice spoke again: 'How'd you survive? It was in the middle of the ocean.'

Bones shook his head. He said, 'It was black as the jaws of hell, I remember dat. The ship's lights was swallowed by the fog, leavin' just the phosphorescence of the path it had churned. And in dat eerie sea glow, great sharks was swimmin'. One nosed me, den passed on. And I hung dere, waitin' for death, makin' deals first with God and then the Devil, and then with God again (for I reckoned by then dat the Devil was on the side of the sharks). I was tellin' the Almighty dat I would give up strong spirits forever if he'd save me –'

Red poked Billy Bones in the ribs, laughing: 'Only strong spirits? Why not give up ale and wine as well?'

'I wasn't *dat* desperate yet,' said Bones mildly, causing raucous laughter throughout the crew. 'No, I'd only promised strong spirits when an empty rum cask came bobbing towards me, so I latched onto it like a barnacle on a ship's arse and rode it all night, and the next day too. The night after, when I was startin' to go crazy from thirst, I was washed onto a soft, lovely beach. Mud Island, dey call it.'

There was a murmur of assent to this: clearly, it was a place known to some of them.

Bones gave up trying to light his pipe and put it back in his bag. 'The funny t'ing is,' he said, 'I reckon Captain Jones did me a favour. Haven't touched the spirits since. I tapped dat cask I'd floated in on, and found it had a good gallon of rum still inside: but I poured it away on the sand. One of dem sacrificial offerings, you know.'

Some of the crew snorted disbelievingly at this.

'Mind you,' Bones added, 'I've had to drink twice as much ale since den to make up for it...'

After the lively cheers to this had subsided, Bones asked, 'So, Cap'n, do you have a place for a good sea cook?'

Red looked about at his crew before answering. 'I seem to recall some bad reports about your cooking,' he said. 'On the *Firebird*, I think it was. Or it may have been on that old tub - the *Tempter*, weren't it?'

'Ah, it'd be the *Firebird*,' said Bones. 'And it were partly my drinkin' – but mostly because I was undercook to the filthiest cook in the empire. He weren't called Jaggy the Poisoner for nothing, you know. I seen him blow his nose into the soup and laugh about it. "That'll thicken it for the scumdogs!" he'd say. And he used to boast about never washing his hands, not even after – well, you can imagine.'

There were groans at this.

Red asked, 'You can cook the usual? Skilly, broth, salt beef and beans?'

'All dat an' more, Captain. Been earnin' me way by it for half me life now. You won't regret takin' me on. And I can do a bit of doctorin' too, if you're needin' it. Was apprenticed to a barber surgeon for a year, up Pembrock way. Look, I brought me instruments and potions –'

He began to move the cloth-covered object from his sea trunk, when there was a plaintive cry from within it.

One of the older crew shouted, 'You got another Tiddles, then?'

Bones nodded and took the cover off, revealing a small

cage holding a grey and black kitten. 'Tiddles Five,' he announced.

'You had Tiddles Two on our voyage,' said old Forrest.

Bones sighed, 'Ah, but he was a grand cat, was Two. A fine ratter an' all. What happened to him?'

Forrest grumbled, 'Captain Jones took him; Tiddles lived in a high and fancy fashion after that.'

Bones' eyes twinkled. 'Dat explains why I was pushed overboard – Jones wanted me cat!' he laughed. 'Tiddles Two knew more tricks dan an acrobat, didn't he?'

'You taught this one any tricks yet?' asked someone as Bones lifted the kitten from the cage.

'Only had him a few days. But look here.' Bones put the kitten on the deck, stroked it a few times and then took a small piece of dried meat from a bag. He made a circular motion with his hand above the cat's head and Tiddles Five responded by doing a back flip, landing on his feet.

'Good cat!' the man said softly, feeding him the meat as the crew clapped and cheered.

'That's decided, then,' said Captain Red. 'Stow your gear alongside the galley. You'll be Cook - and Surgeon too, for we haven't anyone trained.'

Bones made a face, as if thinking. 'Captain,' he said, 'could I ask a favour? You see, what with cookin' and doctorin' and maybe a bit of carpentry (for I've the training for dat as well), I'll be a bit stretched. Could I have an undercook? Is dere a man you could spare? Someone who won't be missed from other duties, I mean: I wouldn't want to upset your running of the ship.'

Red laughed freely. 'Man!' he cried. 'You can have the most useless piece of supercargo I've ever been saddled with, and be welcome to him. If you can keep him from getting under everyone's feet, you'll be doin' me a service. Take him!'

As I looked about to see which scurvy jack tar he had in mind, I realised that every sailor was looking at me – and then Red grabbed me by the arm and dragged me before the new Cook.

Red growled at me, 'This is your master. You'll do as he says, when he says, and as he says. If he decides to beat you to a pulp with a saucepan, you'll take it like a man and then crawl along the deck to light the fire for the crew's breakfast. Understand?'

'Aye aye, Captain Red,' I said briskly, feeling sulky and embarrassed, but determined not to be shown up before Amy and the others.

Bones peered at me, then said with a little jerk of the head: 'He'll do.'

A voice now called from further forward, Madame Helena's voice: calm and authoritative. 'Captain, will this man be suitable for *our* purposes? Can he cook for ladies?'

Bones bowed again, so low that his head nearly touched the floor (I was beginning to hate his simpering, obsequious ways).

'Ah, ladies,' he sighed. 'It'll be my *pleasure* to prepare for you whatever culinary delights take your fine fancy. Beef olives in red wine wid mashed potatoes, minted peas and truffles followed by an iced sorbet to clear the palate - and den, raspberry parfait with a sprinkling of chocolate.'

'We don't have any of that on board,' observed Amy.

'What about hard tack, salted pork and boiled peas, den?' Bones asked with a smile.

The ladies were trying not to laugh, I could see: and I hated the fact that they found him amusing.

'Is that all you can manage?' Madame Helena asked, fixing the man with one of her stares.

He quickly dropped his eyes, but soon regained his cheeky composure. 'I can make a fine broth out of mutton, peas, barley and vegetables,' he said. 'And if you've got salted beef, onions and potatoes, I can cook a hash a man would kill for - and a lady would kiss for.'

I saw Vicky and Sandra sigh and exchange glances, and I hated the man even more.

He added, 'I make a fine bread, an' all. I've brought me own starters: a ball of slow yeast for a heavy bread that sticks to your ribs, and a lighter, sweeter yeast dough for something dat melts between a lady's soft, sweet lips.'

Even Amy sighed at this passage, and I resolved to kill the Ship's Cook at the earliest opportunity.

'It's a shame we have no flour,' Amy said regretfully.

'No flour?' he exclaimed. 'But dere's twenty barrels of it on the quay!'

'Mouldy,' said Madame Helena.

'We rejected it,' said Amy. 'And it was so bad that they just left it there to rot.'

'Ah, so dat's how the wind lies?' asked Bones. 'Now, I heard something about dis in the *Blue Boar* dis afternoon. The local trade was complaining bitterly about a young lady what was too sharp for her own good, telling me what they'd do to her if they chanced upon her in a dark alley.'

Amy blushed.

'Ah, but den they said – each of 'em – as how they'd never met such a girl before and wished she was workin' for dem, and wished their wives or girls had as much sense and guts.'

Amy blushed further.

The Cook twitched his head a couple of times before continuing: 'And Huggs – it was him as provided the flour? – he was grumblin' dat he'd been sure he could pass dem barrels off as fine goods. But no, you'd looked 'em over and noticed what no other ship's master had seen: dat faint water mark along the bottom. And you'd made him turn a barrel over and open it from the bottom. He'd sold a hundred of dem barrels since dat flood at the warehouse, and you was the first to spot that dey was mouldy in part and would soon enough – on a long voyage – be mouldy throughout.'

Amy was bright red now but very pleased, and I was beginning to forgive the man for being a shameless flatterer.

He continued, 'So I says to Huggs – What do you want

for dem barrels? And he sells 'em to me at a third of the price he offered 'em to you. I got the bill of sale in my bag here.'

'What?' Amy asked, recovering herself. 'You bought mouldy flour?'

'No, Miss. I bought flour dat's *part* mouldy. And I'll sell the clean part to you at the price you'd pay for good flour.'

'How?'

'We'll take dem barrels on board. Meself and me young assistant here – a fine lad, if ever I saw one – we'll take off the good flour from the top. I've a good nose for such t'ings but we'll need you ladies to do some sniffing too, for in my experience ladies have a more delicate appreciation of what's fresh and what's not. Anything dat smells mouldy or has more dan its fair share of weevils goes overboard, and den we get the empty barrels to burn for the galley fire. And maybe I'll turn a profit; maybe I won't.'

Red, who had been listening to this, snorted. 'You've not changed a bit, Bones!' he exclaimed. 'Always on the make! Always looking for a bit on the side! And in more ways than one – Madame and ladies, you'll need to watch this man. He has an evil reputation with women.'

Bones looked genuinely hurt. 'If I've had a bad reputation in the past,' he said, 'dat has been with the type of woman for whom culture and sensitivity and taste has no value. I t'ink I know how to behave amongst *Ladies*.'

He bowed again, and this time I think Madame Helena herself had to stifle a sigh.

And thus it came about that I was apprenticed to the oddest, most interesting and most infuriating man I'd ever met (with the possible exception of Captain Jones himself). And within an hour I found myself covered in flour and shaking with laughter as we sifted through twenty barrels with the boisterous help of the ladies, under the amused but watchful eye of Madame.

7 An Uneasy Start

From my diary:

Day 1 - *This is amazing. I never want to live anywhere except on a ship, gliding about the world.*

Day 2 - *I never want to see a wave, hear a seagull or stand on a ship again. I just want to die....*

On the night of Bones' arrival, I made a vow to myself that I would record each day's passage, with perhaps a drawing and sometimes a little poetry (for I was feeling poetic just then, what with my feelings being enflamed by the prospects of adventure and – well - whatever else might come). But "things change quickly at sea", as Captain Jones often told me as he cast the Wind dice, and my diary was never any more than scattered comments.

The first change was to my sleep. My hammock was taken down and moved near to the ugly, smoking iron galley stove. Tiddles Five immediately assumed the hammock as his rightful perch and whenever I climbed into it, weary and aching, I usually found I was lying on him or on some spiky fish bones he'd brought to share with me.

I was ordered to tend the fire, mind the bubbling pots and scrub anything that didn't move. I wasn't permitted to touch the bread dough however, for Bones swore, 'Ah, but it's sure to go sour if a clumsy boy like yourself so much as looks at it!'

I was shutting the stove down for the night when Bones bustled past with a tankard of hot grog for Captain Red. He whistled to me as if I was a dog, and I followed.

We went to the back of the ship – the stern – and climbed

the raised wooden quarterdeck there. Red was standing by the binnacle light, talking with the short, round helmsman, a map in his hand. Around us all was a confusion of shadows thrown by the lights of the ship and the harbour.

'Dis is how you do it,' Bones said to me quietly. He stopped a few steps away from Red and stood respectfully still. After a few minutes, the helmsman turned and asked what the devil we were doing there.

'The Cap'n's grog, sir,' said Bones. The grog was taken from his hand by the helmsman, who passed it to Captain Red.

Bones bowed and led me away. 'You don't address the Captain directly, see,' he said. 'Dat is - not unless he speaks to you first. Like he's about to do now.'

We paused a moment before descending from the quarterdeck and – as predicted – we were called back by Red.

He wanted to know what the devil was in the grog besides rum.

'A dash of ginger, Captain,' said Bones, and then (having been spoken to) he said, 'Which reminds me, sir: dere was two t'ings I needs to tell you. First, I heard somet'ing at the inn today dat might be of interest to us all, about a King's ship dat was planning to sail into dis very harbour at dawn tomorrow...'

The result of this announcement – after a lot of arguing and name-calling – was that Bones was punched by the helmsman "for not telling us sooner", the helmsman was decked by Red for "being too free with your fat fists", and hasty plans were made for sailing as soon as possible after the moon had dropped beyond the hills. As for the second thing Bones had wanted to say, that was forgotten for now.

"At 196 for 220, seek the small harbour on the island of breasted stone."

I'd been ordered to attend an emergency meeting in Red's cabin: the captain and Madame Helena sitting at a table, with me standing before them like a schoolboy required to recite my lesson.

'That's what the parchment *says*,' Red told me, one of his big fingers tracing the words again. 'But we need to be clear about what it *means*.'

'We've already agreed what it means,' said Madame, rather crossly: which crossness I could understand, for we had argued over these words for almost an hour at her house before Red finally gave in and accepted that I knew Jones' intention better than he did.

'I need to check before we do something *stupid*,' he said to her, with equal crossness. He pointed at me. 'How certain are you that he means a compass bearing of 196 and sea miles of 220?'

'It was the way he always said it when he set out his plans in the Game,' I replied. 'You state your intention of the point you're sailing to after rolling the dice, and the other player can challenge it if he thinks it's not possible with that wind and the hazards that lie between.'

'Always?' Red was angry. I knew he hated the fact that he had to rely on the word of a boy, and (worse still) a boy whose experience of the sea was limited to a board game and a few trips in a rowboat.

'Always,' I said. 'And he made me report to him in the same way.'

Red nodded. 'You'd better be right,' he said grimly. 'Now go back to the galley.'

A few hours after midnight, as the tide turned and began to flow out to sea, Bones roused me from my hammock in total darkness and told me to come down to the sick room in case I was needed to help with the wounded.

'What wounded?' I asked.

'Dere's always likely to be a few when you cut and run,' said Bones from out of the darkness he'd already explained was necessary to stop the harbour watch from seeing us leave.

We waited below and had to follow the action of the ship being towed out by sound alone.

Bones whispered, 'Dat's a boat bein' lowered over the side. Hear the ropes creakin'? And dat gentle splash as she kisses the water? Dere's another – and another. Only three, den. Now the splashing of oars - twelve rowers in each, I expect, wid a man at the bow whispering orders. Ropes bein' tied between each of dem and the ship's bow – hear dat sound of a rope bein' pulled through a ringbolt? Oars splashing again... now dem big shore ropes bein' untied – ah, dey dropped one in the water: Red's swearin' in a whisper... gangplank pulled up... slight creakin' as the bow is pulled around, ship turnin', startin' to shift from the quay, makin' way now.'

And I could imagine it all: the dark, elegant ship being towed quietly out of the harbour, with the ship's master Misty kneeling at the front, dropping the line and pulling it back, measuring the depth in a whisper (*One length... two... three... by the mark four and feels muddy... a little to larboard, you flea brains!*).

We were pulled safely out of the narrow harbour entrance, after which the wind caught us, causing the ship to drift sideways.

'Boats in!' was the muffled whisper next, followed by 'Ready sheets!', which I understood was an instruction to prepare to release the sails. But then a shout came from the darkness to our left side – the larboard. Some unseen ship was out there, tucked in near to the shore beyond the ring-shaped harbour.

'Ship there!' came the ringing voice again. 'Name yourself!'

We made no answer apart from the clatter of hurried oar strokes and the sound of men clambering up the rope ladders. I heard one boat being winched up, then a second.

The shouts were nearer now; we must be drifting a little in that direction. And still we delayed setting sail.

'Let the sheets go!' Bones muttered to himself. 'Tow the

last boat – won't do 'em any harm!'

But Captain Red was a man who, once he had a plan in his head, stuck to it like a tick to a dog. A full minute passed before the final boat crew bumped alongside, then began to climb.

We must have become just visible in that half-clouded, half-starry darkness, for there was a louder, angrier shout and then a couple of gunshots, followed by a groan and a splash.

I lost track of events then: hearing shots and shouts and the turning of winches and singing of ropes all at once, and then a new sound, that of a ship surging through water: a most heavenly and stirring sound, and in a moment I was ruined forever for land life and knew I must live on the high seas.

My elation was dimmed a few minutes later when the wounded man – the one I'd heard being shot - was carried down to us. His left leg below the knee was a wreck and there was more blood than flesh.

Bones had already lighted a lantern and fastened it to a crossbeam overhead. He shook his head at the leg and turned to his wooden, ironbound chest. He made the sailor drink something from a bottle, while two others tied the man to a bench. A rope was bound about the leg just below the knee; then Bones picked up a saw.

I was about to run out, but Bones stopped me with an angry glare.

'I want a hot fire in five minutes!' he ordered, so I scuttled away to the galley stove, grabbed the bellows, opened the vents and started coaxing the remaining hot coals into life.

Five minutes later, I'd heated a tin of black tar on the stove and Bones was looking at the bloody stump critically, as if it was a picture he had painted and he was trying to decide whether the colours were right.

He took the boiling tar and applied it to the stump; that woke the sailor, who had passed out after the first stroke of the saw.

'Dat'll teach you to row a bit faster, won't it?' Bones asked him. The sailor laughed weakly, groaned, and fainted again.

That would have been enough excitement for me for one day: but there was more to come. We were chased by that same sloop through the night and most of the next morning, and laughed at her too – until the wind changed.

While we were sailing into the wind, they had no chance of catching us. Our caravel could point "a few degrees more into the wind" than that great, lumbering square-sailed monster. We edged away in elegant zigzags while they swung to and fro in ugly, alternating diagonals. Older sailors looked at the flags fluttering in our masts beneath a glassy sky and murmured approvingly.

But Bones studied the full horizon, shook his head and headed back to the galley. I was mystified when he growled at me to shut down the fire and then started placing everything moveable into the galley chests, which he fastened shut. He even locked Tiddles in his cage.

While I was working up the courage to ask why he was doing this, the first mate Tom shouted down: 'Captain wants to know when the crew's skilly will be ready.'

'Fire's gone out!' Bones shouted back, with a wink to me. 'I reckon it's dis change in the weather did it.'

Tom swore at him, adding, 'What change, you lazy pot scrubber?'

Bones just laughed and said, 'The boy's gonna bring up some cheese and bread and ship's biscuit. Dat'll sit best on our stomachs, see.'

Tom swore some more, then stomped away. When I emerged with the first large panniers of food, I could see him talking earnestly to Red. They were leaning against the starboard rail on the quarterdeck, wind ruffling their hair: then they both suddenly stood up straight, glanced up at the masts and turned about to look behind them.

A moment later, the ship seemed to lose all interest in sailing. We were becalmed.

After a few orders dealing with sails and ropes, the men were sent to collect their paltry meal. I received oaths and cuffs I was sure I didn't deserve, while Bones busied himself with taking food to the ladies.

A line of officers had gathered at the stern railing, some of them peering with telescopes at what I could see without any glass: the chasing ship was now flying towards us across a white-capped sea, her half-lowered sails puffed out in our direction – which meant that the wind was now at her rear, and too strong for full sail. Beyond her, a greenish bank of clouds was growing and darkening at an appalling rate.

Suddenly, all was activity as men were sent to trim sails, secure boats and tie down anything that could be tied down. An order was brought by first mate Tom to shut down the fire.

'Done an hour since,' said Bones with a smirk and a little twitch of his head.

Tom glared at him. 'Then do it again!' he roared.

When the gale hit us soon afterwards, it was like being shoved by a whale. The boat shuddered, tipped up, and skidded forward. Then the wind wrapped about us and drove us lurching towards the horizon: a horizon that soon disappeared behind endless rain.

The rain forced me below decks, and after this I was banned from returning because of the danger that I would be blown away. The ship began to dive and rise, dive and rise again, and continuously wallowed from side to side. I lay in my hammock feeling sick, or on the floor feeling sick. Soon I was actually being sick, miserably and repeatedly.

This went on for hours, until I was too weak even to retch. I slept, woke, was sick and slept again. From time to time Bones would try to make me drink some water, but I couldn't take more than a few drops. And still the wind rose; and still we swilled about in the murky sea.

I heard men above me on deck, dragging things, drop-ping things, winching things in or letting them out. Some sort of net on a line was thrown over the stern: this would be towed behind us, dragging in the water and slowing us. Not that this made much difference, for we continued to race before the wind, often in total darkness.

Once – perhaps a day after the storm hit us – I woke to that place between nightmares and reality. I rose and stag-gered about, convinced that Tiddles was loose and must be caught before he was blown overboard. I climbed onto deck and began to crawl across it on hands and knees.

I continued to call for the cat, shouting against the wolf howl of the wind and wiping the rain from my eyes. I didn't realise I was hallucinating until I saw two identical pale faces looking down at me, followed by one enormous black face. I thought I was back in the Inquisitor's palace with the guard leaning over me, then lifting me gently.

I gave up the struggle for sanity and fell back into the darkness, dreaming of sea monsters that rose from the deeps to torment me, their faces a dreadful combination of Red, Madame and the Inquisitor.

8 Stowaways

From my diary: *I think it's day 4 now. The sickness has gone but I feel weaker than Tiddles. And I'm totally confused.*

When I woke again, I found I was strapped onto a makeshift bed in the galley. Tiddles was curled on my stomach, purring, and a tin cup of water was at my elbow. The ship's motion had returned to normal and so had I.

Bones told me reassuringly, 'I was sick like dat on my first voyage. Never after, though. You might be the same.'

I managed to eat some bread and then commenced my tasks. Casks had to be examined for water damage; the jumbled contents of every cupboard and case had to be tidied; and the crew were calling for hot soup and biscuit.

I was allowed to take food to the ladies (who always ate in their cabin) and waited at the door, eyes down in embarrassment, while they took the trays from me. Then Vicky and Sandra laughed at me and dragged me inside.

'Look how pompous he's become, Madame!' they exclaimed. 'Don't want to know us now, do he?'

Madame looked the same as ever, as if mere natural catastrophes like hurricanes didn't touch her.

She regarded me for a long moment before asking, 'Are you abandoning your friends so soon? Even Amy hasn't seen you since we set out.'

'I've been busy,' I said, looking anywhere but at her.

'He's been sick as a dog!' Vicky exclaimed. 'Poor boy!' She hugged me to her ample bosom, then passed me to Sandra for a second embarrassing squeeze.

'A little,' I admitted unwillingly.

'*We* loved the storm,' said Sandra. 'They even let us lend

a hand at the pumps when the crew was worn out.'

'Amy too?' I asked.

'No, but she was helpin' Bones with them what was injured. One broken arm, one cracked skull – and one boy laid low by seasickness!'

They laughed at me. 'Don't worry, my little lamb,' said Vicky, squashing me with another hug, 'not everyone can be a good sailor!'

Amy came into the cabin just then and gave me a firm hug that made me blush. 'I'm so glad to see you up again!' she exclaimed. 'Everyone's been askin' how you are!'

So *everyone* knew that I had let them all down – that I was the only one who had spent the whole storm in his bed (except for footless Fred, who couldn't be blamed).

Amy squeezed my arm, saying, 'Tom says even the best sailors are sometimes sick at the start of a sea voyage.'

Vicky and Sandra said in chorus, '*Tom* says!' Then they elbowed each other and sniggered.

I bowed to Madame and left, with Sandra shouting after me, 'Hey! Where's my goodbye kiss?'

As I walked back to the galley I was aware of winks, laughs and knowing looks exchanged between crew mates.

'Feelin' better, young'un?' shouted a grizzled old tar from up in the rigging. I nodded and ran the rest of the way.

Fortunately the jokes and jibes passed quickly enough: before the end of the day there were other things to talk about. I suppose I was partly the cause of this. I had taken Captain Red's coffee to him that afternoon and stood at a distance as Bones had shown me, until Red called me over and asked after my health in his usual rough manner.

'Next time,' he said, 'I'll make no allowances! In a storm like that, all hands take a turn at the pumps. I only let you off 'cause Bones said it might kill you, and I need you alive. While *you* was sleepin' cosily, *we* was workin' with scarce a halt for breath, for nigh on three days!'

'Sorry, sir,' I said; then (wanting to show I wasn't a total wimp) I added, 'I did come on deck once. Or – I think I did. I – I - you see that man by the main mast? I saw two of him, side by side, and they both looked down at me and laughed. Then this enormous black man – the King's Guard – picked me up in my dream and carried me back and –'

I had to stop because Red had seized my head with one big hand and turned it back towards the sailor I'd pointed out to him.

'Which one?' he growled. 'The one with the red cap?'

'I think –'

'*Was* it?'

'Yes, sir.'

He swore and called to some of his men.

'We'll do it *now*,' he was insisting.

'But half the crew's asleep –'

'- two nights at the pumps –'

'- boy was likely dreamin' –'

'- nah, *lyin'* more like!'

Several heads turned to look at me suspiciously.

Red thumped one big fist into the palm of his other hand. 'I won't be made a fool of!' he growled. Then he turned to the evil-faced quartermaster, Pitiless Jake.

'All hands on deck. And I mean *all*! Then you'll take ten big lads and search every bolt hole.'

He turned to me. 'You! Jack! You can write, can't you?'

'Yes sir.'

'You'll stand by me and check the names on the ledger, then. But first go dampen down the galley fire. This'll take a while.'

There were whistles, shouts and drumming; then the crew began massing on the foredeck, many of them half-dressed and yawning. The ladies were kept in their cabin while it was searched, then brought forward as well. Madame was wearing her black dress and a veil, as if this was a formal social event – though in fact this proved to be the pattern of her attire from then onwards: she rarely appeared on deck without coverage of every part of her body apart from two white, strong hands.

Captain Red showed no interest in providing an explanation to us. He stood with his back to a mast while sails were trimmed and the crew murmured uneasily. He didn't even turn when the figure from my dream – the large King's Guard - was brought up from below decks, secured in leg irons. More sailors arrived from the depths of the ship, then we heard bangings and thumpings from below as Pitiless Jake's men searched every nook.

We stood sweating in the sunlight for nearly half an hour until Jake's men rejoined us. They were dragging a woman – age unguessable, clothes and body filthy, hair matted. Her face and arms had open sores on them and she smelled like she'd needed a bath for the past year.

The men dropped her arms and stood away from her, a little upwind. She put one hand on a hip and struck a pose that was meant to be attractive.

'Good to see you again, boys!' she croaked. 'Have you missed yer Molly?'

No one answered. The hatches clanged shut. Red finally turned to address the crew.

'I'll show you what happens when orders aren't followed,' he said sullenly. He looked at the men who had brought the woman and jerked his head towards the side. They began dragging "Molly" to the railing.

She screamed and scratched and tried to bite, calling Red every vile name I'd ever heard and a few new ones I hope never to hear again.

'It ain't my fault!' she shouted. 'I was tricked! They paid me! And I only came on board to give a bit of comfort to sailors wot's lonely at sea!'

She caught sight of the ladies and called to them, begging them to 'take pity on a poor sister!' Madame didn't even turn her head, as if the dirty creature simply wasn't there.

The sailors hoisted her over the railing and dropped her into the water. Her curses and screams stopped briefly, then recommenced with added fury as she floated away in our wake.

Bones' voice came in a clear whisper, 'Ah, but it's the sharks I'm feelin' sorry for now...'

Laughter broke out, and continued as the comment was relayed through the group.

Captain Red wasn't laughing however. 'There's three more heading over the side, unless someone persuades me different,' he said.

Dead silence fell, with men looking left and right.

'Here's the first.'

Red pointed at the large black King's Guard. 'How did you get on board?' he called out.

The Guard shook his head. 'Sorry, Captain,' he said. 'I'm not at liberty to tell you that.'

'*It was me,*' said a voice at my side.

The crew turned to stare at Bones.

'You'll recall, Cap'n,' Bones said, his head twitching, 'dat first evenin', when I said dere was two t'ings I wanted to tell you? Well, dis was the second. We never got a chance to discuss it after a certain officer nearly broke my nose.'

Red nodded slowly. He turned back to the guard and asked him, 'Why should I let you stay this side of the rail?'

For answer, the man shuffled across the deck, dragging his irons. He put one enormous hand onto the back of one seaman, and another on a second. Then he lifted them both in the air and held them above his head.

The crew murmured approvingly. I heard them saying things like, 'Did you see 'im on that winch when we had to lift the fallen spar? 'E was amazin', 'e was.'

First mate Tom was whispering into Red's ear, and Red was nodding again.

'You're not a sailor,' said Red as the guard lowered the two men to the deck. 'Why're you on my ship?'

'I'm a hard man to hide on shore,' said the guard with half a smile.

'Someone lookin' for you, then?' asked Red.

The guard shrugged his massive shoulders. 'When an Inquisitor goes missing, somebody gets blamed.'

Red nodded again, then said to Pitiless Jake, 'Remove his irons.'

Jake's face fell, but he smiled when Red added, 'Bones to receive six lashes.'

A clear female voice cut through this exchange, and it was chilling to see how quickly everyone fell silent as Madame called:

'I would like to ask the Cook a few questions.'

Red nodded again.

She said, 'Cook – tell me – how did this come about?'

Bones smiled. 'Ah well, you see – I met dis man in a pub, you know –'

Many of the crew began laughing at this point, cut short by a sharp interruption from Madame:

'Which pub?'

'Ah... I'm not sure I recalls dat. But it was a couple of nights afore I came on board; maybe three –'

'You'll have to do better than that!'

There was more laughter, which dried up more quickly than water dropped on a hissing fire when Madame turned and looked angrily at the crew.

Captain Red said quietly, 'Madame, you'll need to bear in mind that when a man like Bones says he "*met a man in a pub*", he doesn't mean that at all.'

Madame turned back to glare at Bones. 'So you were lying to me?' she asked menacingly.

Bones answered cheerily, 'Why to be sure, dat wasn't in me mind at all! I just forgot dat you was innocent as to the ways of business. It's like dis, Madame: a man don't tell who he spoke with, or when, or where. It's always left to the imagination, see? Much safer dat way.'

Madame fixed him with a steely eye, and I could see Bones wriggling upon the sharpness of her stare, his twitch increasing. She said frostily, 'I prefer to deal with reality, Mr Bones. So tell me: was there money involved? Or was this simply a matter of kind-heartedness?'

'Ah,' said Bones. 'Dat's hard to say. But I won't deny dat dere *might* have been the mention of cash, or something like it, and dere might have been the involvement of a financial man who might be called Nobby.'

A sailor called, 'Nobby the Fixer!'

Bones said, 'Well, I'm not sayin' dat was his real name, or wasn't. But as Nobby says, money is like oil: it makes t'ings move smooth and quick.'

'So money changed hands? How much?' asked Madame.

Bones rubbed his stubbly chin. 'No *real* money was taken or given, Madame. We sailors don't carry coins as a rule. Money's like water, it finds its level and floats us along. If you reach down and try to take a handful of it, you find dere's nothing in your palm but a fleeting wetness.'

Madame glared at him again. '*How much?!*' she insisted.

'Ah - money's like love, Madame. Can you say how much love is given for how much loyalty? Or how much affection for affection returned? Dem t'ings is a mystery.'

'You're trying my patience, Mr Bones.'

'Alright, den. Let's just say dat in dis case, money was like the salt you adds to a mess of potatoes and cabbage, so's to give it taste. A few doubloons, say; certainly no more dan an eagle. The exact amount was left unclear, like the sun behind a mist. You could say perhaps dat a man named Nobby is under more of an obligation to me dan he was before; and dat three nasty hulkin' lumps from Magus is less likely to knock a hole in me sensitive head when next I runs into 'em.'

Madame nearly smiled. She said, with an amused shrug, 'I see. You were in a tight spot, and did some favours to get yourself out of it.'

'Me? In a tight spot? No tighter dan usual, Madame.'

Red laughed now and slapped Bones about the face, but almost gently. 'Shut that lying mouth of yours before it gets you into more trouble,' he advised.

'Yes, Cap'n,' said Bones, with a wink to the crew.

Next, Red ordered the whole crew to pass before him,

one by one. I stood at his side, marking off each man as he named them passing by. When the red-hatted man I'd brought to Red's attention came before me, he asked the man's name.

'Thomas Bast, Cap'n.'

As I marked the man's name on the list, Red nodded to the quartermaster, who took Thomas Bast to one side.

Near the end of line of men, another red-hatted man came forward and also named himself as Thomas Bast.

'I've marked him off already,' I whispered to Red.

'I mind that. Jake – have this one as well.'

The others walked through without incident.

'Well, well,' said Captain Red. 'We have Thomas Bast and his twin, Matthew. I only signed one of you. Matthew is the most useless sailor I've ever served with, and he once tried to cheat me at cards. I would never employ him. So which of you is Matthew?'

Neither twin moved or said a word.

'Put 'em both over the side,' Red ordered Pitiless Jake.

Jake smiled and took both men by the scruff of the neck. He began dragging them towards the rail.

The twins screeched and begged, both claiming that the other was Matthew. Red turned away.

'I'll work for nothing!' one of them cried; Red turned back as if considering.

'Me too!' shouted the other.

Red held up a hand; Pitiless Jake paused.

'We already have an agreement,' he said. 'You'll be paid for one man's toil, and have one man's share of any treasure – one between the two of you. But I'll have no cheating. You'll both work the same watch. And if either of you slacks or misbehaves, both will be punished. Agreed?'

'Yes, sir.'

'Yes, Cap'n Red sir. Very grateful, sir.'

Red said to Pitiless Jake, 'Twelve lashes each. Now.'

The twins were dragged to the main mast and stripped of

their shirts. Each tried to push the other forward, knowing that the earliest lashes would be the hardest. Jake himself seemed puzzled what to do; then he grinned and ordered them to be tied to either side of the mast.

I watched the first two lashes – one each side – before turning away. The groans and cries were bad enough and I didn't want to watch the faces twisting in pain and the blood beginning to run.

Bones was standing at the rail, awaiting his turn. He pressed his back into the rail, as if trying to get as far away as possible from the waiting whip. He saw me looking at him, smiled grimly and changed position a little. He kept doing this – twisting to one side or the other, always with his back squeezed against the railing.

When it was time for his turn, he strode forward, taking off his shirt. He went straight to the mast and placed his hands upon it and his head on his hands. His back showed faint red lines where he had been pressing against the rail; the lines looked like old whip marks.

His six lashes passed with no response from him; after the final, resounding crack he straightened up, took a deep breath and walked steadily back to the galley.

When I joined him in the galley, he handed me a small crock of evil-smelling ointment.

'Put it on the stripes quick as you can,' he said. 'Don't press hard – *ow!* – *not* hard! – and use as little as possible. Dat's right. Don't rub it in. T'anks, Jack.'

As well as his new wounds, he had a network of scars - including several burn marks running down his lower back into his trousers.

'You've had some hard times,' I said.

'Dat's right. And I don't want to talk about 'em.'

'Why were you pressing your back against the railing?'

He laughed and said, 'Dat's a trick I was told by a clever hand named Dempsey. Supposed to make the back numb and take the edge off the lash. Not sure if it really works; but it stops you from t'inking about what's coming next...'

9 Snake Eyes

When the thrower of the dice rolls double one, he may choose to alter the direction of the wind for all players to be that shown on the line between the two dice, in either direction. He can choose whether this alteration occurs before or after his own move. He can also choose whether or not to change the wind speed, using one or both of the dice.

By now it was clear that we had been blown far south of our initial destination, an uninhabited island shown on the maps as Stoney Isle, but known to sailors as Bigtits because of the shape and size of its two rocky mounts.

The ship had turned north as soon as dawn had confirmed the sailing master's suspicions: but as the wind was still from that quarter, we didn't come in sight of the island until night began to fall.

At this point we should have passed up the western side of this pear-shaped island, seeking a cove half way along, shaped as if someone had taken a bite out of the pear. But a shout from the mast top wrecked Red's plans.

'Sail ho! Dead ahead!'

This was followed by a lot of undisciplined running and climbing of crew to various vantage points before Red began shouting and his lieutenants began beating the crew with short sticks, sending them to haul down the sails – in the hopes that the other ship might not see us in the falling light if we took down our white patchwork.

This seemed to me a futile hope. I suppose we were but a few miles away, and we must have been as clear to them as they were to us. Certainly, the other ship – a large square-rigged brig - seemed to change course; she had been heading for the harbour but now turned towards us, putting on more sail and taking full advantage of the wind behind her.

Red then countered his previous order, shouting 'All sail!

All sail, d'you hear?'

He called to the helmsman, 'Mr Jones, set a course due east and pass below the island; then bear north around the other side of it. They won't catch us against the wind.'

As he said this, night came upon us suddenly. One moment I was gazing – a little dreamily - at the two great peaks halfway along the island, seeing their tips set on fire by the dying red blaze of the sun; a breath or two later, I couldn't have told you whether the island itself was still there or had sunk into the black seas.

Sailors must develop exceptional eyesight during their traverses through alternating darkness and pitiless light, for there wasn't the slightest hesitation from the helm. A few men were sent forward, where they peered into the blackness and sent back reports such as 'Land half a mile off.... Think there's surf breaking ahead, a few points to larboard.... Past the reef now, land fallin' behind – near a mile I reckon...'

As we sailed into the darkness, my eyes adapted to the starlight gloom and I could see the island to larboard, swelling gently from the sea and then (as we passed along it to the north) rising steeply. The twin peaks blotted the stars; then their shapes moved together, merged into one and parted once more as we passed along the coast.

The moon rose as we rounded the northern tip of the island and turned west. It lit the island with ghostly gleamings and filled our sails with light.

'Steady now!' Red grumbled. 'Haul in that topsail and mainsail. Reef the others. We don't want those sons of the devil spotting us before we spot them.'

We crept around the northern coast of the island, then eased around its northwest corner. If there was a King's ship waiting for us, she was as hidden in the darkness as we hoped *we* were.

I was called to the captain's cabin when we were about a third of the way down the coast, stealing south in the darkness. Red and Madame were there already, with the parchment spread upon the table. They looked up from their study of it. A lantern was hanging from a beam above the table; it cast evil shadows upon their faces.

Red pointed at the parchment and said to me, 'The first clear instruction here is to seek this island and its small harbour. After that, it's all madness and if you can't tell us what it means, I'll throw you to the sharks. Time for you to earn the right to stay alive.'

Madame Helena said nothing, but gave me a look such as a shark might bestow upon a floundering swimmer.

'Here it is,' continued Red, placing one large, hairy finger on a sentence. '*Follow the eyes a full turn at seven for the first treesure sunken low and springing high.*'

'That must be *treasure*,' Madame added.

This was one of those passages we had talked about in Madame's house, and given up on. Madame had said at the time that it would probably be clearer to us once we'd arrived at the right place.

Red beckoned me to read the passage myself, which I did with some alarm, realising that I hadn't the slightest idea what it meant.

When I told them this, Red snarled at me. 'You're lying!' he shouted. 'Don't hold out on me, boy!'

'Break it down,' Madame suggested. 'The eyes?'

I shrugged.

'A full turn?'

I shook my head.

'At seven?'

I was about to shake my head and shrug at the same time when a large, hard hand knocked me to the floor.

'Get up!' Red ordered, readying his fist for another blow.

'I'd rather stay down here,' I said weakly.

He pulled me to my feet and marched me across the cabin to one of the windows on the port side.

'Look, you useless lump of sewage!' he hissed. 'We're coming near that cove. If we get there before you give me an answer, I'll break one of your fingers. And I'll continue breaking fingers until you give up what you know.'

'But I *don't* know –' I began; then stopped.

The two pointed hills were moving together again slowly. Soon they would line up and there would be one hill to my eyes. A picture dropped into my head – a picture of the hills seen from above, their points lit up by the final blaze of the sun.

'Snake eyes!' I breathed.

Red had drawn back his fist for another punch.

'What?' he grunted.

'It's part of the Game,' I said quickly. 'If you throw the dice and get two ones – they call that snake eyes - you can set your bearings from the line between their dots.'

He tightened his fist again. 'You're talking in riddles!'

'The hills!' I blurted. 'Their peaks are the eyes you just read about – the snake eyes!'

He looked at the parchment again, nodding slowly but clearly puzzled. At his side, Madame was looking at him with undisguised contempt.

She said, 'You position the ship so that the hills are in line. Then you set a course in the opposite direction.'

'Yeah. Okay. But how far do we go?'

I said, 'You go for "one turn" – a turn, like in the game - that's a full day's worth of sailing. And you sail at "seven" which means that you go as far as you could get in twenty four hours with a force seven wind directly behind you.'

Red nodded again. 'And that's – uh – that's –'

'Twelve knots times twenty-four hours. 288 nautical miles,' I said. I knew the Game's tables by heart.

'Got it,' said Red and strode out of the cabin, shouting instructions to his lieutenants. In moments, the ship was turned about and charts were being consulted, compasses flicked with impatient fingers and notes scrawled slowly in the log book by the half-drunk sailing master, in between peering at the page by the binnacle light.

I left the cabin but didn't get very far. A low whistle drew me to the left, where Bones was sitting on a locker. He was fiddling with his pipe and Tiddles the cat was draped about his neck, purring.

Bones said quietly, 'Dey was talkin' loud, so I was listenin'. You did alright in dere.'

'Thanks,' I said.

'Just thought I'd tell you something. Dat Captain Red, he's a proper bully. Now, when the boss is a bully, you can't do much about it. But dere's some things you *can* do, and you gotta do 'em, 'cause a real bully won't just pick on you a little. He'll keep on pushin' till you crack. Each time you give in, it gets worse.'

I sat down next to Bones and asked what I should do. He fiddled with the pipe a little more, almost lit it, and said:

'You got knowledge dat he needs. He's gotta understand he can't have it unless he treats you right. You tell him dat.'

I nodded.

'Beautiful night,' said Bones, looking up into it. 'Don't you just love dem stars? Like God took a handful of light and sprinkled it in the darkness. Dat's one of the great things about bein' a sailor, lookin' at all dem stars.'

'Have you been a sailor for a long time?' I asked.

'Most of me life,' he said. 'The sea's me home now.'

I continued, a bit hesitantly, 'And you sailed with Captain Jones, you said. What was he like?'

'Ah,' said Bones, 'what's any man like? A mystery, I say. Jones was a holy terror. One moment, the best pirate in the world. The next, he'd have some crazy plan. Once he turned aside from a mission for the King and sailed far, far east. We spent a month trading for gold and spices. Cap'n had filled the holds with copper pots and pans for the adults and toys for their children. And dis is the odd t'ing: he gave dem toys away for nothing, one for each child who came and asked. Good stuff, too.'

I laughed.

'Did he really push you over the rail?' I asked.

Bones winked at me. 'I can forgive dat man, and have

done so,' he said (striking his own heart). 'But I don't like to talk about what he did.'

'And do you think he's dead?' I asked.

Bones said with a little twitch of the head, 'Dere's probably only three or four people who can answer dat question. Wait until you find one of 'em!'

I said, 'I think he's still alive. And I don't believe the dreadful things people say about him.'

Bones laughed at this. 'Ah, but you're young and you've only seen his good side!'

'Is there a bad side?'

Bones threw the question back at me: 'You knew him. What do you say?'

I thought hard. 'He can be harsh at times. And proud. But I like him. And I think that in his centre, in his soul, he's a good man.'

Bones looked away, towards the stars again. 'Or maybe he's simply fooled you. Dey say he's like dat.'

This was uncomfortably close to what the Inquisitor had told me. I said, 'The Inquisitor tried to make me think that. But I don't believe anything that man said. I think he was just trying to get me to talk.'

'Ah!' Bones exclaimed. 'You met the Evil One himself! What happened?'

I sat down again and told the whole story. Bones was enthralled by it, and delighted with the outcome. Tiddles seemed pleased as well: he left Bones' shoulder for my lap and lay there purring up at me.

'Ah, dat's a fine tale!' Bones exclaimed. 'You done well, young'un. And it served the Evil One right!'

'But why do the Inquisitor and Captain Jones hate each other so much?'

Bones turned serious for once. 'Dat Inquisitor has a brother - Arthur, ten years younger dan himself. About Cap'n Jones' age, and one of Jones' friends. Dere's even talk dat dey was both members of an outlawed organisation.'

'The Guar –'

'Shhh! Dere's some words you don't say if you want a long life, and dat's one of 'em. Now, dis Arthur, a few years back, suddenly fell in love. And he nearly had a fallin' out wid the Cap'n at the same time. Dis lady – Nerissa her name is – was a foreign princess come to beg the King's mercy for her country. Cap'n Jones had brought her from some distant land in dis very ship, and I think he was a little in love wid her by the time dey came to port. I saw it, 'cause I was on dat voyage, until I was pushed overboard.'

'Was she beautiful?'

'Still is,' Bones sighed. 'I seen her a few times, passin' in her carriage. Anyway, as soon as she laid eyes on Arthur, and he on her, dat was dat. Dey got married, King Arinaeus made a pact of eternal friendship wid her country as a weddin' gift, and Cap'n Jones was best man.'

I asked, 'So he and Arthur stayed friends, even though Arthur ended up with the woman that Captain Jones... um... liked ?'

'It didn't seem to make no difference, and I reckon dat's cos dey was true friends to start wid. But Arthur's brother – the Inquisitor – was eaten up wid envy and rage. You see, he'd made a try for the lady hisself when she first arrived, and 'cause he's a proud devil, he thought dat any woman would love him, mean and nasty though he is.'

'The Inquisitor fell in love with her?'

'Love? What does dat man know of love? She was just something pretty to own and to use, a shiny trinket. But... maybe you're right, and dere *was* love involved. To be sure, he was dat upset when it all fell apart. He thought he was sailin' fast into matrimony hisself, when what happened? His brother Arthur came back from a sea voyage and Jones introduced him to Nerissa. The Inquisitor was thrown over and never forgave his brother, or his new sister-in-law, or Jones who helped bring 'em together.'

'I can't imagine the Inquisitor being in love,' I said.

'Love comes to many who don't deserve it,' said Bones.

He turned his head to look along the starboard railing, where Amy was deep in conversation with Tom. I didn't like the suggestion that the subject of romance could have anything to do with Amy and Tom, and said so.

Bones shrugged and returned to his story. 'When love is spurned, a bad man's heart can turn against everyone connected wid the one who rejects him. Dat man – the Inquisitor – he had his own brother arrested on false charges. Tortured him wid his own hand. Den he had him put in a special prison, chained to a wall day in, day out, wid one visit a month from his wife and child: and he allowed dat visit not from kindness, but just to torment 'em all.'

'And what about Captain Jones?'

'I can only tell you what I've been told meself. Jones was out of the country when dis happened. When he came back, dere was almost a rebellion: but den the King offered Jones a deal. Cap'n Jones was sent off on a final voyage, wid a promise dat if he returned with a certain diamond, Arthur would be released.'

'Oh.' I sat for a while, trying to think this through. Surely the Captain would have brought the diamond back. He wouldn't have let his friend rot in prison.

Bones continued, as if reading my thoughts: 'He brought back the diamond. The King said it wasn't the right time to release Arthur, and dere was one more jewel he wanted. A great ruby. And whether the Cap'n couldn't find it, or found it and hid it away, it's true dat he didn't bring it back and didn't set his friend free.'

'But the King was never going to release him anyway, was he?' I asked.

'Not to my mind,' said Bones. He knocked out his pipe (which he hadn't managed to light in the first place), placed Tiddles on his shoulder like a furry parrot, and went back to the galley, whistling "Storm at Sea".

I sat a while looking at the stars, wondering what had become of Captain Jones, and his friend Arthur, and the Curchan Ruby.

10 Treesure

Upon rolling a double three, the player will draw a fates card. Upon rolling a double four, a fortunes card will be drawn instead. Upon rolling a double six, the Runes of Destiny will be rolled and the player will refer to the list of Interpretations for the rune shown.

It took us nearly two days to cover the distance indicated by the parchment, the wind being fickle and Misty the sailing master's head being sore. We arrived at the likely island as the sun began to sink and passed around it, anchoring at the far side so as to be out of sight of the brig – if indeed the ship was still following us, for we hadn't seen it again.

As the anchor chains rattled out, I was called to the captain's cabin for "discussions". Madame was there, and Red had his first mate Tom at his side.

'Over here,' Red ordered as I hesitated at the door. 'Look at this blasted scribble and this blasted chart and give me a good reason not to knock your blasted head off.'

I crossed the room and peered at the instructions again: *'Follow the eyes a full turn at seven for the first treesure sunken low and springing high.'*

Red spoke with slow menace. 'We've come the distance and direction you told us. This is the only spot of land within the horizon, but it's a full five miles short of what you said.'

I said carefully, 'Captain Jones always told me that the Game wasn't quite the same as real sailing. He said you can't be exact when charting real distances on a ship, because of things like sea currents.'

Red's face turned the colour of his name. He said through

gritted teeth, 'Don't lecture me about the sea, you impudent pup!' And he would have knocked me to the floor if I hadn't dodged to the other side of the table.

Now was the moment I had to do it. I said quickly, 'If you ever strike me again, you won't get another word out of me, so help me God! Not another word!'

An evil smile spread across Red's face. 'No?' he asked. 'Maybe we ought to test that. Maybe I ought to beat the truth out of you right now.' He moved towards me.

I was surprised when Madame spoke in my defence. 'Leave him!' she said sharply.

Red stopped and turned to stare at her.

'He withstood the Inquisitor,' she said and continued scornfully, 'Do you think you'll do better?'

Red weighed his right fist in his left. 'Yes,' he sulked. 'I'd make him talk. But – if that's what you want, Madame....'

'I do. Keep your hands to yourself from now on. And bear in mind that this boy's life is worth preserving. He is not only Jones' interpreter; he is also Jones' heir.'

'What do you mean?' Red asked, his face dark: I knew by now that he hated it when Madame said things he didn't quite grasp – which was often.

She smiled grimly. 'On Jones' death, the properties he owned passed not to the boy's aunt, but to the boy himself. The properties are held on trust by an old friend of Jones. If the boy dies, the properties pass to that friend instead. Of course, Jones might yet be alive; but if not, then this boy has a fine value upon his head. We may need to use that.'

I gaped at Madame, then hung my valuable head guiltily, thinking that by my short visits to a man in prison I had robbed Aunt Emma of her long-expected inheritance.

Red grunted at this and turned back to the charts on the table. 'This island isn't even shown on the maps,' he said. 'It's scarcely a mile across, mostly circular, rising towards the middle. We don't know anything about it.'

He looked to Tom, who said, 'I asked Misty and he just shook his foul, drunken head.'

Misty was an appropriate name for the sailing master, who wandered about in a fog of spirits: I'd not yet seen him completely sober.

'We'll land a small boat on the near beach,' said Captain Red. 'Those in this room, plus – what's the black's name?'

'Jupiter,' said Tom.

'Plus Jupiter for muscle. Bones as well, he's been in these parts before, maybe even on this island, he says. Besides, he's hoping to find some greens to cook. Picks, spades, a couple of empty sea chests, guns. Jack here will make a copy of this part of the parchment and bring that. Tomorrow at first light. Agreed?'

We all agreed. Then Red slowly extended his fist until it touched my nose. He gave me a false smile. 'And Jack is spared further beatings so long as he continues to tell us what he knows: right, Jack?'

'Aye aye, sir,' I said gravely.

Shortly after dawn we were in the jolly boat, being pulled across the flat, grey sea by Jupiter and a second sailor, with Bones and first mate Tom also tugging at oars without contributing much. The island was dark against the rising sun, its sparse, salt-blasted trees silhouetted and its one hill cutting a soft lump out of the red sky.

As we pulled onto the beach – a disappointing mix of rounded stones and grey sand – the sunlight crept about the edges of the hill. Gulls passed overhead and a thousand other seabirds called to one another in the growing light.

The second sailor remained with the boat while the rest of us toiled up the gently sloping stony hill, carrying our loads. My copy of the parchment's clues was in one of the chests, nestled against Madame's black parasol and the veil and headdress she'd taken off once the boat had landed.

After half an hour, the hill flattened. We'd been picking our way between the stones and cursing the low, twisted trees which turned out to be bristling with thorns and surrounded by bloodthirsty flies. Now we came to a short stretch of level ground, with patches of wiry grasses springing out of dark, sandy soil.

About twenty paces beyond this, the hill sank in the middle - almost as if someone had scooped it out with an enormous spoon. The grasses and spiky trees abandoned hope here, and the hollow was mainly rock – some sort of dark, sandy shale where nothing grew except mosses and bright lichens.

We walked down the gentle slope, stepping across small cracks and skirting around some enormous round boulders that looked oddly out of place, like a child's marbles scattered in a graveyard.

Near the bottom was the one feature of the hollow that interested us: the petrified trunk of a tree, broad as two men and standing perhaps five metres high, with jagged stubs of branches protruding a metre or so from different parts of the trunk. We halted in front of it.

'What was that blasted clue?' Red called back to me.

'*The first treesure sunken low and springing high,*' I said. I knew it by heart.

'Treasure, not treesure,' said Red through gritted teeth.

There was a cackle from Bones, who was standing behind me. '*Sure* looks like a *tree* to me!' he said.

My former guard and now shipmate, Jupiter, gave what might have been a deep chuckle or merely a grunt as he set down the bigger chest, with our picks and spades in it.

'I see,' said Madame Helena (fanning herself with a red and black laced fan). 'Captain Jones has made a little joke at our expense. Perhaps his parchment will provide nothing more than a lengthy sightseeing excursion around a series of natural delights and artefacts.'

Red took one of the picks and prodded around the base of the tree. It appeared to be solid rock in all directions.

'What do you think, boy?' he asked me.

I'd been rehearsing my lines for the last few minutes and said them hurriedly: 'The Captain was no doubt making some sort of joke, sir. About the treasure, I mean. He liked puns and all manner of word games and tricks. But I expect there *is* treasure here as well as... ummm... *treesure*.'

'Go on.'

'*Sunken low* – well, that could be the position of the tree, sunken low in this hollow. Or it could refer to the treasure, I suppose. *Springing high* – that's the tree as well. Or the treasure in the tree, high up.'

'Or there may be a spring of water hereabouts,' said Madame Helena.

'With all these cracks and fissures to drain the water away?' Red demanded. But we went on a spring hunt anyway, returning half an hour later to stare at that rocky tree again.

A sea eagle had made an untidy, sprawling nest near the top, and now the bird itself came soaring down towards us, hovered, then flew off. It settled onto a thorn tree on the ridge of the hill and watched us suspiciously.

'*Springing high*,' said Red. 'Boy – we'll have you up that tree now. Search every nook and branch.'

I was lifted onto the lowest branch and began climbing. The petrified bark had been smoothed by hundreds of years of salty wind and rain mixed with eagle droppings, but some of its rocky ridges were still coarse and sharp. Soon my hands were dripping blood.

'I brought a few bandages wid me,' Bones called up to me. 'Want me to wrap 'em round your hands before you go any higher?'

I shook my head and climbed to the next layer, near the top. I poked about the various cracks and crevices, looked into small knotholes and thought about giving up.

'Check out the nest!' ordered Red. I obediently pulled myself up so that I was hanging onto the final stub of a branch by one sweaty, painful armpit. The eagle's nest was a great mound of thorny sticks: no doubt gathered by generations of birds, each adding a layer to the packed, stinking pile below it.

I pushed my free hand into the base of the pile. It was

somewhat damp and I was tempted to not search seriously; then I thought about the trouble that might follow as a result and shoved my arm in up to the shoulder.

Three things happened very closely together then, and I'm not sure about the sequence. There was a shout, there was an enormous clout to the top of my head, and my hand closed on something cool and hard. And then a fourth thing happened: I fell from the tree.

I recall seeing one stubby, frozen branch passing on my left; then one on my right. Then I landed, hard – though not as hard as I was expecting.

Jupiter's big arms had snatched me from the air, and he was holding me now, looking at me with a worried frown.

'You all right, boy?' he asked.

I was lowered to the ground, where Bones took charge and began bandaging my hands with strips of cloth, which stung like fire because of the iodine he sprinkled onto them first.

'Hold still!' he commanded as he dabbed iodine onto the deep scratches on my head. 'Dat eagle got you good and proper,' he said. 'And don't he know it!'

I looked up to the top of the tree, where the sea eagle was now perched, one angry eye fixed on me. He stuck out his chest, flapped his wings and screeched at me: *Gotcha!*

To one side, Red, Tom and Madame were examining the black metal box I'd pulled from the base of the nest. Tom pulled a dagger from a sheath and jammed the point into the front of the box, near to the lock. He pried and twisted at this until the lock broke. Red lifted the lid.

'That's what we came for,' he said with a wink to Tom. He passed the box to Madame.

She poked through the contents. 'Diamonds, mostly,' she said. 'A few emeralds. Some gold coins – Eagles are they? Yes, all of them.'

'One of his blasted jokes,' muttered Red.

Madame continued her inventory. 'A couple of pearls of

no great value. And a slip of parchment. Ah: another little joke. It reads *Here be the treesure*, with the second 'e' under-lined. Well, this is a promising start, Captain. I'll have Amy list and value these items as best she can, and then we'll lock it in the large safe box in my cabin.'

Tom and Red exchanged glances. Red said, 'One of us will need to be present for all that.'

'Of course,' said Madame Helena, snapping shut the lid. 'You can't trust me; and I certainly can't trust you.' She placed the box within the smaller sea chest.

Red looked back up at the tree. 'Reckon there's another box up there?' he asked. 'Or maybe hidden elsewhere around here?'

Madame looked at him frostily. 'The slip of parchment was perfectly clear, Captain. It said this was "the" treasure – or rather, *treesure*. Jones was meticulous about grammar. He would never misuse the definite article.'

'The *what*?'

'The word "the". There's no more treasure here, Captain.'

Bones spoke up. 'Beggin' your pardon, Madame, but we hasn't seen dat slip of paper. Would you mind if we had a peek? Just in case dere was two ways of lookin' at it?'

Madame Helena stiffened with anger and for a moment I thought Bones was about to become eagle food. But - perhaps beguiled by his friendly smile – she controlled herself.

The box was taken up again and opened; Bones picked out the piece of paper himself and studied it. Then he turned it over. Then he held it to the light.

'Dat's right you are,' he said at last. 'All exact as you said, Madame.' He put the scrap back into the box before adding, 'Exceptin' what's written on the back, of course.'

'What?' Madame snatched out the scrap and looked at both sides. 'Oh. I see. Written very faintly, but – yes – it says – *Always ... check ... the other... side, especially with ladies.*'

Red snorted at this and Tom roared with laughter.

'He got you there!' Red exclaimed.

Bones sat on the ground beside me and chortled at this

witticism for some time, while the others argued about which of them should go up the tree again.

'We'll kill that thing first,' said Tom, looking up at the eagle. He pulled a pistol from his belt.

Bones leapt to his feet, exclaiming, 'Don't do dat!'

We all looked at him, puzzled. He looked puzzled himself for a moment before saying, 'Dat's bad luck. Ten years at least.'

'Balderdash!'

Tom pointed his pistol up at the bird. Bones pushed it aside, but gently.

'No need for dat,' Bones insisted. 'I'll go up.'

And in a moment he was climbing the tree as nimbly as a monkey. Tom returned the pistol to his belt with a scowl and glared up at the Cook.

Most of Bones disappeared around the other side of the trunk and Jupiter followed him below, no doubt preparing for a second game of catch.

When he came close to the top, Bones began making gentle, soothing sounds. The eagle stepped around to that side of the nest and craned his neck to peer down at the man.

There was a long pause, with just Bones' crooning to be heard. Then the man eased himself up half a length and crooned a little more. A few minutes later, he did the same again. Then he too pushed his arm into that moist tangle of sticks, bones and ancient excrement.

Shortly afterwards he was climbing down slowly, encumbered by another box, the twin of the first. When this was pried open it disclosed the same contents, with the same two-sided message written on a scrap of parchment.

'So how did you know there was two?' asked Tom, his hand resting on his pistol again.

'Maybe dere wasn't,' said Bones with a cheery wink. 'Maybe dere's three or four, or a hundred. But what I did know was dat dere was something written on the back of dat paper... 'cause I saw it when Madame was readin' the other side!' He laughed loudly, and we all joined in – except for Madame, who wasn't pleased to be made fun of.

We returned from the island in the jolly boat. As we approached the ship, it became clear that something was wrong. There were male shouts and female screams, together with the sort of thumps and clunks that go with the exchange of blows.

Only after several hails from our boat was the rope ladder thrown to us over the side. As we climbed over the rail, we saw three groupings. In one, the three women were standing, their faces red, talking loudly and angrily about something. In another, a few men were sitting on the deck, looking pained. Around them were gathered most of the watch.

The women started towards us, but one of the seated men – Pitiless Jake – leaped up and got to the Captain first.

'Them hussies!' he cried. 'Leadin' the men on! And then kickin' the stuffins out of 'em! Cap'n, I never seen such brazeness! The moment *she* (nodding towards Madame Helena) leaves the ship, they comes for us, with their wiles and their smirks. And then – look at our men!'

The women had been coming to Red; now they ran to Madame instead and began pouring out a different tale. By their version, the men had chased them around the ship and they'd been forced to '– protect ourselves, Madame. You know what men's like. Had to kick 'em in the nethers, that soon slowed 'em down!'

They all ringed us round and the air was thick with accusations, denials, oaths and – from the injured men – groans.

'*SILENCE!*' Red roared at last, holding up one hand. When one of the crew foolishly began again, that hand balled into a fist and the man was knocked to the deck.

'Now,' Red began, 'I want all of you to go back to your duties, apart from *you* and *you* and *you* and *you* and *you*.' He pointed at various sailors, then the group of ladies.

By now, Amy had sidled up to Tom and was whispering something in his ear. Tom's face hardened and he walked over to Jake, punched him in the stomach and then kneed the quartermaster in the face as fell forward.

Red turned to his first mate. 'And what was that for?' he asked angrily.

Tom said, 'He tried to force his vile attentions on Miss Amy.'

Amy had crept back near to Tom, who went to put a comforting arm about her shoulder.

'No!' shouted Red, pointing at Tom's advancing arm. 'I'm having none of that on my ship! You – Tom! – go to my cabin *now*. I'll deal with you in a moment.'

Tom's arm wavered. But a second voice stopped him: more deadly, though calmer. Madame Helena's voice.

'If you so much as touch that girl, your arm will wither and your hand become a claw.'

Tom snatched back his arm as if he had touched live coals. He gave Madame a look of astonishment, then turned upon his heel to march away, hands on hips. The other sailors faded away, but I seated myself by the railing, just close enough to watch without being sent away.

'Now then,' said Captain Red to the women, 'what's all this about?'

Vicky and Sandra gabbled, 'We was in the cabin –'

'– Mindin' our business!'

'– They knocks on the door. Asks us to come for some entertainment –'

'– Music, they says. And dancin'. So of course we went –'

'– Leavin' Amy inside writin' up her diary –'

'– And it was all right to start with. Then one 'em got a bit fresh in the dancin' –'

'– And another put 'is 'ands where 'e shouldn't!'

'– So I slapped 'is face –'

'– He got a kick in the nethers!'

'– Had to put a few of 'em straight, truth be told.'

'– Was all right again after that, we all had a good laugh. Then we heard Amy screamin' –'

'– Ran back to the cabin –'

'– Amy shoutin' about Jake attackin' her –'

'– Then someone pushed Jake –'

'– Someone pushed me an' all –'

'– All hell broke loose, kickin', hair-pullin', shoutin' –'

'– Amy cryin' 'er eyes out –'

Red held up his hand again to silence the two women. He looked to Amy. 'Miss Amy?'

Amy said agitatedly, 'I was writin' at the table when your quartermaster came in and leaned over as if to see what I was writin'. Then he grabbed me and put his foul face to mine and tried to kiss me, and that's when I started screamin'. He tried to pull me up from the chair but I got away and ran out the door, him chasin' me. And then the others came and the fightin' started.'

'Including you?' asked Madame, with a hint of surprise.

Vicky answered for Amy: 'No, Madame. She just stood there, bawlin'!'

Red looked at Pitiless Jake, who had risen from the deck and was rubbing his broad face. 'Well?' Red asked.

Jake shook his head, looking bemused. 'I knocked on the door and Miss Amy said to come inside, so I did. I asked if she wanted to come to the dance. She said no, she didn't dance with sailors. She said she might dance with officers though, and gave me a look. I said I was an officer, and would she like a dance? She laughed and said she might, and gives me another of them flirty looks. I says, what about now? She stands up and starts to dance with me. Then she pushes me away and laughs in my face. I puts one hand on her shoulder, friendly-like, and she starts screamin' and runs out the door. It was still open.'

Red growled, 'The lady says you grabbed her.'

Jake held out his big, meaty hands. He swore and said, 'If I'd grabbed her, would she have got away?'

Amy was staring at him with her mouth open, her face as pale as her sun-bleached hair, looking as if she wanted to say something but was too shocked and astonished to start.

Jake sneered at her: 'Yeah, go on: act like butter wouldn't

melt between them sweet little lips! You been givin' Tom the come-on, and me, and a few others I could mention, lookin' all shy and cute, but flirtin' like a real tart. But you just want to tease us, don't you? I hate hussies like you!'

There were murmurings from the other men gathered on the deck. Red turned to them next.

'What have you got to say for yourselves?' he asked.

The men shrugged their shoulders. Yes, they'd got a bit too friendly. But they thought Vicky and Sandra wouldn't mind. And yes, they'd been kicked and scratched and slapped, but that was okay.

'She's got a mean uppercut, that one,' said a sailor admiringly, nodding at Sandra.

'And that Vicky kicks like a mule!' laughed another.

Vicky and Sandra laughed back and shook their fists at the men. Their eyes twinkled; they clearly hadn't been much bothered by the incident.

Captain Red exchanged glances with Madame Helena. 'All right,' he said. 'This is what we'll do. You men - including you, Jake - six lashes each. Tom will give them out - no, not Tom; second mate Jimmy instead. I'll deal with Tom myself, and the ladies I'll leave to Madame. But if any of you - ANY, ladies included - give me trouble in this way again, I'll throw you to the sharks. I'm not joking.'

Madame looked at her girls, who all hung their heads. She said, 'You've behaved despicably - all of you. Yes, you as well, Amy! You're not to leave the cabin today or tomorrow. After that - well, we'll see.'

The sailors dispersed and the women went back to their rooms, soberly and slowly. Madame smiled as she watched them go, and it occurred to me that she was pleased to see them in trouble. Perhaps it simply amused her.

'It won't happen again, Madame,' said Captain Red.

'Oh, but it will, Captain,' said she. 'However, you and I are prepared for it and we will use it for our own purposes. I always welcome the opportunity to clip wings...'

11 Battle stations

Friendship, how frail it is! And the prettier the mouse, the shorter her intention span. (From the collected works of Bunstropple, mouse and philosopher)

Madame was about to turn and walk back to her cabin, when a shout from the mast threw us all into confusion:

'Sail! Sail there! Port bow! Comin' fast!'

Heads turned, necks craned and men began running along the deck. Red hurried to the rail, reaching for his telescope – but there was no need of that, for the approaching ship was already near enough for us to see that it was probably the same brig we'd met the day before.

Red swore and turned to peer up at the lone figure in the tops. 'Jimmy!' he shouted to his second mate. 'Who the hell put one of the twins up there as main lookout? That brig must've been in view for half an hour!'

The second mate came running up, as did Tom - who had decided that waiting in the cabin for the Captain's wrath was no longer a top priority.

Red and Madame exchanged glances. She pointed to the sea chest containing the two treasure boxes and he nodded.

'Tom, take the chest to their cabin. Madame will stow the contents in their safe and give you one of the keys. Madame, pile a few ladies' chests and clothes against the safe to hide it. Jimmy, come with me!'

With another glance to the approaching ship, Red charged along the deck, shouting orders. He stopped when he came to Bones, who was overseeing the loading of empty water casks into the jolly boat – still tethered off our right side, towards the beach and away from the brig.

'What the hell are you doing?' Red roared. 'We've got an attack to prepare for, and you're *getting water*?'

Bones winked at him. 'Of course, Cap'n,' he said. 'And

why else would we be here? Not lookin' for treasure, dat's for sure. Dere's a stream of fresh water dat empties near where we beached this mornin', right? And we're low on water, right? So what better explanation for bein' here?'

Red thought for a moment. 'Carry on, then!' he said crossly and hurried away to make sure the larger cannon were being prepared properly.

Bones shouted after him, 'And I tole dat new sailor – the big one – to hide himself among dem barrels. Dat all right?'

Red just waved him away, and soon the jolly boat was being rowed slowly across to the beach on our right, arriving there as the brig came close enough to hail us – approaching bow to bow to our left, trapping us against the island.

'*Firebird*!' called one of the brig's officers through a cone. 'Stand away from your guns!'

Our cannons were out and charged; so were theirs.

Red shouted back (he needed no amplification), 'Stand away from yours first!'

The brig dropped sail and its anchor chain went rattling down into the deep. We were within a hundred metres, our guns glaring across at one another. A boat was lowered from the brig and set off towards us, with what looked like a party of soldiers and a few officers in it.

I went back to the opposite side - the starboard railing – and stared across to the beach. Bones and a few sailors had taken the boat beyond the place we'd landed at that morning and had pulled it into the mouth of the tiny creek itself. They pushed the casks out into the water and floated them upstream, one by one. But the first object they sent overboard – hidden by the row of casks – seemed larger than the rest and didn't bob to the surface in the same way...

I came back to the port rail and watched the visitors climb the rope ladder. There were arguments about the armed sailors before four of them were allowed up over the side with their guns.

I would have retreated into the galley then, but Pitiless Jake strode up and grabbed me by a shoulder. 'Cap'n says you're wanted!' he said grimly, giving my shoulder such a pinch that it made my eyes water.

I was led up to the visitors, wiping my eyes and trying to look self-assured. Heads turned and a familiar, sneering voice called out:

'Here's the little coward now! Got your Release with you, coward? Or are you hiding behind some lady's skirts again?'

It was the Inquisitor's boy, clad in a red velvet cloak tipped in gold braid, as if he were an admiral. He had a large, red, admiral-style hat on as well.

'That hat doesn't go with the cloak,' I observed. 'And it doesn't go with your face either, because the hat and the face don't have horse crap on them like they did the last time I saw you.'

I was pleased to see how angry this made him. For a moment I thought he was going to fling himself at me, and I had a fist ready for him if he tried that. But he controlled himself and smirked at me instead.

'Your friend is dead!' he hissed.

'I could say the same to you,' I suggested, 'if you *had* any friends.'

This time he did fly at me, but a large arm barred his approach.

'Not on *my* ship!' said Red, pushing the boy William back into the group from the brig. 'If you children want to fight, do it somewhere else.'

'I'm ready,' I said. 'Handbags at dawn?'

There were some snorts of laughter from the sailors nearby and this made me reckless.

'I'll fight you any time, any place,' I promised. 'Just don't bring your Nanny with you,' I added, looking at the officer standing behind William.

The "Nanny" wasn't too pleased with that. He stepped forward and introduced himself:

'I am King's Captain Alvez of the King's Ship *Barquetine*. Your Captain has agreed that we can search this ship for traitors and contraband. You will produce the document that His Excellence William has referred to. And you will be questioned by us, if necessary.'

Red nodded to me and I went to search my sea chest, praying that I'd actually brought the Release with me. A soldier accompanied me and seemed amused at the oddities I pulled out of my trunk – including the decorated box of the Game of Pirate and sketches of Omar Vlstg.

'You like mice?' he asked, puzzled.

'Omar is a seeker of truth and a disciple of the great mouse philosopher Bunstropple,' I explained.

'Oh,' he said.

When I returned with the Release, the boy William snatched it up as before and read through it greedily.

'There!' he exclaimed. 'He is "*to be given free passage within the Kingdom*". But we aren't in Albion now! He can be arrested!'

The King's Captain took the parchment and studied it. He passed it back to me, saying to William, 'It also says he may "*come and go at his pleasure*". That means we have no power to detain him outside the Kingdom.'

William pouted. He said petulantly, 'But it doesn't say that *exactly*. We could interpret it a different way!'

The King's Captain shook his head and bowed to me. I felt I'd wronged him now.

'I'm sorry I said those things,' I said. 'I was upset. Captain Jones was my good friend... and like a father to me.'

The Captain's eyes met mine. 'Was?' he asked softly, then bowed once more and turned away, giving quiet orders to his men.

I stood there a long time, stunned. There was something in how he said that, and the look he gave me, that told me he believed Captain Jones was alive. More than that: the Captain was safe, and Alvez was pleased that it was so.

The searches continued for a couple of hours, in which time Bones had returned with the filled water casks. While they were being winched up the side, he was questioned by one of the soldiers in the galley, where I was making the day's soup.

I saw Captain Alvez walking past; he stopped and peered at the Cook. Bones' head was twitching occasionally as he answered the soldier, and he was tossing bits of meat into the air for Tiddles to leap up and catch. The Captain asked uncertainly, 'Billy Halfbones?'

Bones screwed up his face in a fit of remembrance and exclaimed, 'Alvez! You was on dis ship yourself! The greatest actor of villains and scoundrels a sailor's ever seen!'

There followed a lot of shaking of hands and slapping of backs, and stories of old times. Bones told again his tale of being pushed off the *Firebird* by Captain Jones, and Captain Alvez laughed.

'Serves you right, you rascal!' he exclaimed.

The boy William came up just then and was introduced to Bones as "an old shipmate". William didn't offer to shake hands and actually yawned in Bones' face. I could tell that Bones was a bit offended, and wasn't surprised when he asked William in an innocent manner:

'So – have you heard from your old master the Inquisitor? The talk was dat he'd run away wid a young friend.'

'What?' William cried out. 'Who?'

Bones pulled out his pipe and began fiddling with it. 'Dat name. On the tip of me tongue, but – ah – I can't recall. Someone from the King's court, a foreign boy. Dey said he'd gone back to the boy's own country wid him.'

The boy William looked at Captain Alvez. 'Have you heard of this?' he shouted. 'Why didn't you tell me?'

Captain Alvez shook his head. He looked at Bones and smiled. 'Your Excellence,' he said to William, 'you have to bear in mind that this man makes up tales all the day long.'

'Dat's true,' Bones agreed. 'I've told some tall ones in me time. But dis one I heard the day after His Inquisitorship disappeared – from a man who knew someone who said he'd been paid to take a party of four out to one of dem foreign ships at night. One of dem looked like the Inquisitor, one was dis foreign boy, and den dere was two big men – one of dem black, one white.'

'That's it!' shouted William. 'One of those foreign ambassadors! Or more likely, one of their ugly little assistants! They were always calling on him, trying to use him, flattering their way into his confidences and the King's.'

Bones interjected, 'Aye, suspicious dat is. Foreigners, hey? Can't trust 'em, can you? I expect they took advantage of the Inquisitor. I've heard he's a trusting man, in his own way.' Bones managed a quick wink in my direction as he said this.

William's eyes widened. 'Maybe – maybe he was kidnapped! That would explain it! He *didn't* abandon me, of course he didn't: he was lured on board and then *taken!* And that's why there's no clue about where he is! They put him onto a boat at night – they sailed away – no one would know! We must get back to Magus! Now!'

Captain Alvez sighed. 'Yes, your Excellence,' he said.

William raged, 'I'll have them check the lists of every foreigner at court! One of them will have left suddenly around that time! We'll track them down! Oh, they'll regret this!'

Captain Alvez asked, 'And the treasure, your Excellence? The King's orders were to recover whatever treasure was indicated by Jones' manuscript.'

'There *isn't* any treasure!' shouted William. 'Or if there is, Jones has it himself and is far away, laughing at us!'

King's Captain Alvez nodded his head. 'That may be so,' he said - with a smile to himself that only Bones and I saw.

Our ship's officers had gathered to salute the *Barquetine's* Captain as he prepared to leave the boat. His crew were going over the side and he was having a final word with Red, when the boy William – who had been kicking moodily at a railing post – suddenly announced:

'This isn't right, you know! I'm an Excellence now. You haven't received me with the proper honours!'

The two captains exchanged a glance. Red said, 'I'm not

familiar with the honours an Excellence receives.'

Captain Alvez said quietly, 'William here was awarded the status of Excellence, third class, as recognition for his – ah - *services* to the court.'

William burst out, 'Third class is the highest that *can* be awarded to someone of my age. Otherwise it would have been a higher grade.'

'A third class Excellence,' continued Alvez, 'should be received and despatched with a single gun salute.'

'No!' exclaimed William, striking the rail in agitation. 'That's the *minimum* requirement! It can be more at the captain's discretion. At the ceremony to honour my award, I received two guns – an ordinary salute and then a salute with streamers.'

'Streamers?' asked Red.

William's face reddened. 'How *ignorant* you are, Captain!' he exclaimed. 'First you don't know the proper forms for addressing an Excellence (you should always say, "Yes, *your Excellence.*" or "Streamers, *your Excellence*?"). *Then* you don't know how to salute a ship with an Excellence on it. And *now* you don't even know what *streamers* are! They are tiny rolls of paper that are shot from a cannon into the air. They unroll and make a celebratory pattern that falls slowly to the ground. Or sea. Or deck of a ship.'

Red and Captain Alvez exchanged glances again. Red said slowly, 'Well, *your Excellence*, I'm sure we can arrange something of that sort. Perhaps not exactly streamers, but certainly a single gun salute followed by a celebratory salute. I'll ask my men to prepare something appropriate.'

'Your reply is noted,' said William, with a proud toss of his head. 'I shall be standing on my deck to receive the salute as we pass your ship.'

'*Your* deck? The foredeck? Or do you mean the aft deck above the captain's cabin?' asked a puzzled Red.

'Above *my* cabin,' said William. 'An Excellence takes precedence over a mere ship's captain.'

Captain Alvez's face did not change, except that his eyes

hardened. 'Of course,' he said. 'Those are the rules, even though most Excellences do not insist on them. I share a cabin with my lieutenants and we dine once a week with his *Excellence*. At his *excellent* expense.'

Red roared with laughter at this, but stopped under William's glare. He said to the boy, 'Well then, *your Excellence*, I suggest that your ship should set sail before ours, and sail towards us slowly, passin' half a cable's distance away. As your bow comes to ours, we'll fire a salute from a bow cannon. As your stern deck passes our stern shortly after that – you standin' there alone in your fine red coat and hat – we'll fire streamers from our stern chaser. Agreed?'

William nodded regally. 'Your compliance is welcome, Captain, and I will report upon it favourably at Court.'

Then he swept over the side, but paused – unable to leave without some low shot at me. He sneered, '*You'll* never get a send off like this, you cowardly traitor!'

I thumbed my nose at him: but he was probably right.

Within moments of the boat setting off back to the brig, our men began readying sail, positioning the bow and stern cannon and taking up the slack on the anchors.

Red was on the rear deck, in close discussion with Pitiless Jake who was cranking the cannon to the correct angle. Bones was there too, and he signalled to me to come over.

'Leave it to me, Cap'n,' Jake was saying. 'Done this afore. Half a cable's distance, right? This'll be the elevation, then. Waterproof wadding, then half fill it only. What've you got, Bones?'

Bones turned to me. 'Where'd you put dat cask of pork dat went rotten?'

'Just inside the first hold, on the right,' I said. 'You wanted it for shark bait.'

'Let's fetch it up. And Jake - could you send some navvy to find us a few empty buckets?'

We carried the heavy barrel between us and unwrapped the canvas we'd strapped around it. An unholy stench drove us back.

Bones stuck a peg on his nose and waved us away. He knocked the lid off the barrel and used the buckets to empty the thinner liquid over the side. Lumps of pork and bones went over the side as well. A thick slurry of rotting meat and fat was left in the bottom.

'Dat'll be perfect!' crowed Bones. He poured it into the two buckets, then sent the ruined barrel over the side, too.

I watched, mystified, as Jake dropped a package of powder into the cannon, then two layers of canvas that Bones cut to size from the sheet we'd wrapped the barrel in. He stuffed some cotton wadding onto this and pounded it with a rammer. One more layer of canvas followed, a bigger sheet this time so that it extended out of the end of the cannon. He nodded at the buckets of stinking slime.

'Let's have 'em ready, but don't put 'em in until the last moment.'

He poked a spike through the fuse hole near the base of the cannon, sending a slight puff of powder out of it. He cut a length of fuse and measured it against his little finger. 'Three seconds,' he said and pushed it carefully into the fuse hole, giving it a twist.

A few minutes later, the *Barquetine's* sails were loosed and her capstan was run round, pulling her anchors smoothly from the shallow water. She was under way.

Bones and I were leaning on the port side railing of the rear deck, peering forward at the brig as she slowly processed towards us. The *Barquetine's* officers stood in her bows and saluted our officers as they approached. Our bow cannon spoke, sending a flash but no ball. Our men waved their hats and cheered.

Now they moved alongside us, their left side to ours. As their bow passed our stern, Bones and Pitiless Jake removed their hats and bowed extravagantly, then picked up the buckets of stinking pork slurry. Their officers noted the gun and the buckets being poured into it; I saw them point at the cannon, nudge one another and laugh.

Our stern was now opposite their midships. Jake had a lighted taper in his hand and was counting as he watched the ship pass. *One – two – three – one – two – three – one –*

The rear deck was coming; his Excellence William stood there alone (apart from the man at the wheel, a little forward of him and half-hidden by the sides of the booth that protected him from winds). William was facing us, his bright red coat and golden epaulettes catching the sun, with his ridiculous, showy red admiral's hat on his head.

'One – two – three – *now!*'

Jake lit the fuse. William was coming opposite us. He raised one hand in an imperial salute.

The cannon roared. A dark, stinking rain sluiced him, the deck and his cabin. Fragments of rotting pork and slimy gobbets of rancid fat covered him from hat to pointed toe.

We waved merrily.

'Sails away! Anchor up!'

We were away within half a minute, by which time the *Barquetine* was a hundred metres off and picking up speed. I could see William running forward, shouting; men scattered from his stench, roaring with laughter. I expect he was demanding that the brig turn back and punish us; instead, it went even faster.

We passed around the island to our right, stopping at the far side of it to send a boat to collect the large, black figure waving from the beach. We sailed away at some speed, in case captain of the *Barquentine* decided to chase after us.

After an hour with no sign of pursuit, Red shortened sail and we watched several floggings, starting with the twins and ending with Pitiless Jake himself. Then we sped away into the beckoning horizon.

After cleaning the pots that evening, I went and found Jupiter. He was sitting against some barrels, working his way through a mess of ropes – checking for flaws, then cutting and splicing where necessary.

'Coil that one for me, boy,' he said. I settled next to him and began winding a thin, tangled hawser.

'What happened at the Inquisitor's?' I asked.

He shook his head. 'I can't tell you that.'

I tried to think of another way into this subject. 'Do you know if Jones got away?' I asked. 'Or was he really recaptured, as the Inquisitor said?'

Jupiter shook his head. 'I'm not talking about that either. So stop asking.'

'Is your son safe? And your wife? I really want to know, Jupiter. After all, you put them at risk for me. And I still don't know why you did that.'

'Yes. They're all safe.'

'What about the other guard?'

'Saturn and his family are safe, too.'

'Good. I was worrying about them. But why did you -'

He growled, 'Hush, boy. I did it because your father was a good man. I owe him a lot. We all owe him a lot. If we'd stood with him the way we should have, he might still be alive and Albion would be a better place. Me helping you was my way of standing with him now: me and Saturn and some others you'll never meet. We still stand, boy.'

I sat a while in thought before saying, '*The guard still stand.* I said those very words to the Inquisitor. It shocked him. And it scared him, I think. He went pale.'

Jupiter laughed, a deep throaty chuckle. 'You told the Inquisitor that? Boy, you've got courage.'

'Tell me about the Guardians.'

Jupiter grumbled to himself a little before signalling for me to sit closer to him. Then he said quietly, his eyes fixed on the rope he was mending:

'The Guardians believe that God is sleeping, and while he sleeps we must care for the world. There are four ages of mankind, boy. First there was the Garden, where we lived at peace with one another and with all creation. Then came the Revolt, a mighty battle in which God allowed himself to be defeated so that we might learn what the world is like without him. We're now in the third age, the Sleep of God. The final age begins with the Awakening.'

I asked, 'So while God sleeps, the Guardians look after everything? But if God is sleeping, who appoints them?'

'We're all Guardians, boy. This world is the responsibility of every man, woman and child. Most of us don't take that responsibility seriously. But some of us stand up and try to do what must be done. Whatever the cost.'

I was suddenly bitter and said, 'That includes my father and mother, of course. But it wasn't just a cost for *them*, was it? It was a cost to me as well. That's not fair. Why should I have to pay? They could... they could still be here. I could have grown up with real parents. We could –'

Jupiter grabbed my shoulder roughly and pulled me around, until his face was centimetres from mine.

'You don't know what you're saying!' he growled. 'Sometimes the price you pay is high. Sometimes there's a price for others, too. But some things matter so much, you *have* to do them.'

'Nobody has to –' I started sulkily.

He interrupted: 'I won't let you spit on the memory of your own father! Don't you think he agonised over his decision? Jack: he would have done anything to keep the three of you together, *anything*. As would your mother. But they couldn't betray their calling and friends and beliefs just to make sure they could live in a big house with a nice back garden and a few children playing on the lawn.'

'I didn't mean –'

Jupiter silenced me with a look. He said gruffly, 'There may come a time when *you* have to make a choice between your honour and your own safety. When you come to that time, you'll understand the choice your father had to make. Until then, you keep your stupid mouth shut.'

'Sorry.'

Jupiter released me and continued working on the ropes.

'Please tell me more,' I said. 'I need to understand. Just like your own son – like *he* needs to understand.'

Jupiter gave a deep sigh. 'Okay, Jack,' he said. 'The Guardians stand up for the rights of all people, but especially the weak, the poor, the oppressed. They speak out. They care for their fellow men and don't stop caring. They might even fight, where there's no other option.'

'But they can't win,' I said.

'Maybe not. They believe in the equality of all men and women, so they're hated by every man who has authority or money or feels he's important. The powers in this world are stacked against the ordinary man and woman.'

'You sound like the Captain,' I said. 'He said it was a bad world. He also said you have to work with the world the way it is. But I'm not sure the world is really all that bad. Albion isn't, anyway.'

Jupiter shook his head at me. 'We all grow up thinking a man becomes rich or famous or powerful because he deserves it. No, boy. The top hundred people in Albion are up there with all their money and properties and privileges because the King likes them. He likes them because they tell him how great he is and laugh at his jokes and wink at the evil things he does. The next thousand people are chosen by those first hundred, in the same way. The next hundred thousand are chosen by the thousand.'

I found myself repeating my aunt's words: 'But these are men of quality – breeding – good family. They're not like... common people.'

Jupiter laughed, saying, 'You see a rich man being driven down the road in a big carriage and you think his silk cuffs make him a good man? He's no better than the man begging for a scrap of bread by the side of the same road. Boy, I've met beggars of more honour and nobility than the King himself. And I should know.'

'But the Guardians can never succeed,' I said.

'Perhaps not. But they have to try. They can do a lot of good, even while they're being dragged to prison. They can teach men to live in peace, to act honourably and live honestly. And the Guardians of old had the stones of power.

That brought them some protection.'

'What?'

Jupiter smiled broadly at me. 'Didn't you know? Your father had the Curchan Ruby.'

'Before Captain Jones did? You mean my father stole the Ruby, too?'

'Hush! Of course not. He was given it by the people of Curchan, so he could use it for our own land.'

'What?!'

'There are four gems of power and one wooden staff. The staff was destroyed long ago, and no one knows where the stones lie. Except that the Ruby was said to be here, then there, then known to be in your father's possession. That's why the King had your mother put in prison: to lure your father from his hiding place so they could take the Ruby from him.'

I said, 'But if my father had the Ruby, he could have used it against the King. He could have ruled – everything!'

'That's nonsense, boy. The Ruby only gives power that fits the user. Your father didn't want to rule anything; just to bring peace and fairness and happiness. Him using the Ruby to fight the King would be like using a handful of flowers against a sword. In any case, when your father was captured, the Ruby wasn't found on him.'

I said, 'Just as they didn't find it when they captured the Captain.'

'Yes. And so your father and mother were executed, just as the Captain would probably have been executed if you hadn't gone to see him one last time.'

'Only... probably?'

Jupiter looked at me steadily. 'Maybe there's others who would have tried to save the Captain as he was led out to be hanged, boy. But the King would have been expecting that, and a lot of good men and women would have died as a result. You done good, son.'

He patted me on the shoulder, rose and walked off. I knew not to question him about it again.

12 Mermaids

The cards of Fate and Fortune bring individual reward and tragedy, such as items of treasure or the loss of a sailor. The Runes of Destiny generally control the greater matters, such as bringing fair weather or foul, good health or the plague, crews that are happy or mutinous, ships running aground, good food and plenteous water. The Rules set out how each of these affect the progress of the ship.

This time, interpreting the instructions didn't get me into trouble. We had gathered in the usual way, except that Misty the sailing master had also been dragged in and was sitting at the captain's table, smelling of rum and trying to focus on the charts laid out there. He had the air of a man wandering down a long street after a hard night's partying, wondering which house was his own.

'Madame,' invited Captain Red, indicating the parchment she was holding.

She read it slowly, for Misty's benefit I think:

Follow the Mermaid until you glimpse the Rock. Anchor before you founder and follow the mermaids' silver summons to worship.

'Well?' asked Red, looking at me.

'The first part is from the Game,' I said. 'The Mermaid is one of the compass points at which you can place your ship when you start. It's exactly southeast.'

'Aye,' said Red. 'I recall you saying that, back in the house. Misty, if you set a course due southeast from the centre of that island we were on, where do we hit land?'

Misty moved a rule across the chart nearest him, swivelled it about while muttering to himself, then gave a confused shrug. 'Not for days, Cap'n. There's a cape around four hundred sea miles southeast; until then, there's just empty sea.'

Red swore. 'Does the blasted parchment give us an idea of distance?' he asked. 'Glimpsing the rock? Anchoring before we founder? Do those have a meaning, Jack?'

'No, sir. I've never heard them used in the Game. Or at any time with the Captain.'

'Four hundred miles is a long way to sail without certainty,' growled Red.

Madame said quietly, 'The instructions say to travel until we *glimpse* the rock. Might that be a considerable distance before the cape?'

Misty shook his head. 'It's not a high cape,' he said. 'See it from fifty sea miles, maybe. And if we travel in a straight line, we'll have holed ourselves afore then. There's isolated rocks aplenty, too small to show on this chart. Best to go round 'em, further south.'

'What?' Red walked over to Misty and picked him up, then slammed him against the cabin wall and held him there by the throat. 'You fool!' he shouted in Misty's face. 'It's one of *those* rocks he'll be meaning. Not something a few hundred miles off!'

Misty gurgled something in reply; Red eased his grip of the ship master's throat, but didn't remove his hand.

'I – I,' said Misty hoarsely. 'I think – no – let me look at the – the charts again.'

He was allowed to sit again at the table, where he began tracing a course with a dirty finger, mumbling to himself. 'My head,' he said finally, putting his hand to the back of his head. 'You've hurt my head. I can't think.'

'I'm going to hurt your head a lot more,' warned Red. He held a meaty fist in front of Misty's eyes.

Misty nodded. 'Somewhere here,' he said, waving at a blank area of the chart, 'there's a region of troubled water. Shallow. Sea bed that's almost land, or land that's fallen below the waves. Some big rocks. If I lie down a while, I'll remember it better. It's about a day and a night away. We have time. My head. You shouldn't have –'

'One more word,' said Red coldly. 'One more word, and I'll break your skull like an egg. Go lie down. And if your breath smells of rum at any time in the next two days, I'll find a punishment that will cure your thirst forever.'

Misty nodded once, then hurried from the cabin.

Red turned and looked at me steadily. 'There some that can take their rum,' he said. 'And there some that the rum takes. You make sure you stay the right side of that line. Misty was once the sharpest pilot and master mariner you ever saw. Now he's less than useless. He's a liability; and pretty soon he'll be shark food.'

I nodded, wondering that Red should care to give me fatherly advice. Then he put one large hand slowly about my neck and squeezed, just enough to let me know he could break it if he wished.

'You think we need you?' he asked quietly. 'We need you only so long as you give us what we want. We need you less than we need Misty, and in a few days he's goin' over the side. Rum's done him in, and here's my point: rum does in a lot of galley boys. Oh, I seen you sippin' the grog, lad. And I seen you gettin' above yourself with the ladies. Others has told me that, too. You take one sip too many; you touch with as much as one finger; you do anything that muddles your mind and interferes with your judgement, and you're dead. You understand me?'

His fingers tightened their grip a little. I tried to nod. He released me and gave my face a gentle slap.

'Go back to the galley,' he said.

I looked at Madame. She had an odd look on her face, as if she was enjoying this.

'You won't get a kind word from me,' she said crisply. 'I agree with the Captain this time.'

I hurried away, feeling miserable.

Once in the galley however, I found comfort in my routine tasks. I tidied, fed Tiddles, then began preparations for the evening meal. Bones wandered in, looked at my face, then patted me kindly on the shoulder.

'You're a good lad, whatever dem bastards say,' he said with a wink. 'Even so, Cap'n says no grog for you dis week, so no grog it is. Look upon it as one of dem religious duties. Good for you an' all. I've had no rum dis many a year and don't miss it. I miss beer and a good glass of wine more. Ah, well.'

Then we sat and talked and laughed for half an hour, at the end of which I felt good about myself again, even though we mostly talked about the ship's rats. Bones had a way of taking a subject and making it serious and funny at the same time. He seemed in love with every detail of life, as if facing death at sea had made him capable of extracting whatever was lively and good from the world.

He described some of the different types of rat: pack rats living in the woods; wharf rats that were brown and easiest to train; the black rats that were common on ships; furless mole rats he'd come across in one of his shipwreckings.

I told him about Omar Vlstg and the mouse philosopher Bunstropple: he listened open-mouthed with pleasure, and laughed at my account of Madame and the Omar invoice until tears coursed down his cheeks.

He told me about some rats he had tamed and taught to thieve from a captain's cabin, then about the time he'd fired rats from a cannon into a ballroom full of fancy ladies and their escorts. ('Well, dey had been rude to me, 'cause I was just a ship's cook and dey had eyes only for some rich Admiral and his snooty white-coated lackeys. So I paid the crew for each rat dey caught; and lad, we had our revenge. Dem ladies was paradin' about wid fancy mink furs about their necks, and a moment later dey was wearin' furry rats as well. Most of 'em alive and a bit angry, hey?').

The next day we travelled peacefully across calm seas,

then hoved-to overnight, fearing we might come upon the promised rocks in the darkness. At dawn we pressed on and it was on the afternoon of the second day that we arrived at the place we guessed was our destination, anchoring a few sea miles short of Cursed Rock, pretty much northwest of it.

Cursed Rock was a towering black spur that rose from the sea like the enormous forearm of a man shaking his right fist at the heavens. Where it left the water, it was as broad as our ship, narrowing slowly as it rose to a height well above our mainmast. It ended in a great lump strangely like a fist, palm upwards – you could even imagine the thumb and the four clenched fingers, except that its little finger was a stump pointing slightly to the left.

The rocky arm pointed east, as if cursing the rising sun. We had sailed towards it from the northwest and therefore the arm slanted to our left. Between ourselves and this angry peak, the sea appeared to boil; it was in ceaseless agitation, covered with foam and waves, with occasional spurts high into the air.

Misty the sailing master was dragged forward from the cabin he shared with Tom and some other officers.

'The Boilin' Sea,' he muttered, scratching his matted beard with filthy fingers. He smelled of rum again and his eyes were red. 'Wide shelf of rock this side of Cursed Rock, not more'n a fathom deep in some places, so the water boils across it. Not safe half a league to the north or south either. There's rocks aplenty and the charts don't show 'em.'

Red said drily, 'Good of you to warn us, Misty. You were supposed to be at the helm two hours ago. I only brought you on this voyage because you know the southern seas.'

'I'm not well,' Misty groaned. 'Had to lie down.'

Red shouted over his shoulder, 'Bosun's mate!'

The man - one of Pitiless Jake's evil friends - ran over and put a big hand on Misty's shoulder.

Red growled, 'Tie Misty to the bow railing – starboard side. Get the twins to wash him down with a couple of buckets of sea water every half hour. Leave him tied there until the sun has burned the rum out of him.'

As Misty was being dragged away, Red turned to Tom and ordered, 'Go search the officers' cabins now, including their sea chests. I want every drop of liquor, hear me? Whoever it belongs to! We need Misty sober for a few days; after that, he can drink as much as he likes, so long as it's sea water.' He gestured with his head towards the ship's railings and the hungry sea beyond it.

"Follow the Mermaid until you glimpse the Rock. Anchor before you founder, and follow the mermaids' silver summons to worship."

We were at the bow railings this time, looking forward. The evening sun behind us cast the shadow of the masts far across the troubled sea. I was holding my nose against the smell rising from the ship's open toilets below, the "heads"; Red seemed not to notice it, being long accustomed to squatting over a hole that emptied more or less directly into the sea; Madame as ever seemed determined not to react with weakness to any external forces.

'Summons to worship?' asked Madame. 'Something to do with churches or temples perhaps: I don't see any of *those*.'

'Mermaids?' asked Red, staring into the water before us but talking to me.

'It means nothing to me,' I said. 'The only mermaid reference in the Game is the southeast marker. And there isn't anything in the Game about worship. Well, not exactly.'

'Out with it,' said Madame frostily.

'The bell,' I said. 'It's one of the pieces in the Game. And it's meant to be a ship's bell, of course. But don't they use bells to call people to worship? And I seem to recall the Captain telling me that the Game's bell we were using was shaped like a temple bell from one of the strange lands he'd visited.'

She said, 'That's a very poor connection. And you could

read it differently: that it's the mermaids who are doing the summoning. They're said to have voices of silver, like bells ringing beneath the waves.'

'Perhaps that's what it means,' I said. 'But if – instead - it was the mermaids going to worship, they would be summoned by a bell underwater, wouldn't they?'

Red sneered, 'In an underwater temple, rung by an octopus wearing a red cape and a funny hat, right?'

There was a croak from the railing a little further along, where Misty was still tied. 'Underwater!' he called to us hoarsely. 'That's it!'

'That's *what*, you drunken sot?' shouted Red.

Misty beckoned us over. 'The Boiling Sea,' he wheezed. 'It's all because there's land just below the water. Used to be an island.'

'So?'

'An island with people. A drowned world. We once took a boat into – into the middle. There's houses beneath the waves. Other buildings, too.'

'A temple, maybe?' asked Madame.

Misty shrugged. 'Hard to say. Might be.'

Red was nodding his head. 'Stands to reason,' he said. If there's people, there's some damned religion - and that means some big building they gather in.'

'Probably with a high tower,' said Madame. 'Probably the highest building, perhaps nearest the surface.'

'Aye,' said Red. 'With a bell in the top, for the purpose of bothering honest men with its janglin'. We'll find that bell tower and have a look in it.'

Madame added, 'It would be a fine place to hide treasure: a place unusual enough to appeal to Jones.'

Misty gave a pathetic cough, to remind us he was suffering. Red looked at him, then shook his head. 'You'll stay there until nightfall,' he said. 'And you'll be grateful it ain't until dawn.'

Shortly after dawn, three of the ship's boats were rowed

carefully into the foaming waters of the Boiling Sea. One boat had everything likely to be needed for diving and recovery of underwater treasure: ropes, nets, two crowbars and – surprisingly - the yellow-haired twins Matthew and Thomas.

A second boat was there to stow any booty and was oared by the strongest men on the *Firebird*, including Jupiter of course; the third held Red, Misty, a couple of rowers and myself.

Misty was more sober than I'd ever seen him, and his grey whiskers weren't as matted and greasy as they'd been before several buckets of sea water. He was leaning forward in the bows, shading the surface with his hat.

We were heading south of Cursed Rock, hoping to come upon the drowned city. We'd been zigzagging about this course for nearly an hour now, with the three boats a stone's throw apart so that we covered more of this broad expanse of troubled sea.

A large albatross passed far overhead; cormorants dived about us; gulls called us names as they passed. I peered into the depths, thinking that if a man could fly, then the land below would look like the sea bed I was gazing upon: remote, unreal, untouchable like the soaring clouds.

Misty shouted excitedly: 'Starboard! Take her starboard, there!'

The rowers obeyed and soon I saw it too: the outline of a long-decayed house some fifty fathoms below us. Had it been on level land, I could have run there in fifteen seconds; here, it was unreachable.

Misty stood and waved the other boats in the direction we were facing – nearly due south. We settled again to watch the drowned world passing below us.

We were in an untroubled stretch of water now, looking down into what was once a pleasant valley. I could see the markings of an old river bed, with the remains of a square, squat building half across it: a water mill, no doubt. There were outlines of small dwellings nearby, then nothing for a few minutes as we followed the track of the river.

'Ah!' Misty breathed, to himself rather than Red or me, 'It comes back to me! The river will curve left in a little – there it goes – and the main part of the town will appear.'

Soon we were passing over rows of dwellings lost long ago to the sea: most of them visible only as a discolouration on the sea floor where their walls still protruded, or where their collapsed roofs had become a source of nutrition and support for the more exotic seaweeds and corals.

Misty continued, 'And here's the main part of the town on the other side of the river, climbing what must have been a lovely green hill. Maybe with a crown of oaks and beeches at the top?'

We bore a little right, which was south or maybe a little west of that. The houses were nearer to the surface now: I could see ruined walls and the outlines of what had once been orchards and gardens and front lawns. At one time people had lived there. Children had played ball in that park and mothers had called to them from the doorstep. Men had worked those fields, maybe gathering with their friends in that bigger building to talk and laugh and drink some odd concoction made from grapes or fermented grains. A lost world haunted me in this watery vision.

'There 'tis!' Misty shouted, gesticulating to the sailors to pull a little to the left.

A tower rose through the blue-green waters, dappled in the watery colours of this underworld: rusty red-orange, deep purple of waving anemones, scaly whiteness and blackness of the shells, shockingly vivid pinks and blues of the corals and every mixture of brown, green and orange imaginable in the waving weed.

Perhaps the tower was the only structure that had been built with particular care, for all its stones appeared to be in place. It protruded from the middle of a round, domed building that was perhaps twenty metres across and was covered with multicoloured seaweeds. The tower's sides flared gracefully from the dome, thinning quickly from about eight metres across to around five, then rising twenty metres into the clear water. It reminded me of the stem and bowl of a large wine glass upended upon the sea floor.

The scene below us was not as clear and static as my description suggests. There was a continuous agitation of the water's surface that caught the light of the sky and distorted every vision; and there seemed to be erratic currents beneath us, causing the edges of structures to waver and even disappear beneath the dappled mosaic of light and shadow from the sun, crisscrossed by the patterns cast by the waves and our slowly moving boats.

The top of the tower was five metres below the surface; not too far to dive down to, but far enough to make it difficult for anyone to stay there for more than a few seconds, I thought.

The boats dropped anchors at different points around the tower, then were rowed to just above it. We tied the boats together before shortening the anchor lines until they were taut; we were now fixed in place.

Matthew and Thomas stripped to their breeches, shivering in the light wind that danced about us. Then they began breathing slowly and deeply, their eyes fixed on the water. After several minutes, Thomas – the one twin regarded as an able seaman – signalled to Red.

They lowered themselves into the water. Each twin was given a cannonball stitched into canvas and fastened to the end of a thin rope which had been coiled in the bottom of the boat and tied off at a ringbolt. Each took one last, long breath and disappeared into the water.

The rope ran out quickly, then stopped. I peered over the side and could see that the twins had landed on the top of the tower, setting down their weights there. Then they began searching about, swimming in and out of the windows of the tower, starting at the top and slowly working their way down.

As they descended, their shapes became distorted by the

shifting currents and finally disappeared into darkness.

I found I was holding my breath as I watched – but soon had to stop. The twins however carried on. Several minutes passed before one of them could be seen rising through the dappled light. Matthew it was; he held onto the side of the boat, gasping. His face had turned a light blue but it quickly returned to its usual reddish tinge: the twins were very fair-skinned and never tanned like the other sailors.

A full minute after Matthew, Thomas emerged and swam to the boat.

'Mermaids!' he exclaimed through chattering teeth. 'I saw mermaids!'

'You're full of it,' Matthew said, rather angrily I thought.

'Nah – there was two of 'em! And they was callin' me!'

Red was listening to this with impatience. He demanded, 'Never mind all that! What's there to see in the tower?'

'Nothing, Cap'n,' said Matthew.

'Nothing yet,' said Thomas. 'But we didn't look all that close. Barely peeked into some of the rooms.'

'*I* was lookin' close,' said Matthew sulkily. 'Doin' my job, instead of chasin' skirt. All in your head, anyway.'

'Wasn't. And there wasn't no skirt – they don't wear clothes. All loose and free and they lookin' right at you, just beggin' to be touched. Pretty faces, too. Not long hair though, not like in the paintings.'

'You're touched,' said Matthew. 'You always stay down too long and it turns your head.'

Thomas began, 'I saw – '

'Silence!' shouted Red, thumping Thomas on the top of the head with an angry fist. 'Get ready for a second dive.'

The twins climbed on board again and went through the same procedure as before – a routine I later learned was common amongst divers for pearls and sponges. The twins had grown up in a small fishing village and had been doing this since they were small.

They retrieved the cannon balls that had been hauled up and I realised now that the weights helped them to cover that first five metres quickly, as well as providing a line back to the boat should they need it.

The twins dropped over the side again. They were both gone for longer this time, though once again Thomas was back much later than his brother.

'I seen 'em, too,' Matthew said to us quietly while we were waiting for Thomas. 'Not clearly, though. Too far down for me. I don't like it when the water's dark and icy.'

Misty shook his head. 'Dangerous,' he muttered. 'They ain't human, see. They don't think like us.'

'Some says they's witches,' added one of the other seamen. 'Witches what's drowned and now does their evil spells under the water.'

'I heard that too,' said Misty. 'They enchants a man further and further down, then ties him to the sea bottom for to watch him die. They gives him a few bubbles of air now and then, so that he lasts for hours - days even.'

Red said brutally, 'There's no such thing as mermaids. And if anything that looks like a mermaid sticks its head out of the water, I'll shoot it off.' He motioned at the gun tucked in his belt.

'They only puts their heads up to sing,' said someone.

'Nah, that's Sirens.'

'Same thing.'

'Isn't.'

Thomas surfaced now, his face a dusky blue and fixed in a starry-eyed smile. He clambered into the boat and lay gasping in the bottom.

'Report!' ordered Red.

'Nothing again,' said Matthew. 'Searched every corner of the top room. Nothing but crabs and an eel.'

'And a big old bell hangin' from the top!' Thomas corrected him sharply. 'Expect you didn't see that, though.'

Matthew snapped, 'Yeah, I saw it but I didn't need to talk about it. It's a temple, you idiot! Of course it has a bell.'

'You didn't see it,' sneered his twin.

'I saw a lot more'n you did. I was searchin' the rooms

while you was chasin' water hags.'

'You're jealous!' cried Thomas. 'The mermaids was callin' me, but they didn't want you!'

'Leave off,' said Matthew. 'They was ugly anyway.'

'Oh, no they wasn't! And they was tryin' to persuade me to stay with 'em! There's this cave at the bottom, with a greenish light comin' from it. And they was makin' signs like to say I'd be able to breathe. I nearly went, I did.'

'Liar.'

Thomas thumbed his nose at his brother. 'Like always,' he said, 'I'm top dog. We goes into a bar and who takes a pretty girl home afterwards? Me! Matthew here just gets whatever ugly old tarts I leave behind. And mostly he don't even get that! Ha!'

Matthew flew at his brother, punching and kicking until a couple of seamen pulled them apart.

Red slapped Thomas across the face. 'Finish your report!' he growled.

Thomas hardly blinked at the slap: like many of Red's crew he was accustomed to it. He said now, 'Aye, Cap'n. Nothin' in the top four rooms. There's another couple rooms below that; we can do them next. Did come across an old sea chest, all fallin' to pieces. Nothin' there but a skull picked clean.'

Red looked sullen now. 'Down you go again,' he said. 'Look in the bottom rooms. While you're there, Jack's goin' to think about this. He's goin' to think so hard that the answer's goin' to pop out of his head before you get back. Right, Jack?' He put his hand on my shoulder and gave it a harsh squeeze.

I said, 'Aye, aye sir.'

Just then Misty called, 'Listen! They're singin'!'

We listened, then shook our heads apart from Thomas, whose face was shining. 'They's callin' for me,' he said softly. 'They wants me.'

I leaned over the side of the boat and peered into the depths. Perhaps there *were* some womanly shapes below –

or perhaps they were merely shadows or my hopeful imagination. I leaned out further – half out of the boat - and placed my ear to the cool water.

There *was* a song. Something haunting and thrilling; something eerie, frightening and yet alluring. I tried to take my ear from the water but couldn't. I felt myself being drawn in by that music of pure silver; and for a moment it seemed that everything was upside down, that I was deep beneath the water and rising towards the bright surface. I understood suddenly that this sea below us was in fact the wide sky; it was my true breath. There was a terrible, savage beauty within it, a beauty that was calling me home.

A horny sailor's hand hauled me back, and the spell faded like a dream on waking; yet still I heard those silver voices calling. I was coughing seawater from mouth and nose, while the others laughed at me.

'I heard them!' I choked out.

'You're a weakling,' said Red crossly. 'A fool to your own imagination.' He slapped me across the face; that brought me fully to my senses.

He said to the twins, 'Matthew – Thomas – bottom rooms and then the bell room again. You've missed something. Jack's missing something, too. Jones' instructions have to mean... something.'

'Unless the treasure's gone,' wheezed Misty. 'No silver 'cause someone's been and took it. Only mermaids left.'

'And a bell!' I exclaimed.

They all looked at me.

I said, 'A silver bell! Is it silver?'

Matthew and Thomas looked at each other. 'It might be,' said Matthew.

Thomas shrugged. 'I'll go and see,' he said. 'I'll scrape it with my knife.'

'If it's a large bell, it won't be pure silver,' said Misty. 'That'd be worth a fortune.'

'It ain't that large,' said Matthew. 'I could probably put my arms around it.'

'Could be silver, then. Make a lovely, clear sound if so. Not that you'd hear it underwater…'

While we were still talking, Thomas dropped into the water with his cannonball. We watched him land on the tower, then disappear into the top window. A minute later, he half-emerged, but seemed to be pulled back into the tower by something. Another minute passed before he shot upwards and latched onto the boat.

'Silver!' he shouted. 'Bright as anything under the crud!'

'You took your time,' growled Red.

'Met a friend,' said Thomas with a wink. 'And then we –'

'Stow it,' said the Captain. He reached down and grabbed Thomas, dragging him into the boat. He said coldly: 'Put your clothes on. Matthew can do the next part by himself. You're goin' back to the ship.'

Thomas's face fell. He sat in the bottom of the boat, breathing heavily and looking moody while Red discussed his plans with Misty.

'The sea's quiet just now.'

'Aye,' said Misty. 'And it should stay like that for a few hours at least.'

'Good. We'll secure the bell with ropes; we can tie them to whatever ringbolts or arms they hung it by. Matthew can go down and check that out in a moment. Then we'll need some way of breakin' it loose from its mountings. A couple of turns of chain about the main support – is there a beam that goes across above the bell? We'll move the ship closer and use the smaller anchor chain, payin' it out from the ship by boat.'

Misty nodded. 'Yeah – take up the strain usin' the capstan on the ship. Oughta bust the beam clean out of the wall and – hey!'

Thomas had seized a cannonball and thrown himself out of the boat. I was still sitting at the side and watched the silver turbulence of his swift passage until he was lost to view halfway down the tower.

The crew grabbed the rope that had secured the cannonball; but he had untied it as he sat in the boat's bottom.

Matthew stood up, cursing his brother and reaching for another cannonball. Red knocked him to the bottom of the boat.

'You're stayin' put!' he shouted.

'But Thomas –'

Red said, 'Thomas is dead. If the water bitches don't kill him, I'll flog the skin off him when he returns.'

'He'll not come back,' said Matthew, trying to rise from the bottom without coming close to Red's fists. 'He was always goin' on about mermaids and what he'd do if he found one. He – he ain't quite normal, sometimes. If I don't go down there and drag him back –'

'Tie him up,' said Red to a sailor; and in a moment Matthew's hands were tied together and fastened to one of the boat's benches.

There followed an hour of preparation. The *Firebird* was pulled carefully by boats into the Boiling Sea until it could anchor perhaps a cable's length away from us. A second anchor chain was dragged out from it and lowered until it touched upon the top of the tower.

Meanwhile, Matthew had been untied and his tasks explained to him.

'I ain't goin' down there alone, not into that tower,' he said stubbornly, flinching in expectation of a broken jaw. Red however simply laughed at him.

'Feared of the water girls, hey?' he chortled. 'I wasn't turnin' you loose without a minder anyway, in case you follow your brother's bad example.'

So another sailor dived down with him; they couldn't stay underwater for long, but finally they were able to report that the bell had been secured by ropes to two of the boats that bobbed quietly above the tower.

Then the two men spent half an hour securing the anchor chain to one side of the beam that supported the bell. When all was ready, Captain Red waved back towards the ship and we could hear rhythmic shouts as the men turned the capstan, winding the cable in until it pulled tight. Then they spent some time on the other side of the ship, drawing the *Firebird* away towards the anchor it had earlier dropped some fifty metres further back.

The near capstan began its rhythmic cranking once more; the chain that ran to the tower was lifting out of the water and humming with the tension upon it. Then there was an odd, muffled sound: I suppose the sound of something rending apart beneath the water. The chain went slack, while the boats suddenly dipped.

Red had raised his hand as soon as this happened, and the capstan on the *Firebird* ceased its turning.

'Let's see what we've caught,' Red ordered the sailors in the boats, and they began pulling in the ropes that were tipping two of the boats to one side. After ten minutes of heavy work, a large dark object came into view, cloaked in seaweed: it looked like the monstrous, hairy head of some beast, half human and half sea monster.

It was too heavy to lift safely into a boat, so we ended up towing it to the *Firebird*, where they lowered a net and winched the bell – or monster – on board.

When I got up on deck, Madame and a few of the officers were already gathered about the object, which was now clearly a bell standing on its broad base, a little above waist high. Tom cleared off some of the weed with a cutlass and scratched at the metal.

'Reckon that's silver for sure,' said he. 'And there's plenty of it. Weighs as much as Jupiter, and that's a fact.'

He scraped more weed from the outside. 'Look at this,' he called, pointing with his cutlass at a raised pattern he had uncovered.

We peered at it in turn. The shape was womanly, with hair flowing about her shoulders and her body tapering to a broad fish's tail. A mermaid; but there was a crown upon her head, an orb in one hand and a rod in the other.

'That's bad,' said Misty. 'We've got a bell from a temple dedicated to the sea goddess. The mermaids'll be chasin' us to get it back, turnin' the men's heads with their singin' and their beauty. They -'

Captain Red took out his pistol and made a show of priming it.

'On second thought,' grunted Misty, 'I expect a lot of seaside temples got bells like this one. Means nothing.'

'Right answer,' said the Captain, putting his gun away. He said to Tom, 'Might be copper inside, though. Turn it over.'

The inside of the bell was completely clogged with weed and crusted with shells. But a little scraping showed that the bell was likely to be pure silver throughout.

Tom was pushing his cutlass into the belly of the monstrous thing, prying out the weed and swearing at the anemones and sea urchins that stung his hands.

'What's this?' he called, pointing at a head-sized lump attached to the end of the bell clapper, wreathed in slime. He swung at it with his cutlass, dislodging something largish and roundish that rolled across the deck before coming to rest by a mast.

Red swore and grabbed it – whatever it was – by the yellowish weed growing on one side of it. He flung it overboard, far into the water.

'None of you is to tell Matthew,' he said, pointing at us in turn. 'In fact, none of you saw that.'

'Saw what?' I whispered to Jupiter, who was looking solemn.

'The head of his brother,' Jupiter whispered back, making a sign across his chest and turning away.

13 Cursed Rock

From my diary: *Everything seems to be settling into a pattern. We follow the instructions, sail to a new point, retrieve the treasure. There's another six clues I think; at this rate we'll be back home in a month, with enough treasure to keep everyone happy.* (The diary  breaks off here and is not resumed for several days).

The next directions were: *Hand high, spy where the finger points.* Back in Madame's house, we had debated the meaning of the phrase for hours, with Red fuming and Madame looking at me with some coolness as I insisted that the phrase made no sense to me at all.

However, now that we were in sight of Cursed Rock, it didn't take long to figure that this was the hand referred to.

The *Firebird* had been pulled back from the Boiling Sea the same day we'd recovered the bell. We sailed north a ways and anchored far enough from the hidden rocks to ensure we wouldn't be driven onto them by a sudden squall. But the next morning we crept back until we were a few hundred metres from the Rock.

As a boat was being prepared, I was summoned to the Captain's cabin, where Red awaited me alone.

'Alright then, pot scrubber: earn your keep,' Red growled at me. He moved five bottles from the table – the hoard taken from Misty's trunk – and spread out the parchment.

He said, 'It says here "*Hand high, spy where the finger points. Be black widowed there widdershins and fight the black gulls for their booty.*". Madame and I think we have to climb that evil lump and look along the fist – the pointing finger on the fist, I mean - for sight of land. Yes?'

I nearly shrugged my shoulders but realised that, with Madame absent, I might get a fist in my face for this. Instead I said carefully, 'I can't think of another explanation.'

'You'll call me Captain when you speak to me!'

'Yes, Captain.'

'And the black widow? It's as you said back at the house?'

I read the sentence again and nodded. 'You'll be going around a coast to the left, widdershins - counter-clockwise, that is. I think you have to keep close to the shore, very close. Then – I don't know what the rest means... Captain.'

'*Fighting the black gulls for booty* – doesn't that have a special meaning? Think, boy!'

'Not that I know of, Captain Red, sir. It might mean something to me when we arrive.'

Then an unusual thing happened: Red smiled at me. A little grimly, but still a smile.

'You've done all right so far, boy. Been a surprise to me. Been a surprise to us all. Back to the galley, then.'

'Aye, sir,' I said and scooted out of the cabin before he found a reason to change his tune.

In the galley I came upon Bones poking at his chest tattoo with a needle. Unusually for him, he appeared to be totally absorbed and didn't hear me come in. He put the needle away quickly and replaced the cork in a bottle of black ink he'd been using.

'It's fading,' he said. 'Can't have dat.'

'Oh,' I replied, wondering why it mattered to him, or why he thought he had to explain it to me. 'You're not going up on the rock?'

Bones looked agitated. He sat down in a corner of the galley and took Tiddles onto his lap. 'No good would come of it,' he said softly. 'Dat rock has a curse on it, for sure.'

'I don't believe in curses,' I said, a little primly.

'Oh no?' asked Bones. 'You only say dat because you've not been in the jungle at night, or deep in a cave, or lost on an island and heard the banshees calling and felt a ghost's hand touch your neck.'

'Did you... did that happen to you?' I asked.

'Dat, and more. But dere's more'n ghosts to worry about. Men take their own curses to dat rock.'

He said nothing more to my questions and spent the next hour teaching Tiddles to jump from one hand to the other.

I went up on deck and watched the preparations for climbing the rock. Red didn't go; he sent Tom and one of the better foretop men. Their boat was rowed across to the far side of the rock and was secured to some warty lumps that rose from the sea there. The two men clambered out, cursing the foaming water that soaked them to the waist.

They had ropes but didn't use them. Though steep, the rock was broad and gently rounded. The men were able to climb directly to the top, where they stood in the dip of the great fist, peering forward.

I imagined Captain Jones' visit here, perhaps two years ago: saw him walking calmly to the great, clenched hand, scaling the bent fingers and then sitting on the knuckles, staring out to sea, thinking – what was he thinking about? How to hide the Ruby? Or perhaps, how to destroy it. Perhaps he was holding it in his hand; perhaps he leaned out over the dark waters and let it drop, seeing it hit the surface and disappear forever.

Or perhaps he'd hidden the Ruby up there. Suddenly I was convinced that this was what he'd done: he had found a crevice in that mighty fist and tucked the jewel into the angle of the angry fingers. So clear was this vision that I nearly called out to the climbers; then I realised the madness of this.

If Captain Jones couldn't trust himself with the Ruby, how could Red be trusted with it, or Madame Helena? I had a new, disturbing vision now: of ghostly armies marching, screams in the night, families dragged from houses and roped together as slaves.

So I watched quietly as the men climbed a little higher,

took out compasses and sighted them along the pointing half-finger. They seemed to compare their results, then climbed down again.

I set off back to the galley, as subdued now as Billy Half-bones himself.

Before I got to the galley, first mate Tom grabbed me by the ear and marched me to the ladies' cabin, where Amy was sitting at a table with Madame. She flashed a big smile at me, then passed me a new accounting ledger and a pen.

'We're listin' the treasure,' she said. 'A copy for Madame and one for the Captain, see.' She took up her own pen and opened a second ledger.

Tom and Madame each produced a key and unlocked a cupboard. I took a seat beside Amy and wrote a copy of her every line, while Madame carefully emptied two boxes of "Treesure" onto the table and tallied the takings. Vicky and Sandra crowded about us, exclaiming at the jewels.

'Diamonds,' Madame Helena said. 'Thirty-two small: around half a carat each. I'd price those at twelve crowns apiece for now. Another ten which are a full carat. Forty crowns each. Six which are two carats or more. Probably a hundred crowns apiece – no, make it a hundred and fifty.'

Tom leaned over the table, counting the diamonds slowly and nodding his head. 'Look good on a cute ring, that one,' he said to Amy. 'D'you fancy it?'

Amy blushed and concentrated on writing.

Madame produced a velvet bag and dropped the diamonds into it. She pulled the drawstring tight and placed the bag into one of the boxes.

'Emeralds now…'

This went on for half an hour, followed by a few minutes of copying out the details of the silver bell that had been stowed in the ammunition room: height, thickness, circumference, weight and estimated value. Tom whistled at the figure: eight thousand crowns. Then Madame locked the treasure boxes in the sturdy cupboard safe built into the wall of the cabin. Tom stepped forward and turned a second lock with a separate key, which he took away with him together with my copy of the ledger. He stopped at the door and gave Amy a long look before striding away, whistling jauntily.

Madame said to me, 'I need you to make a copy of the ship's cost ledgers as well, for the Captain to put in his waterproof safe. Amy will show you what to do. Come on, girls: time for our constitutional walk on deck.'

She swept out of the cabin with Vicky and Sandra in tow, leaving me with Amy.

I settled to my work, but I kept thinking about the glances exchanged between Amy and Tom. I looked up at Amy: she was standing at the small cabin window, gazing out. I imagined she was sighing occasionally as well.

Finally I couldn't stop myself. 'It's not right,' I blurted out. 'You and Tom. You shouldn't.'

She turned around and looked at me sternly, folding her arms across her chest. 'What business is that of yours?' she asked in a cold, offended tone.

'None,' I admitted. 'But I care about you. I don't want you to do anything foolish. I don't want you to get hurt.'

She laughed scornfully; and it was the first time she'd expressed any feeling like that to me. It was like being punched in the stomach.

She said, 'Tom's the only one likely to suffer. I'll be fine.'

I said, 'But – he's not worth it. He's just a seaman. He's half a pirate, too.'

She continued to speak coldly and firmly: 'He's tall and handsome. He's second in command of a ship. He's got a house in the city bigger than the one you live in. He's a smuggler with links to the Royal Court. Why'd you think Minerva was after him? But he doesn't care about Minerva any longer. He sees how special I am.'

I was hurt by her coldness and reacted unkindly: 'Why stop at the first mate? Why not go for Red?'

Her eyes went even colder and her body stiffened. 'You

think I'm just a common little tart, do you?'

I tried to retreat from the insult. 'I didn't mean it that way. I was just… suggesting… that it's the logical conclusion of what you just said.'

Amy smiled, but icily. 'Maybe I'll do that, then: I'll set my bonnet for the Captain. I've seen him lookin' at me. Men are easy to catch: show them your body, look into their eyes, touch them on the arm, flatter them a bit. Never fails.'

I had no answer for that. 'I didn't think you were like this,' I said weakly.

She said, 'You don't know me.' And she was right. I had a sweet, innocent, selfless version of Amy in my head: just as I used to have an idealised version of Aunt Emma.

She continued, 'A year ago I was plump and pimply and men ignored me. I used to die of embarrassment when I talked to a man, knowin' he would be nice to me for a bit and then walk off with someone pretty like Minerva. But I'm prettier now, and a lot wiser. I've realised I can be the one in charge. I can make them want me. I'm good at that.'

'But you can't want *them*. Not Red and Tom.'

'How do *you* know what I want? They're big and strong and manly, and they've got a bit of money. And they're *important*. I like that. It makes me feel good, havin' them chase after me. Every woman gets excited if the captain flirts with her. She doesn't feel the same if it's the boy who cleans the galley.' She looked at me mockingly.

'I thought you cared – I mean, I thought we were friends.' My words sounded pathetic, even to me.

'Did I ever say that?' she asked in a flat, unfeeling voice.

There was no answer to that, either.

She continued, 'What gives you the right to tell me what to do? Think you're my father, do you?'

'I just think – it's wrong.'

She treated me to another icy smile. 'Ah, so that's it? You know about right and wrong, and I don't? You're full of compliments today: I'm not just a tart, I'm a *stupid* tart.'

'It's not about being clever. It's about –'

'Grow up,' she said. 'Love isn't just a bit of fun: it's a competition. Friendship is, too. The other person has something you want: so you try to get it. I used to be the one that always lost, always got used by others; now *I'm* in control, and I can use them instead. I like it better this way.'

Her argument was completely logical. But I still wanted to say that it was wrong somehow – that it was cold and loveless and unsatisfying like the calculations on the desk before me. Fortunately, before I could dig a deeper hole for myself, Madame and the others returned.

I wasn't awake when we arrived at our next destination; the ship had eased north of east across a quiet sea under a full moon, and I knew nothing about our arrival until Bones dragged me out of my hammock an hour after dawn.

'Put dat coffee pot on, lad,' he ordered cheerfully. 'Cap'n wants to see us both on deck as soon as it's brewed.'

I shook the dreams from my head – uneasy dreams, where the ship's rats had kidnapped Omar Vlstg, Amy had cut a hole in her cabin floor and leaped into it with Tom, water was running in through the hole, and Captain Red (a huge red-furred rat dressed as a pirate) was running along the deck shouting that the ship was sinking....

On deck, the sun was rising over the island to our east: if indeed it was an island, for it stretched across our full horizon. A small group stood at the bow, peering through brass telescopes.

'Misty says it's not inhabited, unless you count the birds,' said Captain Red, waving a large, hairy hand towards high stony cliffs that rose like a great wall from the water.

'How the devil would he know?' asked first mate Tom irritably.

'He's only going from what the charts say and what he's heard from other seamen,' said Red.

'And what he makes up,' said Tom.

Captain Red pointed to me. 'Jack thinks we go around the

island counter-clockwise, huggin' the shore. I don't know why. Perhaps this way we'll come across something that's not shown on the charts. The charts are nearly useless anyway - like a child's drawing. Jack's goin' to stand here at the bow, and you're goin' to stand with him, Tom, and make sure he does his job. I'm not sailing around this island more than once, so he'd better see whatever's out there on the first pass.'

'I'm not a bloody wet nurse,' said Tom through clenched teeth.

'You are today.'

Tom turned away, muttering something about slitting my throat if I annoyed him.

Captain Red turned to Bones, saying. 'I don't like the look of this coast or the weather, so if we do go seekin' treasure on that island, I'm leavin' most of the officers on board and you're comin' instead.'

'Aye, sir.'

Red continued, 'I want you to get together the equipment we might need. If we understand Jones' blasted notes at all, there's climbin' to do, because the gulls he mentions will nest high up on those cliffs. Get one of the foretop men to help you choose what's needful – ropes, pulleys, blocks and so on. And we'll probably want some muscle, so the black – what's his name – he's to be released from his watches and told to stand by. Tell Jake that.'

'Aye, sir. Will do dat.'

Bones hurried away and I settled myself at the larboard bow railing while the ship's anchor was loosed and we turned south, following the coast.

It was a dull day for me, staring at an unending wall of rock. By lunchtime we had passed the southern tip, then turned sharply to port to follow the coast, bearing east of northeast. More rock, more seabirds launching themselves into the stiffening breeze, more bitter taunts from Tom.

'Bit of a show-off, aren't ya?' he asked me. 'Think you're better'n the rest of us, just because Jones let you bring him cakes once a week?'

'It's not like that,' I said quietly.

'You'll call me SIR, damn you!' A blow to the side of my head from a fist nearly as large as Captain Red's, knocking me to the deck.

'Yes, sir.' I got to my feet again.

'Givin' yourself airs – makin' out you're somethin' special – suckin' up to Madame – lookin' all lovesick at Miss Amy: oh, I seen you doin' it. But she don't need a little boy lustin' after her sweet flesh; she needs a man. You keep away from her, you hear me?'

'Yes, sir.' I knew better than to disagree.

Mid afternoon, we came to a section of uneven coastline that looked down onto a seabed spotted with rocks - as if some enormous sea maggot had gnawed bits out of the cliff face and then spat them into the water. Misty kept two men busy with lines to measure the sea depth and another two looking ahead for rocks, while he muttered over a couple of charts, making tiny notes on one of them.

Hours passed. We cleared a little point and turned hard left to follow the line of the sea cliff, as we'd done a dozen times already. The rocky cliff rose above us, dizzying in its height. It made a broad circle around to the right again and we followed it, an endless span of mottled brown and grey and black rock that made my eyes ache. But then –

'What's that?' I asked, at the same time as Misty. Some of the rock seemed to move against another part of the cliff, like one piece of paper sliding over another.

'It's a channel,' Misty said, wiping his eyes and peering left and forward. 'Wide enough for a ship, though I wouldn't want to chance it.'

Tom hurried away to alert the Captain, giving me a final smack with a horny hand to the back of my head. Soon we were anchored and staring into a gap between two high walls of rock.

To understand what we saw, you need to imagine a bay

shaped like a large letter 'G' with the inner swoop exaggerated: G. The part near to us – the right side of the G – was about half the height of the cliffs behind it, but it was difficult to see that this was a separate curve of rocks, promising a hidden bay behind. If we'd been sailing at a sensible distance from the cliffs so as to avoid the outcrops of rocks speckling the sea, we would never have noticed this bay.

My eyes were smarting from the sun's glare and my head was pounding, so I retired to my hammock and soon fell asleep with Tiddles purring on my chest; but an hour later I was dragged out again, by Pitiless Jake this time.

'Here's your reward for bein' the girlies' pet,' he grumbled, tweaking my ear. 'Cap'n says fill a sack with enough biscuit and cooked meat to feed six men for the afternoon. And put some in for yourself: you're goin' with 'em.'

A little later, I staggered onto the main deck, dragging a sack and cursing Captain Red under my breath. But he seemed not to care about my aching head.

'That boy's as lazy as a legless dog!' he said to Madame, who despite the heat was dressed in all her dark finery, veil included, with a black parasol dangling from one arm.

She said nothing, but raised her veil to peer at me.

'He'll be all right,' Red grumbled, pulling me round by the ear and looking at my red face. 'Just had a little too much sun this morning.' He turned and shouted, 'Bones! Jupiter! Over here!' Then he asked Tom, 'Which are the foretop men you've chosen for us?'

'Taylor and Stephens. I'll fetch 'em.' Tom too tweaked my ear before he walked off, as if it was a new fashion.

Bones glided over to the Captain as soon as Tom had gone and began speaking with him quietly. But Red shook his head and swore profusely before demanding:

'How dare you? Who's Captain here – you? Or me?'

Bones persisted, 'It's just dat – Cap'n Red, sir – the last time, dem ladies was put in a spot of trouble.'

Red's face darkened. 'Every man on board knows I'll flog the skin from his back if it happens again!'

'Yes sir, Cap'n sir. But like I said, dere's also some of the men –'

Red exploded, 'Think I don't know my own crew? Don't know who I can trust? Not another word, Bones!' And he strode away, shouting at the men who were lowering a boat over the side.

Bones shrugged his shoulders and winked at me. 'Can't win 'em all, can we lad?'

'What were the men saying?' I asked.

'Oh, just the usual mouthin' off,' Bones said. 'Probably means nothing. Cap'n will have heard as much as I have... if his mates has been doin' their jobs properly, dat is.'

He glanced further forward, at first mate Tom and second mate Jimmy laughing with Pitiless Jake. He shrugged again and went to the galley to collect some carpentry and doctoring gear, whistling "Storm at Sea" yet again. I was beginning to hate that tune.

Our boat moved smoothly into the channel, which was as wide as four ships and a few hundred metres long. The cliffs on either side were steep but not shear: they could probably be climbed if you didn't mind holding onto slippery rock at a height far above the ship's mast.

Halfway to the back of this bay, the cliffs to our left dropped a little in height and then apparently finished a little further on. Those to our right curved round in front of us to the left, with those two opposing cliffs apparently encircling a secluded inlet. Once we were past the end of the cliffs to our left, we would see more; there might be nothing but a rocky dead end.

I was sitting in the rear of the boat next to Madame. In front of us were the two foretop men with an oar each, and Bones between them. Beyond them were Red and Misty, leaning over either side and taking soundings: I suppose they wanted to discover whether the channel was deep enough to bring the *Firebird* through. At the very front, Jupiter was pulling two oars through the water as if they were matchsticks.

'Ease off a little!' Red called out testily. 'We don't know what we'll find beyond this spit of rock.'

Jupiter rested his oars and we drifted past the final lumps of the left hand cliff, then turned left into what looked to me (peering between bodies) like a broad cove.

Just then an explosion made us jump. It was followed by a deep shout:

'Surrender - or we'll kill the lot of you!'

Several hands moved towards belts or grabbed at weapons in the boat's gunwhales; hesitated; stopped.

The large boat to our left – still half hidden by the rocks - was bristling with guns and behind the guns it bristled also with the serious faces of a dozen pirates.

'Easy, men,' Red said to us quietly. 'Hands off weapons but not too far off.' He raised his voice and called to the approaching boat:

'Parley, then!'

'Parley my ass!' came the laughing reply. 'I'll give you Parley: we talk and you listen!'

Red stood up and laughed back at them (and despite my dislike for him, I had to admit this was impressive). 'In that case, you'll be talking *out* of your ass!'

Their boat had drawn level now: about the same size as our own but loaded with men and weapons. Their leader – a lean, bearded man with a large hook nose and one eye - pointed at Red. 'I know you!' he exclaimed. 'One of Barley's men, weren't you? What happened to old Barley?'

'I killed him,' said Red. 'Who's your boss?'

For answer, the man jerked his head back at the large ship we could now see moored at the far left of the bay. A large red and black ensign was fluttering in the breeze. As it folded and unfolded, I could just make out the outline of a black skeleton, lying on its back in a sea of scarlet blood.

'I see,' said Red grimly. 'Well then: let's not keep Death waiting.'

14 Captain Death

If a player does not call into a port within 7 days (ie 7 turns) of their previous landing, their ship will suffer a loss of 10 men each day until they reach a port. They must then rest in port for one day for each loss of 10. Once a ship has lost 80 of its crew, it is treated as sunk and the player must start again from the beginning.

Jupiter bent to his oars again and we followed their boat back to their ship, the *Tombstone*. It was a caravel like our own, though larger and sporting more cannon on the fore and aft decks.

As we glided along, Bones moved back to sit between Madame and myself. He spoke to Madame quietly; she made little reply but nodded her head gravely at times. I wasn't happy that the word "death" was repeated often. I was even less happy when I glanced across at the other boat: it was filled with the faces you see in nightmares – distorted by scars, some lacking ears, eyes, noses; all lacking the any sign of mercy or humanity.

We climbed a rope ladder and cowered on deck. Their equivalent of Pitiless Jake – an obese, red-faced man with a hook for his right hand – herded us towards the Captain's deck at the stern, striking us with a long, heavy stick if we didn't move fast enough.

The Captain's deck was raised well above the main deck, and he was waiting there at a railing that overlooked us.

The lean, bearded pirate (they were mostly bearded) who had accosted us came forward and bowed to the Captain.

The Captain looked in our direction. 'You're *dead*,' he

called down to us, in a voice that was itself oddly dead –
cold, dreary, bitter; deep and cold as the ocean. 'You're
dead, do you hear me? In a moment I might order your
stomachs slit and your guts dragged out for the seagulls to
rip apart while you scream in torment. I might throw you
into the ship's bilge for the rats to gnaw your living flesh. I
might drag you behind the ship as shark bait. Or I might
send you back to your own ship, with or without the eyes
and limbs you came with.'

His accent wasn't rough and common as I expected, but
as cultured as Madame's or the Inquisitor's.

He looked at us in turn. His face was broad and flat and
lifeless. Only his eyes had life – a restless, angry searching
that stabbed at us. His hands lay quietly on the railing; his
left hand lacked a thumb and his right lacked the final two
fingers. He was tall and had once been a big man; but his
wide shoulders were now bony and the stringy flesh hung
loosely on his face and neck, like a corpse's.

Those eyes pierced each of us in turn until they came to
Madame, standing at the edge of our group, nearest the
starboard railing. Captain Death frowned.

'Kill –' he began.

Madame spoke out, her clear voice cutting across his
command:

'Captain Death, I am pleased to make your acquaintance
at last. Morgana told me I would find you here today.'

I saw his hands clench the railing. He choked out: 'She's –
but she's –'

'Dead ten years last month,' said Madame crisply. 'The
dead speak, Captain: and they expect to be heard.'

'*No!*' But I could see that he was rattled. His hands were
still on the railing, clutching it so hard that the knuckles on
his remaining fingers showed white against the dark tan of
his hands.

'Morgana wished me to remind you of a promise,' said
Madame, in a voice that reminded me chillingly of the Inquisitor: insistent, cruel, punishing. 'She said you are not

released from it.'

Captain Death nodded once.

'She said that your brother awaits his revenge. Skin for skin, eye for eye, and the worm that dies not in the fire.'

The Captain shuddered. His deep voice came hoarsely. 'Witch!' he cried. 'Witch as she was herself!'

His right arm trembled as if he was trying to raise it, but his hand would not let go of the railing.

One of his men – a wild-eyed fellow with white hair and half his nose gone – pulled a pistol from his belt and pointed it at Madame from across the deck. Madame turned to face him, and there seemed to be a smile beneath her veil.

'Witch!' cried the man as he shot her.

The pistol roared; there was a dull metallic sound; Madame staggered but then stood up straight.

She took a step forward. She raised her right hand and made a clawing gesture towards the seaman. 'I have your heart,' she said calmly. 'Can you not feel my fingers closing about it? You feel it pounding within your chest, throbbing as I squeeze the life from it. You can scarcely breathe. You feel death pulling you down, down, down...'

The man gave a cry and fell to his knees, clutching his chest. His pistol clattered to the deck. His face was contorted with pain and terror.

I looked at the groaning sailor and then back to Madame, seeing the ragged spot of torn dress in the middle of her chest where the bullet had struck; the man gasping for breath, his eyes rolling; Madame's glittering eyes behind her veil. I didn't notice Captain Death coming down to the main deck, drawing his own pistol.

I *did* notice that he fired it: I felt the wind of the shot as it passed by my head, and the explosion made me jump.

For a moment, I thought he had shot Madame; but then I saw the blood on the sailor's chest. The man sprawled sideways, still alive but bleeding badly from a wound near the left shoulder.

The Captain's voice was oddly triumphant now. 'Ha!' he

exclaimed. He walked up to the groaning sailor and kicked away his pistol – not that it would have been any use to the man unless he could reload it with one arm.

'Have you forgotten?' the Captain roared at him. '*I* am death here! *I* decide who lives, and who passes into the waiting darkness: not some wild fool of a deckhand frightened of beasties and boogies and bad-tempered grannies!'

He took a second pistol from his belt and held it against Madame's head. 'Have you any further messages from the other world before I send you there?' he asked grimly.

Madame's voice was as calm and chilling as before. 'Between the fire and the ice there is no rest, Captain. *They* are waiting for you: you've seen them, haven't you? There is no peace, there is no escape, except one. You held it for a moment and have not been able to forget its touch against your fingers; and it is within your grasp once more. I bring you news of the Ruby.'

The hand grasping the pistol trembled. 'You lie!' he cried.

She said, 'I have information provided by Jones, who took the Ruby from Curchan.'

'Where is this information?' he cried hoarsely. 'Give it to me now!'

'Where, Captain? Why, half of it is within this head that you hold a pistol against.'

The Captain's face screwed up in an agony of fevered thought. 'No!' he cried at last. 'He would not have done that! He would not trust it to a woman!'

Madame shrugged. 'Of course not,' she said mildly. 'He surrendered the instructions to a friend, the day before his execution. We took the manuscript. We are chasing about the world – into this very bay, indeed – to retrieve his treasures: including the Ruby.'

'Ha!' Captain Death replaced the pistols in his belt. He turned and pointed at the bleeding man. 'Throw him to Satan!' he ordered.

Four men took a limb each and carried the sailor to the starboard railing. He was begging and cursing as they swung him once, twice, then threw him over the side. There were a few long seconds before the splash. Then we heard him calling weakly as he thrashed about in the water. I turned back to look at Captain Death, who was listening for something with his head turned to one side; so we all listened with him.

More splashing; then the sound of the man trying to climb the anchor chain with one hand, falling back, cursing, calling to us. Then a cry of terror.

'Satan's coming!' was murmured between Death's men, and most of them crowded to the railing to watch. I was swept along with them and saw something I wish I'd closed my eyes to.

The man was still hanging onto the anchor chain and trying to climb it, pathetically, making a few painful centimetres before his arm failed him and he slid back into the water reddened with his blood. Beyond him...

Beyond him, further out in the bay, a large grey fin passed calmly through the glassy sea, cutting beautiful arcs through the clear water. Beneath the fin, dappled with reflections on the water's surface, a long muscular body flexed slowly, driving that fin forward. A great grey head, awful yet beautiful, moved to and fro, seeking something.

The shark passed the sailor once, hardly turning its head: just checking. I could now see that it was twice the length of a man, with twice the girth too. It turned lazily in a wide circle to the left, straightened and surged forward.

The sailor tried to scream but his lips seemed to be frozen with fear. He snatched at the anchor chain again; his body shuddered as the shark struck; his hand still gripped the chain; the shark returned and snatched what was left of him, shaking the limp body from side to side. A minute later, the only signs of the sailor's struggle were patches of red that slowly drifted towards the shore.

'Satan's been fed!' shouted the gross-bodied quartermaster. 'We're safe for today!'

Captain Death spoke grimly: 'He's still waiting for *you*,

Hulky. One day – one day soon…'

All fell silent again as the Captain turned back towards Madame. 'My cabin,' he directed.

Madame inclined her heard towards Red.

The Captain shrugged. 'Bring who you like. Hulky – have them all searched for weapons first. Not the lady.'

A couple of men came to prod and poke us all over. They took especial care to search Jupiter, and one of them gave the King's Guard a slap across the face – then stepped back nervously in case Jupiter should react. But the guard had no doubt experienced treatment like this many times and wisely made no response.

Red and Madame followed Captain Death back to his cabin while I waited on deck with the others, feeling the sweat trickle down my back and telling myself that this was because of the heat and not from fear.

I'd thought of our own crew as pirates but now realised that they were pale ghosts in comparison. These men were the real thing. Each face had serious scars and most were missing body parts – an ears, an eye, half a leg, a hand. Every remaining eye had a glint of cruelty, every voice mocked us, sneered at us, promising us no mercy. One of them took a knife and began poking at the timid foretopman Stephens.

The big man Hulky – their quartermaster - called out: 'You! Black boy! Come kiss my feet!'

Jupiter glanced at Bones, who nodded briefly. Then he walked forward and dropped to his knees. He bent forward as if kiss the top of Hulky's big leather shoes.

Hulky smiled and swung one heavy foot upwards, catching Jupiter in the mouth. The guard rolled to one side, holding his mouth and groaning.

'Yeah,' said Hulky, with a soft, evil laugh. 'You look big, but you're soft, aren't you? Come kiss the other foot now.'

I turned my head so I didn't have to watch the second kicking.

Hulky was laughing again. 'C'mon,' he gloated. 'Kiss my hand next.'

He held out his right hand – not a hand at all but a wicked brass hook on the end of his fat arm.

'You doesn't want to do dat,' a voice at my shoulder stated quietly.

The big pirate turned to stare at Bones. 'What did you say?' he menaced.

'I t'ink you understand me,' said Bones. 'Her Ladyship has a special likin' for Jupiter here and doesn't want no holes in him. Besides dat, Jupiter's quite happy wid the seven holes he's got already.'

There were a few quiet chuckles from the watching crew for this. But Hulky didn't smile. He came forward, rocking from one large leg to the other, and stood before Bones. 'And what about yourself, old man?' he asked. His voice had that soft and evil quality about it again. 'Does Her Ladyship care what happens to *you*?'

Bones looked the man in the face, not at all frightened. 'Ah well,' he said. 'Dere's only one way to find out.'

I saw the quartermaster's fat face turn red. His remaining hand clenched and unclenched. He raised his hook and placed it against Bones' neck.

'I'll deal with you later!' he said between clenched teeth.

'Dat's what the ladies always tell me, too,' Bones replied cheerfully.

A chorus of laughs broke out among the other pirates, but stopped as the big man turned to glare at them. It occurred to me that Hulky wasn't well liked, and Bones was playing upon this.

As our two groups – pirates and half-pirates - stood looking at one another, there was a shout from a man up in the masthead.

'Signal!' he shouted. 'Not sure what it means!'

I looked over to the cliff top that overlooked both this hidden bay and the sea outside it. Several men stood up there, waving. They must have been there all along: they would have seen us approach and drop anchor before sending our boat into the channel. They would have alerted their own ship, which is why there'd been an armed welcome awaiting us.

Whatever they were trying to report now, it didn't make sense to those on the *Tombstone*. Soon one of the lookouts was descending a steep zigzag path, dislodging stones that skipped down the steep slopes and thumped upon the shore or kicked out into space to land with a splash in the bay itself. The sailor pushed a small boat from the beach and began rowing across to the ship.

At this point, Captain Death came striding from his cabin, followed by Madame and Red.

'Shipmates! Gather by!' he ordered.

While the crew were hurrying across to him, he began in his dull, grave voice: 'Madame Helena –' (wave of an arm) '– and Captain Red here - and their crew – these are now our comrades for the purpose of plunder, pleasure and piratery. We will combine forces: boat with boat, brain with brain, brawn with brawn, bastards and bitches together. What say ye?'

His men obediently raised a cheer, apart from quartermaster Hulky: a fact observed by his Captain.

'Hey!' he called out. 'Hulky's sulky! Why the evil looks? Are you setting yourself against me?'

Hulky shook his head. 'Not I, Cap'n.'

'Then let's see you raise a cheer, Quartermaster.'

Hulky reddened before calling out: 'Men! Three huzzahs for the Captain's plan!'

The third cheer was dying as the lookout clambered up the rope ladder and over the railing. He crossed to Captain Death and touched his forehead. The Captain gestured to him to speak.

'They's gone, Cap'n' the man said hurriedly. 'Headed straight out to sea, then turned north along the coast. Lost sight of 'em just afore I came to report.'

'Oh ho!' exclaimed Captain Death, looking at Madame and Red. 'What becomes of your parchment now, hey?'

'It is in my head,' Madame replied stiffly. 'Do you wish me to recite it to you? It begins: *At 196 for 220, seek the small harbour on the island of breasted stone. Follow the eyes a full turn at seven for the first treesure sunken low and springing high. Follow the Mermaid until you glimpse the Rock. Anchor before you founder and follow the mermaids' silver summons to worship. Hand high, spy where the finger points. Be black widowed there widdershins and fight the black gulls for their booty....* Rest assured, Captain: I will provide the whole document, one clue at a time, as we agreed.'

Captain Death sneered at her, 'And your shipmates have it all in writing! What's to stop them from finding the treasure before we do?'

Red stepped forward suddenly and grabbed me by the scruff of my neck. 'This!' he cried. 'This landlubberly excuse for a sailor! The boy understands Jones' twisted mind as none other! He it was that visited Jones each week. He –'

Madame snapped, 'The boy knows much that is useful. I know much that is hidden to all others. And the rest of our group are competent sailors; you need us all.'

Captain Death stroked his beard. 'But your crewmates – why have they bolted?'

Madame said, 'Perhaps they were spooked by the gunfire. Perhaps – but what does it matter? Let us finish our business here, then set sail after them. That is what I offer: a chance of treasure and perhaps the Ruby itself, but first we must rejoin our ship.'

Captain Death looked at Red shrewdly. 'What say you?'

Red's eyes were smouldering. 'They've mutinied,' he said through clenched teeth. 'My first mate saw the silver bell and the boxes we recovered: I should have known it would turn him. I expect they'll try to solve the next couple of clues; but they'll fail. Only four of 'em can read and none of 'em knows these waters. We'll find the ship in the nearest large port, every man drunk.'

'And every woman ravished,' added Captain Death, with a sly wink.

I shuddered, thinking of Amy at the mercy of both Tom and Pitiless Jake. Perhaps Amy would be protected by Tom; but I doubted he would be so sweet and gentle now that the ship (and everyone in it) was under his command.

'Aye,' continued Death in a grave, hollow voice. 'The women are doomed. And the treasure on your ship is beyond our grasp, unless we give chase now and have considerable fortune, for the *Tombstone* rides low and heavy like its name.'

Their quartermaster Hulky said suddenly, 'Bird in the hand, I say. Seek the treasure here.'

Captain Death nodded. 'Aye, that's my mind as well.'

Red looked at Madame, then growled, 'We might not be able to find the treasure here. At least we can be sure of the treasure on the ship. You've got enough cannon on this ship to scare the *Firebird* into surrender with a single shot. And they won't go far, I swear it.'

Hulky repeated sullenly, 'We ain't goin' until we've looked here. Bird in the hand.'

Death said, 'I agree with the Quartermaster. Let's bide a day here seeking the gull's booty: a *bird* in the hand indeed, hey? And if your mutineers are as stupid as you suggest, Captain, we'll find them easily enough. There are only two ports nearby: they'll put into one and be drunk there for a week.'

I saw Madame's eyes flashing behind her veil and thought she was about to do something drastic, when there was a shout from near to me:

'Cap'ns both! Might I say something?'

It was Bones, looking unusually serious. Perhaps he too was thinking about the ladies.

The two Captains exchanged glances and Red said something to Captain Death.

'The Cook!' exclaimed Death, waving his arm again. 'The Cook wishes to tell us something! Is it about the best way to make soup? The many uses for pepper? What's on the menu, Cook?' He dropped his voice to a whisper as dry as ashes from a cremation: 'Is it a *lively* dish? Or are you stirring up your own death?'

His right hand moved to rest on his pistol.

Bones knuckled his forehead respectfully. 'I'd be honoured to cook for you, Cap'n. But just now dere's more pressing matters at hand, and I was wonderin' whether dis talk about fightin' gulls for booty… well, if dere might somet'ing important about dem bein' black, y'know.'

Death looked interested - and his hand moved away from the pistol.

'What of it?'

'Well, Cap'n, dere isn't any black gulls, not dat I ever saw. But in dese parts, dere's big bats as black as a coffin's insides. I seen hundreds of dem last night. Anyway, Cap'n sir, bats live in caves. Like dat one over dere.'

He was pointing away, towards the rocky cliff that stood between us and the sea: part of the upright of the '𝐆'. If I squinted at it, I could see what might be holes – or might simply be shadows in the late afternoon sun.

Death thought the same. 'Bats there may be, Cook – for I seen 'em myself at dusk and dawn. But I can't see where they're roosting, not from here.'

'Poop!' exclaimed Bones (he used a coarser word, which I don't repeat here).

'What?'

'Bat poop, Cap'n sir: guano dey calls it. See dem three rocks close together, pokin' out from the water? Go up from dem, about two thirds of the way up the cliff. See a sort of green and white mess? And above dat, a hole not much bigger dan yourself?'

'I see it,' declared Madame, who had raised her veil.

'It's worth trying,' said Red.

Captain Death was still peering across the bay. He took up a small brass telescope and looked through that. He shook his head. 'The eye of faith, brothers: that's what I need. Some has it, some has it not. So tell me, faithful Cook: how is it that your eye sees what mine only squints at?'

Bones laughed. 'I saw it as we came past it in the boat, Cap'n! I'm half guessin' which blur across the bay is the right one.'

Death looked at Bones, considering. 'We'll take a closer look then. But if you're right, how shall we get up there?'

He addressed this question to Bones, as if he had suddenly raised Bones' importance in his own mind.

Bones puzzled for a moment. 'A careful man could do it, Cap'n,' he judged. 'You can see from here dat the rocks to the right ain't so steep. I've climbed worse.'

'I take that as a promise to climb it yourself, then!' said the Captain.

Bones objected, 'Dat was when I was young! Perhaps one of the foretop men dat came wid us – or one of your men –'

'No, no! The honour's all yours, Cook!' exclaimed Death with a hollow chuckle. 'And the risk!'

'Wait a minute,' said Bones.

We all looked at him. He was weighing something up, looking at the cliffs opposite. His head twitched twice.

He said, 'Alright den: I'll do it meself. But I'll need Taylor and Stephens to come wid me part way and fasten me wid ropes, so if I fall it won't be far.'

Death looked at him gravely, then nodded.

The Captain ordered the ship to move across the bay, and while it crossed I saw Bones and the two foretop men in worried discussion, pulling out ropes and hooks, swapping them for others, and finally adding some marlinspikes and three club hammers.

By the time we had drifted to a halt at the far side of the bay, it was clear that there was indeed a narrow cave, shaped and angled like a cat's eye. A scum – green, white and black – spilled over the edge and splashed upon the rocks below.

A boat took the three men the final ship's length to the

base of the rock, where they found something to tie up to, well to the right of the cave. Two pirates sat in the boat while Bones, followed by the foretop men, climbed the steep rocks, zigzagging upwards until they were a couple of metres above the cave and several to the right of it.

Now came the difficult part. A marlinspike was pushed into small cracks in the rock and hammered in until it was firm. A rope was attached to this and Bones wrapped it once around his waist before tying some sort of running knot in it. He then eased himself to his left and down a little before being passed a second spike which he hammered in as before, then secured the rope around it before passing it once again around his waist.

He repeated the process twice more, while the foretop men secured the original spike with a second rope and spike, then secured themselves to the two spikes and found a place on the rock where they could sit and brace themselves so that they could support Bones' weight if he fell.

Bones eased himself to the top of the cat's eye and hammered in a final spike. He lowered himself slowly to the floor of the cave.

'Dat stinks!' he shouted to us cheerily, then disappeared.

For half an hour not much happened apart from a large amount of guano being pushed out of the cave, splashing in the water and sending a strong stench across to us.

Then Bones shouted. A minute or so later he came to the edge of the cave, dragging with difficulty a box about the size of a small child.

There were cheers from the ship at this. The pirates clearly liked the idea of obtaining treasure without any danger to themselves, or any work whatsoever.

'Dat's all!' Bones called. 'Only guano besides!'

He bound up the box with more rope and lowered it slowly down the side of the cliff to the waiting boat, his face red with effort. Then he retraced his path back.

The box was lifted onto the ship and was being prised

open with a crowbar as Bones pulled himself over the railing. A few of the pirates gave him a short cheer, which was then mightily repeated when the lid flew off to reveal bars of gold and silver packed in sawdust.

'Count 'em!' ordered the Captain. 'Quartermaster, bring your book and record the booty!'

The haul was four bars of gold and six of silver, each bar weighing around 150 ounces.

'One thousand, five hundred ounces near enough!' exclaimed Death. 'Four shares to the captain, two to the first mate, two and a half to the quartermaster, one to each of the other officers and the rest equally to the crew.'

'The quartermaster gets more dan the mate?' I heard Bones whispering to the first mate, who said nothing but the look that passed between the two of them said much – though I didn't know then *what* was being said.

'And *our* shares?' asked Red suddenly.

Captain Death stroked his beard. His eyes were gleaming with lust for gold. 'We'll discuss that,' he said. 'Aye, we'll talk. Won't we, Quartermaster?'

Hulky laughed, with a wink to the other pirates. 'And the talk goes like this: *It's our ship; our gold.* Am I right, men?'

Before the men could respond, Bones raised his voice: 'We're all ship hands here. Every man has a share, every man a vote. Dat's the Law among free men.'

Hulky walked over to Bones and punched him in the face. It was meant to be a hard punch, but Bones saw it coming and stepped back; the quartermaster drew blood, however.

'Here's Law for you!' the big man hissed. 'My fist!'

Bones wiped his face on his sleeve. 'And here was I t'inking dat Pirates was free men!' he said gravely. 'But we're wastin' time fighting when we've got a ship to chase and a parchment to recover – and fine ladies to save.'

'Aye!' came from Red, and 'Yes!' from Madame – who had been quiet during all this, as if waiting for the opportune moment.

Captain Death nodded, then looked to his quartermaster. But Hulky shook his head.

'The men always gets a double rum ration after we takes a prize,' Hulky grumbled. 'Double ration and a half day's rest as soon as we're to safety, which we are.'

'That's true,' said Death, looking only at the quartermaster. He added softly, 'But it's also true that there's another prize fleeing north. And there's the matter of honour.'

Hulky's face was dark and stubborn now. 'I speak for the men, Captain,' he said. He turned to the crew and glowered at them.

Captain Death stroked his beard again. 'Do you now?' he asked softly, then turned on his heel and strode back to his cabin, signing to Red and Madame to come with him.

'Is this mutiny?' I asked Bones, looking at Hulky leaning against the rail as he gave orders to his cronies.

Bones replied, 'Dis? No, it's how t'ings is done on most pirate ships. The Captain decides what to do and where to go and who to fight; but someone – usually the first mate, sometimes the quartermaster or another – deals wid the men. He sets the watches, agrees the prize shares, says who gets to sleep where. He can even ask the crew to vote the Captain out. And if he's an evil son of a sea dog, he can make your life a living hell. I knows all about dat, lad.'

'We're doomed, aren't we?' I asked. And as soon as I said that, I realised how frightened I was.

Bones looked all around, peering up at the masts and along the decks at the pirates going about their duties. Then he nodded.

'Seems dat way,' he said. 'But don't give up hope, lad. Always a chance, hey? We just gotta keep our heads down for a while. Especially now dat the evening is comin' on and dem pirates will be knockin' back the rum. You stick close to me, okay?'

He patted me on the shoulder; then we stood at the railing and watched the darkness gather.

15 In Pursuit

A mouse's tail may seem ugly; yet it is a wondrous, graceful appendage with uses that astonish an open mind. It exists for balance; for grasping, feeling and measuring; for the display of feelings, social position and prowess; for comfort on a cold night when we curl up within a wisp of grass. Mice, never judge by appearances but seek the beauty that the eye cannot see. (From the collected works of Bunstropple, mouse and philosopher).

The rum was being passed around now, though we weren't offered any. 'Come wid me,' whispered Bones.

He led me to the galley, where a fat, lazy-looking man sat on a chair drinking grog from a steaming mug.

Bones addressed him: 'Dis lad here is galley's mate to me on the *Firebird*. While we're on board, would you like him to work for you?'

The Cook slurped the rest of his grog, wiped his mouth on his sleeve, and nodded. He pointed at the floor. 'Start on that,' he said. 'Work your way up from there. And keep cleanin' till I tells you to stop.' Then he fell asleep.

I found a scrubbing brush while Bones fetched a pail of water. He brought Jupiter with him. 'You try to keep outta sight, hey?' he whispered to the big man. 'Help the lad wid dat floor, maybe.'

There wasn't much room in the galley itself, so I took the pots and pans on deck and began cleaning them there. They were filthy: not just from today's grime, but thick with food and dirt and slime from meals long forgotten. The pork and beans of yesterday would have tasted of the fish from the day before; and this morning's oatmeal would have tasted of them both, and worse.

As I cleaned, I studied the crew who were drinking steadily. As soon as one ration of rum was drained, Hulky shouted for another. His own draughts went down in one gulp, but seemed to have little effect on him.

After perhaps half an hour - the sun hesitating just above the ridge of the island now - I saw Bones approach Hulky, knuckling his forehead respectfully. The man swiped at him with a broad hand but missed: perhaps the drink was working on him at last.

Bones kept talking to him quietly, and after a while they walked off together into a dim, secluded space next to the galley, cluttered with casks of rotting food. I moved my pots closer to this alcove and listened.

'- talk it out man to man,' Bones was saying. 'For I can see dat it's your word what matters here, not the Captain's and for sure not the Mate's.'

'True enough,' said Hulky.

'And I t'ought we might come to an arrangement, like. You see, I'm wantin' to keep dat other ship in sight. And if we sits here much longer, it'll be too dark to set out; den dere's no tellin' when we'll catch her.'

'Why do I care?'

'Ah, dat's where I t'ink we could make a deal. I have me own bit of treasure on dat ship. It's worth as much as one of dem bars you saw today. Half for you, if we set out straight off.'

Hulky laughed. 'You think I'm stupid?' he asked. 'A dirty ship's cook rich as a gentleman? You got nothin'!'

'Maybe not,' said Bones. 'But maybe I has. What have you to lose if you gets the men ready to set sail? Only a night's drinkin', dat's all!'

Hulky laughed again. 'I know your game,' he said. 'You just wanna use me. Well, I'm not playin'! You think I'm doin' this for a few glasses of rum? I can have a keg of it any time I like! No, I called the men off watch 'cause I don't like the way your scummy crew are actin' – you included. I don't *want* to catch your ship: I think you're tryin' to trick us into a fight with it. Oh, you're a devious son of a dog - but I saw through you the moment I laid eyes on you.'

Bones said in a hurt voice, 'You got me all wrong, Hulky.

I told you me reasons for catching dat ship. And dere's a matter of honour too. Dere's ladies on dat ship. And me cat. I got promises I made –'

Hulky was roaring with laughter now. 'The noble cook!' he shouted. 'Wants to save the *ladies* and his *pussy cat!* Well, you can kiss 'em both goodbye!'

Bones voice was so soft now that I could barely hear it: 'Well, you can't say I didn't give you a fair chance.'

I heard the quartermaster swear softly.

Bones said, 'Aye, dis will blow a big hole in you, sure enough. So no quick movements, right? Put your hands behind your back and Jupiter will tie 'em for you. Den we're gonna treat you fairer dan you treated us, but you're gonna be kept quiet until we've caught up wid our ship.'

I heard Jupiter walking across from the galley: but before he got to the quartermaster there was a scuffle, an explosion, and the sound of a heavy body falling.

Men came running – some of them not as steady as others – and a fair group of us gathered about Hulky's large, still body.

'I'm sorry about dis,' Bones was saying, 'but dere wasn't another way to deal wid him. Maybe you'd better take me to the Cap'n now.'

The first mate was poking at Hulky with his boot. His face was strangely contorted and I realised he was trying hard not to laugh. 'He's dead!' he said finally, turning a nervous chuckle into a cough.

'Satan's gonna be pleased,' said someone from the back of the group and there were several snorts of laughter, quickly stifled.

'Cap'n pleased an' all,' muttered another, with a hysterical, rum-fuelled giggle.

Bones was holding out his pistol. 'Suppose I oughta give dis to one of you,' he said.

'Keep it,' said the first mate. 'As a – as a keepsake –' and then he laughed aloud before walking away.

Bones set off for the Captain's cabin, followed by a wary group that kept looking at one another, as if unsure which of them were Hulky's supporters.

Bones knocked respectfully at the door. When it opened he said with a straight face, 'Beg pardon, sir, but I seem to have killed your quartermaster.'

Captain Death's face showed no reaction, as if Bones had commented on the colour of the railing.

'In that case, Cook,' he said gravely, 'you'll have to be acting Quartermaster until the crew have an opportunity to appoint a new one.'

There was a murmur from the men.

'Ah, but Cap'n, sir,' said a horrified Bones. 'I couldn't do dat.'

'*Quartermaster!*' the Captain addressed him sharply. 'Is the ship ready to make sail?'

'Ah – well - yes, sir, it is,' said Bones, looking back at the men he was now representing. 'Dere's just the matter of feedin' the sharks, sir. Den we can go…'

Six pirates struggled to lift Hulky's body over the rail. It made an enormous splash and disappeared for a few seconds before bobbing up next to the ship.

As before, we crowded to the rails – even Madame and Red this time. We watched for a minute or so. The small island that had been Hulky rose and fell with the swell of the sea; that was all. Some of us turned back, disappointed.

Then there was a sudden groan; and Hulky lifted his head from the water.

He looked up at us and we stared back. His face broke into an evil smile and he seemed about to talk. But a movement caught his eye and he turned his head towards the darkening bay.

He watched it all the way, paralysed with terror: the blunt snout and high fin moving directly toward him, steady as an arrow. All the way, until the shark rose from the water, turning slightly to one side, and closed its jaws about the man's head.

One twist, and Hulky was left floating there, headless, his arms still twitching.

'What a way to go,' muttered a comrade.

'Satan claims his own,' said another.

Other sharks appeared and dragged the corpse away. By the time we had raised sail, there was nothing left but a trail of blood.

While the ship was being readied to sail, there was a meeting in the Captain's cabin of the *Tombstone*: Death, Red, Madame and myself. We could hear the crew rushing about on deck and the first mate shouting orders, then dropping his voice to exchange words with Bones, the boatswain and the two sailing masters (our Misty and their one-eyed Buster).

'The next clue, then!' Death called to Madame. 'Let's see if you truly know what's in that parchment!'

Madame joined her hands behind her, like a child reciting a piece. '*Follow the plough. What fate and fortune are crafted of, there seek your fourth, sweet fortune beyond the fourth fate.*'

They turned to look at me and this time I began confidently, 'The important words here are –'

'Silence!' roared Captain Death. 'We don't want to know that yet!' He lowered his voice. 'What we need to know is what *they* made of the clue.' He nodded his head forward, towards the unseen ship we were pursuing.

'That's easy,' said Red. 'They won't understand a word of it except the reference to the plough. They'll take that to mean heading due north, and they'll hold that course until they reach land.'

'Or until they grow thirsty,' said Death.

'In fact,' said Madame, 'they might not follow the clue at all. They might think what they have is adequate.'

'No!' Red insisted. 'They'll gamble on finding it. Tom might be happy with what they've got, but Jake won't and nor will Jimmy. They'll think it worth their while to try one clue. *Then* they'll give up.'

'Or they might skip this clue and go onto the next?' asked Death.

Madame shook her head, saying. 'Each clue takes a bearing from wherever the previous treasure is found.'

'They're all linked,' I added. 'Every clue to the next.'

'The shin bone's connected to the thigh bone… the thigh bone's connected to the hip bone…' murmured Death, raking his fingers through his beard and peering out through the cabin's porthole before turning back to look at me. 'Well, then – we'll hear the boy's interpretation.'

'The plough should be the north star,' I said. 'It's also the marker for North in the Game. As for what *fate and fortune are crafted of*, there are fate and fortune cards in the Game: thin, wooden cards.'

'What kind of wood?' asked Death, his cold eyes piercing mine.

I hesitated. 'I'll have to go look at –' I began, then fell silent: the game was back on the *Firebird*.

'You mean you can't remember?' Red roared at me, his fists tightening. 'You played that game with Jones every week and you don't recall what you played *with*?'

'I *will* remember,' I promised. 'I can almost see them – in my head. They were dark – no, I think very light – no, that was the spinning compass. Ah – I remember – the fortune cards were light, the fate cards dark!'

'Made from what tree?'

I shook my head. 'I don't know.'

'Who else has seen these cards?' asked Madame.

'Only Amy,' I said.

'That's no help to us just now,' she said bitterly.

'Perhaps there will be only one kind of tree on the island,' I suggested. 'Or maybe the type of the wood isn't important anyway. Then it won't matter that I can't recall it.'

Death said evenly, 'Or maybe it *does* matter, and we'll have to stab your eyes with a red-hot spike, to make you remember. In my experience, that usually works.'

'The final part,' said Madame sharply. 'What of that?

There seek your fourth, sweet fortune beyond the fourth fate.'

I drove from my head the image that Captain Death had planted there. 'The fourth fortune – I suppose that just means this is the fourth treasure in the parchment. As for the fourth fate, the fate cards are numbered, though they don't come up in that order, because they're shuffled.'

'And you can't remember *that* either, I suppose,' Red said scornfully.

I said, 'The first is the loss of an item of treasure, I know that. The second, a broken rudder. Third, the hand of an ugly maiden in marriage. Fourth – I can't think straight when you're looking at me like that – fourth is something to do with... to do with another person. An old man. No, an animal: that's it, an animal. And the animal is – just a minute, fifth is prison... and *sixth* is the animal: a rabid dog. That means fourth is something else. I think if I write this down, it will come to me.'

'Something else will come to you if that fails,' Red observed dryly. 'And it'll have a large boot attached to it.'

'No matter!' exclaimed Death suddenly, slapping a table with his hand. 'We head north for now. We won't reach land until late tomorrow: enough time for the boy to ponder the clues.'

'He knows the answers already,' Madame said crossly. 'We went through all these before we set sail. He even checked the game to see which the fourth fate card was. He said then that it was –'

'Drowning!' I exclaimed suddenly. The card had come to mind: a figure under water, tangled in weed. 'And the cards are made of... no, I still don't know that.'

'You don't know much, and that's a fact,' said Death. 'But it'll do for now, and we'll leave those eyes of yours unpierced for a few days... unless we find that you've misled us, of course.'

He turned from staring at me to a study of Madame. 'Your pardon,' he said, crossing suddenly and putting his hand upon her large chest. She didn't move as his hand felt about.

'Ah. I thought so. Metal.' He rapped upon her chest with a knuckle; there was a dull noise.

Madame said quietly, 'And below that, a layer of felt. Please remove your hand now, Captain. *That* part is flesh.'

Captain Death felt about a little longer, then sighed and took his hand away. 'At least *that* is real. Not much else.'

Madame's laugh was short and cruel. 'All I've told you is true, Captain. And if you wish to talk with Morgana herself, that can be arranged in this very cabin.'

His eyes smouldered at this – though whether from fear, desire or anger I couldn't say. He turned away and fetched charts from a cupboard, which he laid upon the table. 'The boy can go,' he said harshly, and I went.

On deck, all was bustle and purposeful cooperation. I saw Jupiter forward, working alongside the pirates; our foretop men were up in the rigging; Bones was pointing something out to their sailing master as we edged across the bay, which was now totally in shadow.

We left the narrow channel and turned left, soon steering dead north. The sun had already disappeared behind the high ridge of the island and it wasn't long before it fell into the sea, leaving us to sail beneath the moon and stars.

At least we had the advantage of two sailing masters, though it was clear that both of them had been at the rum. They pored over the charts together, exchanging stories and laughing riotously. I fell asleep to their laughter, swinging from a hammock rigged in my galley.

My galley. One of Bones' first actions – in league with the first mate - had been to send their cook to join the deck-hands and place me in charge of the food.

'Number three soup, I'd suggest, young'un,' he said to me. 'Dere's even some half-decent greens in the locker to your right.'

He had been training me on the *Firebird*. Each recipe of his had a number, and I'd learned each by heart. Number three soup had dried peas, barley, shredded meat and whatever vegetables could be found. You cooked it for at least two hours, with three times the amount of water to the solids. If any spice was available, one tablespoon per large cauldron.

When they tasted the evening meal, the pirates were surprised and grateful. Even their Cook was pleased. Then Bones announced something that pleased them even more.

'I've been going through the accounts book,' he called across the main deck as the crew lined up for seconds. 'Wanted to make sure I'm treatin' you all fair, dis not being my ship an' all. Now, dere's a few t'ings I t'ink is only justice to do. First, Hulky's own share – I'm putting dat back into the pot for the *Tombstone's* crew.'

There were murmurs of approval at this.

'Second, I notice dere's been a few small mistakes. Dere was three bits of plunder dat's on Hulky's private list and in one of his chests, what didn't get onto the main list at all. So I'll share dat out as well.'

A few catcalls and cheers.

'Den we has dat treasure I shifted a mountain of guano for. We'll share it out to everyone here, includin' me and your other new shipmates.'

Grudging acceptance, with a few growls of dissent.

'Lastly, dere's about fifty bits of paper from lads dat owed him money. Here dey go.' And he flung the scraps overboard.

Almost all the crew shouted and stamped on the deck in delight now.

Bones said cheerfully, 'Glad to be of service to you black-hearted sons of the devil. Now, while you're all in a good mood, I'll read out the new list of watches agreed wid mate Johnnie here. Dere's a few changes, but you'll see we tried to make it fair.'

I fell asleep recalling all this. At the back of my mind I knew there was something I ought to be recalling instead, but I was too weary to think of it.

16 Pondering

There was once a mouse who read a human magazine instead of making a nest from its ripped-up pages. Herein she learned that females must continually alter themselves so as to approach perfection. First, the whiskers must be shortened – or sometimes extended; then they must be thinned or else made to appear thicker; finally, they must be curled and coloured, or bleached and straightened. Before this, she had been the happiest of mice; now she spent so much time changing to meet the latest fashions, and so much energy worrying about it, that she lost the simple enjoyment of life. Ah, fellow mice, learn from this: good literature liberates; all the rest should be chewed to shreds. (From the collected works of Bunstropple, mouse and philosopher).

I rose at dawn to get the porridge started and make coffee for the officers. We were moving along gently, for the wind was slow. As the sun played upon the sea and warmed the unseen lands to north and east, the breeze strengthened.

We were alone on the water and it stayed that way throughout the day. Number one pork (with root vegetables) went down well, as did number two soup (like number three but without dried peas and with some crumbled biscuit as thickener).

As the sun passed overhead, land appeared on the north eastern horizon – a low, symmetrical mound, like a drop of water on a flat table. It was clearly well-known, for the lookout called its name immediately:

'Land on the starboard quarter! Scum Bay!'

Many hands crossed to the railings, looked at that distant blob and sighed deeply.

'Prime drinkin' spot,' said the ex-Cook to me (he was hiding from his deck work in my galley and getting under my feet). 'Prime dancin', too. Loadsa pretty girls. And pretty boys. And some gamblin'. And lots of knifin' and shootin'.

Great place.'

I made a mental note not to go out partying with the cook, and continued with my rearrangement of the galley. I'd already thrown over the side several boxes of evil-smelling powders and grains liberally spiced with rats' droppings and urine; taken half an inch of grease off the stove; replaced the ancient and rancid cooking oil with a newer keg from the hold; and killed vast populations of insects that had made the galley their home.

The cook was found and sent back on deck, and I got on with preparation of supper: number four stew (salt beef plus weevilly biscuit and something I was sure must be field beans, which I boiled with the rest of the greens). After a few hours the lookout called again, and it was land due north this time. I went out on deck to see.

Ship's master Buster was on the foredeck with Death, agreeing our destination. It was the obvious one – an island about ten nautical miles wide and three deep. Apparently, the only uncertainty had been whether we would come across a small, uncharted island on the way there.

'Not a good place to hide treasure,' said the first mate to Red as they stood apart at the railing nearby, peering forward. 'Too near Scum, really.'

Scum Bay was out of sight now, south and east of us, but only a few hours away in a good wind.

'But plenty of places to do the hiding,' Red grumbled. 'Do we look high, or low?'

The island must have been volcanic, for there was a severe peak in the right hand side and a smaller one crumbling away to the far left. Between them, the land fell and rose several times.

'Not low, I think!' Death called in response. 'That middle part is swamp. The rain runs off those peaks and gathers in great pools in the middle of the island: pools writhing with snakes, hazy with mosquitoes and stinking with the corpses of drunken crews who left Scum in the dark and took a wrong turning.'

He looked at me and added softly: 'Perhaps our young guide has remembered the meaning of the clues?'

'I need to do something in the galley,' I said.

Having earned a few minutes' thinking space, I fussed with the pots until there was nothing more to do – and no more time to ponder either. I set out the food for the crew and went forward to where the captains were still studying the island, now very near.

Madame was there as well, and for the first time I saw her fretting. 'No sign of the *Firebird*,' she remarked. 'Could we have passed her on the way?'

'Not likely,' said Captain Death. 'Either she sank, was lost or turned aside – or has been here and gone again.'

'Here and gone,' judged Captain Red. 'Back to Scum Bay.'

'Aye.'

'What are we to do, then?' asked Madame sharply. 'Stand here staring at the island until it's too late?'

They all turned to look at me.

'Wood,' I said. 'Captain Jones said they came from two types of tree, the... no, I can't remember what they were - but if you suggested some trees, I might recall.'

'Birch, beech, elm, oak, ash, hazel, cherry, yew?' Madame shot at me. 'Pine, spruce, willow, chestnut, cypress?'

'Mahogany, deal, ironwood, teak, fir, hickory, maple, cedar, gum?' suggested Death.

These names – and the others they recited – all tumbled through my head without striking a chord.

'I'm sure there was something about colour,' I said. 'Birch bark is very light, isn't it?'

'And a few hundred trees are dark,' Red observed grimly. 'I'm sure we talked about this at the house. Madame made notes about it.'

'– Which are on the *Firebird*,' she said. 'Along with much else that is of value.'

Captain Death said briskly, 'We'll hold our course to the island. And we'll keep an eye open for unusual trees... or drowned men! Or is that a useless clue as well?'

And so we did: wasting two precious hours poking about in the shallows, rejecting this tiny inlet and that bay, scraping past outcrops of rock, with the crew cursing Captain Jones, his parchment and his ignorant young friend.

Finally, with night about to fall, Death called it off. He turned the ship about and set a course for Scum Bay, on the chance that we might find the *Firebird* there.

But there was to be another uneasy twist for me: as the ship settled onto its southeastern course, he had all hands piped up on deck. Then he made me stand facing them with my back against the mainmast while he berated my memory, my courage, my intentions and my parentage.

'Such a boy!' he cried. 'Cooks well, don't he?' (Contented murmurs at this). 'Couldn't climb a ratline to spare his life, though. Wouldn't know North if you shoved a compass up his arse. And the little bastard has robbed us of our treasure. Well, if it wasn't for the fact that my stomach is easier than it's been for a year, I'd shoot his head off. As it is, he'll only have to play the Game.'

He turned to me suddenly. 'What's your favourite fruit, boy?' he asked. His eye gleamed.

I thought fast but falsely, thinking that whatever it was, it was going to be inserted into an orifice of his choice. 'A – a grape, sir!' I answered.

The crew hooted with laughter at this. Death simply smiled. 'Well lad,' he said, 'I don't think we have one of those on board. What about a raisin? That's a dried grape.'

'I threw them all overboard,' I confessed. 'Half of them could have walked to the railings by themselves.'

'Ha! What's the next biggest fruit we have?'

'Plums, maybe?' I asked. 'Prunes?'

Death looked at the ex-Cook, who shook his head. 'I think there's some apples, sir,' he said to Death.

I couldn't help but groan at this.

'An apple!' the Captain shouted. 'Fetch me an apple, someone!'

The apple was duly fetched and placed upon my head as I stood against the mast. Then Death paced away seven long steps, turned, and pulled out his pistol. 'Now, young lad: ain't you pleased we didn't have no grapes?' he asked.

The ship was rocking a little – up and down, side to side. The pistol swung with the movement, then became steady. It seemed to be pointing straight at my forehead, though in the gathering dark this was difficult to judge.

'Don't move, lad. Don't even breathe...'

I knew about pistols: they were so inaccurate that most duels – conducted at twenty paces – ended with both men missing the target. The barrels were scarcely straight and the bullets never round. In any case, the bore of the barrel was generously sized so that the shot could be dropped into it with ease: and therefore each bullet rattled about randomly when discharged.

I took a deep breath and looked Death in the eye. I saw him smile; then there was a flash and the apple leapt from my head.

'Got it!' he crowed. 'One hundred and three out of one hundred and twenty, by God!'

'And he was drunk for half of those,' I heard someone mutter. Death pretended not to notice.

'He's a good lad, isn't he?' he asked the crew. He came forward and clapped me on the shoulder. 'Didn't flinch like old Bob did, hey?'

'Didn't get his head shot off like Bob, neither!' one of the men shouted back.

'Aye, but I had a headache that day. Right, men: back to quarters. And when we get to Scum, maybe we'll have a little fun. But only after we've recovered what's rightly ours: the *Firebird*, her treasure, and the fair maidens that come with her!'

'Arrrrr!' shouted the crew in a fully piratical fashion, with an intonation that made me fearful for Amy and the others girls.

We glided into Scum Bay under moon and stars. I expect there were reefs and rocks and tricky tides here as for all harbours: but this place was so well known to the men that the two sailing masters were left to doze peacefully throughout, Misty's hammock swaying next to Buster's.

'There's the *Firebird*,' I heard Captain Red whisper to Death, both standing near the wheel. 'No one showin' on deck.'

Death chuckled. 'Aye, and there's room for us nearby. Mason – steer small, will you? We'll tuck in within a cable of her.'

There were the usual commands before the ship dropped anchor. No one looked out from the *Firebird*; no one shouted across.

'My cabin!' ordered Death, and a small group made their way there: the Captains, Madame, Bones and the tall first mate Jenkins. I tried to creep close enough to listen, but the Bo'sun gave me a kick – and then another – which persuaded me to return to the galley.

I heard about it fairly soon anyway, when Bones came and whistled me out on deck. 'You'll be in the third boat wid me,' he said. 'The first two boats will be full of armed men, wid Cap'n Red to guide 'em; Madame and I are following in the third to secure the treasure and save the ladies from – ah - further *unpleasantness*, you might say.'

'And why am I coming?' I asked.

'To keep you out of mischief here. Get your jacket on. And take dis old hat – pull it down over your forehead. Dat's better. I've got a short cutlass for you to wave about, but I'll give you dat just before we goes on board 'cause you'll probably just cut yourself wid it otherwise...'

The three boats moved off quietly through the dark waters. The first rowed onwards, as if for the shore, while the other two moved lazily. I peered forward and could just see the first boat turning right, passing in front of the bows of the *Firebird*, before disappearing into the gloom. Our boat held back while the middle boat made for the stern of the ship (the part nearest to us). A shout went up:

'*Firebird*! Hail there! Message for the Captain of the *Firebird*!'

Two faces appeared at the rail. 'Cap'n's not here!' shouted one of them. 'What's the message?'

'Can I come aboard? I'm first mate of the *Tombstone*, with a message for whoever's in charge of your stinking, rat-infested pile of –'

'Easy now! We be fond of our rats, hear?'

Pirate mate Jenkins laughed. 'Who's in charge there?' he asked.

The man at the rail shouted back, '*I* am. Newly promoted second mate Barber. The others has buggered off. Fancy some hot rum? Come on board if you do.'

'Thank you kindly,' returned Jenkins. 'Throw me a line, then.'

There was a splash of a rope ladder hitting the water; then Jenkins made quite a noise climbing up it. I heard a distant commotion as he was pulling himself over the railing, two men from his boat following him.

It was soon over without a shot, and with scarcely a shout. Our first boat had gone to the other side of the *Firebird* and its crew had climbed aboard while our second boat was keeping the men in charge busy.

So – less than an hour after entering the harbour - I was back in the *Firebird's* galley, making coffee and hot rum.

I took the drinks aft, to the cabin that had once housed the ladies. Red took his rum and pointed to a corner. I went and stood there next to Bones, listening.

The man named Barber was speaking; I remembered him as a cheerful, thoughtless deckhand who did what he was told without questioning or grumbling.

'It was Jake and Tom and Jimmy – and that miserable git Forrest. They waited until you was outta sight, then Tom ordered us to raise sail. We went north for an hour, then they hove-to and called a meetin'. Treasure, they said:

enough for every man to buy his own cottage and set up as a gentleman. Half of it in the ladies' cabin, the other half not a day's journey north. So we all cheered of course and said we'd do it.'

'What about the girls?' Madame asked.

'They'd locked themselves in, and the first man that tried to break inside – which was Forrest - got a bullet through his head. After that, Tom and Jake asked for a parley, like. Went in without weapons, hands in the air, sayin' they would let the ladies go free in return for the treasure that was kept in the cabin.'

'My girls wouldn't be tricked that easy.'

'Ah, but Tom had got one of the cannon moved so that it pointed at the cabin door. Said he would blow them to hell and back if they didn't parley. So they had to talk. Well, you can guess what happened: the men jumped on 'em, first chance they got. Got beat up proper.'

Madame leaped up in a rage. 'I'll kill them!' she cried. 'And I'll kill the lot of you for standing by!' She moved towards Barber, who recoiled, holding his hands before his face and crying out:

'No, Ma'am! You's misunderstood! It was the *men* what got beat up! Tom's privates was kicked to a pulp, and Jake has a bullet in his guts!'

Madame controlled herself with an effort. 'And?' she asked.

'And – and – the other men tied up the girls and then they was goin' to – you know – have their way with 'em, to teach 'em a lesson, like – but Tom and Jake, they swore that if they couldn't have their own pleasure with the women (bein' so beat up as they were), no one else would neither. And then Jake got this smile on his face and whispers something to Tom, and Tom smiles too and they said they would take the girls to town tonight, into Scum. They said they was gonna sell 'em as slaves. That's what they're doin' now.'

17 Scum

Whence come these strange longings for justice and love: for the lion to lie down with the lamb? My fellow mice, this is a furry mystery and yet the mystery must have a meaning. In this brief life we see nature always at war within itself; but we feel – nay, we know - that the whole universe is designed for peace, and one day I will embrace the cat as my beloved friend and will not fear her claws. (From the collected works of Bunstropple, mouse and philosopher).

'This is what we'll do.'
Captain Death was speaking. His eyes were as wild as ever, but calculating and hard: like the stones on the abacus

I'd used when doing the accounts with Amy, only a few weeks beforehand but seeming like an age ago.

We were back on the *Tombstone* now, in Death's cabin: some of his officers, Captain Red and Madame - and myself handing around food and drink. Other pirate officers were in charge of the *Firebird*, with Bones to assist them and cook a hasty meal.

'We'll take three of the bigger boats,' Death said. 'I'll go with some of my men in the first, plus Madame. We don't want them to spot us straight off, so she'll dress as a lady of the night. She'll be able to point out Red's old crew and the women. The second boat – from the *Firebird* - will have Captain Red and whoever he wants to take with him. Red, you'll hang back while we look for the mutineers. If they try to make a run for it, they'll run straight into you. And if you hear a fight starting up, you can come and help out. Agreed?'

'And the third boat?' asked Madame.

'That's for any men we capture or maidens we rescue. The four men who go out in it will stand guard over the three boats until we return, or come find us if we don't.'

'Who stays behind on the ships?' asked Red.

'My man Jenkins will be in charge of the *Firebird*, helped by Bones and whoever you trust from your old crew. Snakeye here will stay on the *Tombstone*. Yes? Good. We go in half an hour.'

He turned to pirate mate Snakeye – a one-eyed sneering man who seemed evil even for a pirate – and said, 'I'll need ten of our men, fully armed; send them to get the two cutters ready. And while we're in Scum, keep the crew alert and ready to move out. Not a drop of rum, hear? Or I'll have that other eye of yours later tonight.'

Not wanting to be confined to one ship's galley or the other, I kept quiet; I had my own plans. I sneaked away to my hammock and studied the few scraps of clothing I had, then went to the galley. I was teasing a cold lump of charred wood from the fire when the ex-Cook came in, demanding to know what I was up to.

'Cap'n said fire t'be left out!' he said drunkenly, wagging a fat finger at me. 'You disobeyin', hey? Makin' yerself some hot grog, maybe?'

'No. I was just… making sure it was all shut down.'

The Cook winked. 'I caught ya,' he whispered. 'But that's between you an' me, hey? Maybe you was even settin' fire to the ship, but that don't matter. You an' me, we're mates. Haveta stick together, us cooks.' He put an arm around my shoulder and I smelled the rum on his breath.

He added, 'Cap'n says I gotta fetch a keg of rum from the stores. Look – I got the key. Gimme a hand.'

I followed, wishing he would move a little faster, for the landing party would be leaving in a few minutes. He looked all about him before unlocking the spirits store and choosing a keg. He didn't lock the store afterwards, not until I reminded him. I was becoming suspicious now but it was too late to start asking questions that would just delay us further.

'Take one end, boy!'

The kegs weren't large, but they were heavy. Usually you rolled them most of the way and only hoisted them when you had to; but I didn't want to waste time by arguing.

We carried it quietly to the galley, stopping in the shadows when men were passing.

'Don't let the crew see,' the Cook whispered. 'Cap'n's orders. S'prise for later.'

As soon as we'd dropped the keg in the galley, I snatched my piece of charcoal and dashed away, ignoring the Cook's call for me to help him with something else.

The night was dark and everything was being done by the light of a couple of shaded lanterns. The boats had already been drawn up to the side of the ship; I watched to see which one Madame clambered into and waited until the last man was descending the ropes to board it. Then I slid down too, settling myself next to Madame herself.

'All in,' growled the burly pirate who had preceded me.

'Cast off then,' said Death quietly. 'Straight to the landing, men. Don't act suspicious. Let's have a song, Brocky my lad: as if we're out for a bit of fun, hey?'

Oh, those Northern ladies are fair
But they don't let you get anywhere:
Give me fast Southern girls
With their sweet Southern curls
And their sweet Southern mothers besides!

Madame turned her head towards me: but my hood was as shadowed as her own and I congratulated myself that no one knew I was there.

She turned back to Death, seated on the other side of her. 'Captain – ' she began.

'I know,' he cut her off. 'He can stay. Every game needs a

pawn that can be sacrificed.'

Her voice showed amusement: 'Just so long as it isn't the queen who is turned over, Captain.'

'A little turning over is good for a queen,' he said, also amused.

Oh, those Western ladies have charms
But they never just melt in your arms.
Give me Southern delight
By day and by night
And their sweet Southern mothers besides!

The crew guided the boat to a stone jetty and tied her up. We clambered out and waited for the other boats, whose oars I could hear splashing softly in the calm waters.

Soon we were all gathered on the landing. Four men settled onto a stone block there, placed their pistols in their laps and lit their pipes. One of them had a shaded oil lamp beside him.

Death took up another lamp and whistled to his band, who moved off. I joined the men at the back; one of them held a lantern too. Apart from these two small pools of light, we were lost in a sea of darkness.

'Send the boy up front!' Death called, and I was snatched and pulled forward from pirate to pirate. Death's strong claw of a hand clasped my shoulder. He whispered:

'Now, lad: you stay with me unless I order you elsewhere. And if I tell you to do something, you do it immediately without asking why. Understand?'

'Yes, Captain.'

'Good. Because the first time you fail, I'll kill you.'

'Aye, sir.'

'That's right. Madame – I'll trouble you to come round my other side and lean upon me, as if you're a drunken floozy sodden with lust.'

'Unlikely, Captain,' she said coolly.

'Lust for the gold in my pocket, that is,' he replied.

'I can do that,' she said. She crossed over and hung upon his arm, stumbling as they walked and giggling at odd moments. It would have been embarrassing if she hadn't been so good at it.

Oh, those Eastern ladies look shy
But they're cold and they're hard and they're sly.
Give me girls who are flirty
And naughty and dirty
And their sweet Southern mothers besides!

We came to what seemed to be a main street. There were people moving about left and right, with lighted doorways beyond them and confused music troubling the air - and a few shouts - and a scream or two for contrast.

Death called back to one of his men, 'Blackguts first, Jonnie, or Lady C's?'

'Blackguts is closer,' said the man. 'May as well check there.'

We waited until Red's group came up. After a whispered discussion, we turned right and pushed past a gathering of men standing about a drunken fistfight that was going on in the darkness. Soon we came upon a building to our left, with oil lights hanging from the ceiling inside, giving us a glimpse of someone dancing on a stage beyond a dark, troubled sea of piratical heads.

'Wait here, all of you,' whispered Death, passing the lantern to one of his men; then he and Madame staggered through the open doors and were lost in a milling crowd.

A few minutes later, they were back.

'Let's try the Lady's,' Death murmured, and I heard the message being relayed along the group. We retraced our steps, past the remnants of the drunken fight, past the turning on our left to the dark road from the landing, and onwards into a more lighted part of town: that is, light spilling from perhaps twenty windows rather than ten.

We came to a second bar, from which came a lot of noise:

a fiddle, some husky singing, tables being banged, and distant cries of pain, pleasure and anger. Death and Madame disappeared again but returned almost immediately and beckoned us inside. Again, I heard a message being relayed behind us.

Death looked at me carefully as I stepped into the half-light of the saloon. I'd rubbed soot on my face and in my hair: I looked foreign and dirty. He pushed my hood back and nodded at the torn red bandana I'd tied about my head.

'You'll do, boy. Come sit over here.'

It was a wide room, with big wooden pillars every five or so paces which held up the two floors above and provided a place for pirates to carve their names, crude messages and even cruder pictures. We moved to the left of the room and found a place near the back and therefore not too far from the door. We settled to the left of a pillar, sitting on rickety chairs at tables so stained and sticky that they might never have been cleaned.

I sat beside the pillar itself, peering around it curiously. There was a central, raised stage at the front of the room, where a lady was standing and singing in a heartbroken fashion. She didn't seem to have enough clothes on, but no one was complaining.

To the left of the stage – our side – there was a large door covered in green fabric, and standing in front of that door was a tall and broad yellow-skinned man wearing no shirt. He had a big, close-shaved head and a mean look in his eye. His torso was decorated with tattoos, crisscrossed with scars and rippling with muscles. He had knives and a pistol at his belt, but I couldn't imagine he would ever need them.

From time to time someone would approach him. He would either nod for them to enter by the green door or else would give them a cold stare, when they would turn about and walk away very carefully.

The lady on the stage had stopped her miserable singing and she seemed to have lost more of her clothes. She hurried away to the green door and was allowed through.

'Over there,' I heard Madame whisper. 'Far right, near the front.'

'I see them,' said Death. He signalled to his men by the door and two of them came forward. After a brief conversation, the men eased away towards the far side of the room.

Meanwhile, a scrawny old woman brought us beer and spirits on a tray, pinched my cheek, and dropped the coins Death gave her into a leather bag. She returned a few minutes later with some olives and stale bread; pinched my other cheek; sighed sadly; then disappeared from our lives. I still wonder who she was, and how she'd ended up there.

We sat through a song by a different woman who managed to keep all her clothes on. Then a fat, oily man mounted the stage and shouted for our attention, which he mostly got. His voice was loud and self-important:

'Tonight, my friends, we have an unexpected auction. Not ship's treasure this time: but *human* treasure! Not merely slaves, but *lady* slaves! And we've got some right beauties for you, lads. Three of 'em!'

He beckoned to his left – our right – and I saw Amy, Vicky and Sandy being pushed up some steps onto the stage. Their faces were grim and their hands seemed to be bound behind their backs.

The man leered at them. 'Ain't they something? Turn around girls, let's see you from all angles.'

The women gave him sharp looks and wouldn't turn, so the man went up to Amy, grabbed her by the shoulders and forced her around in a circle. He discarded her and moved towards Sandra; but she and Vicky suddenly swung a leg each, perfectly in time, and booted him off the stage. A table collapsed beneath him with a clattering and crashing of dirty plates, glasses, weapons and the shouts of angry pirates.

There were roars of laughter, cheers and clapping. Then

the fat man staggered up the stairs onto the stage, wiping blood from his forehead. He had a knife in one hand.

The girls backed away until they met the wall behind. The man waddled after them shouting curses, the knife held forward. He was closing in on Amy when Tom leaped onto the stage and belted him in the face, knocking him to the floor.

I thought for a moment that this was sudden evidence of a restored gallantry; but Tom shouted:

'Damage my property, will you? I'll break your damned neck if you do!'

The man rose unsteadily to his feet, leaning against the back wall. He wiped his face with a handkerchief, then held up one hand until the catcalls and laughter subsided.

'Gennlemen!' he called, not speaking so clearly now. 'Your bids for the slaves!'

'I'll have the two that beat you up!' shouted someone, and the bidding for Sandra and Vicky went on for a few minutes, ending up at something like thirty crowns each. But before the man could declare the sale complete, there was a banging on the stage boards and we all looked to the left, where a tall, glamorous woman with flaming red hair was standing at the open green door, pointing towards the girls with a silver topped cane. Silence fell.

'They're mine!' she said sternly. 'Eighty for the two together. I need some new girls who are strong enough to work with you scoundrels. Send them over to me.'

'And the other girl, Lady C?' the oily auctioneer asked with a leer. 'I'll throw her in for another twenty.'

'No thanks,' the Lady said. 'She wouldn't last a week.'

A couple of big men climbed onto the stage and steered Sandra and Vicky across to the green door. They went through; the door shut; the large bouncer resumed his position in front of it.

At this point, Madame rose from the chair next to mine and walked towards the front. I lost sight of her amongst the crowd and during the turmoil of what happened next.

Amy was being pushed forward. 'What am I bid for this gorgeous, unspoilt girl?' the fat man asked with a knowing wink. 'Maybe she won't last a week, but it'll be a week to remember!'

No one bid. They all shook their heads.

'Too skinny,' said one.

'Too bossy!' shouted another.

Still the auctioneer cajoled and finally one evil-looking decrepit old pirate stood up.

He croaked, 'What with my own diseases, I don't reckon to last the week myself!' he proclaimed to laughter. 'Give you a crown for her!'

At that I stood up and shouted, 'Five crowns!' though of course this was an amount I didn't have: and a moment later, a look of absolute rage from Captain Death told me that I had possibly ruined everything.

There were odd stares in our direction, before Death stepped forward from the shadows and called out, 'I said five crowns!'

'I'm not selling her for that!' a shout came back from the other side: Tom again. 'I'll kill her first!'

'Ten crowns, then: and that's all you'll get.' Death was staring across the room at Tom, his face expressionless.

The auctioneer looked from one to the other. Tom must have nodded, for the man clapped his hands. 'Sold at ten!' he exclaimed. 'Send the lady over there!'

I heard another voice I recognised: Pitiless Jake's. 'Wait a minute!' he shouted. 'Where's your money first?'

'Back at my ship,' boomed Death.

'That ain't good enough!' Jake said sullenly.

Death took two steps forward and turned to glare across the room. 'You're strangers here,' he called. 'I'll make allowances for that.' Then he roared out: 'Does any other man here doubt my word? The word of Captain Death? If so, speak now – and die now.'

His hands rested on the butts of his pistols. Not a man

moved; then someone whispered to Tom, and Tom spoke up: 'I'm told you're a man of your word. At your ship, then, in an hour. Where are you anchored?'

'The *Tombstone* is next to the *Firebird*. Meet me there and I promise you'll get what's coming to you.'

Meanwhile, a helpless Amy - her hands still bound behind her back - was being conveyed in our direction. This seemed to involve being passed from man to man, pinched here and fondled there, with many a quip and critique.

'Changed me mind! I'll give eleven for her! The bow ain't anything to leave port for, but the stern's nicely rounded!'

'Hey – look at dem eyes –'

'Cute little mouth. Worth a crown just for a kiss –'

A pistol went off near my ear and I heard Captain Death's voice through the deafened ringing that followed: 'Hands off! That's *my* woman now! If you wanted a feel, you should've bid for her yourselves!'

A man at the table next to ours chose to ignore Death's warning shot into a pillar (most of which – now that I looked at them – were decorated with bullet holes). He slid his hand up Amy's dress, getting a fair way beyond the knee before Amy was snatched away by one of Death's long, wiry arms; then the matching arm drove a knife into the offending hand, transfixing it to a table.

The man groaned and grabbed at the knife with his free hand; he got a punch to the face for that. Captain Death placed his hand on the protruding haft of the knife again. He turned his head and spoke to Amy:

'Here's the first advantage to you of being acquired by a Gentleman: you can choose how many fingers this despicable pissbucket will lose.'

I saw Amy redden and her chin go up. 'I won't be made a part of this evil!' she cried. 'If you're a gentleman, you don't need my advice! And if you *are* a gentleman, what are you doing here in the first place?'

Death roared with laughter. 'Buying women for my

young apprentice, that's what!' he exclaimed. Then he gave his knife a twist and severed two of the man's fingers.

He slid the knife back into its sheath and turned again to Amy. 'Have I earned a kiss for saving you, girl?' he asked.

'I only give kisses to those I care for,' she said quietly, staring him down.

'Ah – you mean young Tom over there!' winked Death.

Amy blushed a deeper red. She tried to kick Death but, not being practised at it like Sandra and Vicky, merely overbalanced and fell over.

'I understand,' soothed the Captain as he watched her struggle to her feet (rather difficult to do with your hands tied behind your back). 'You loved Tom; but he didn't care for you and sold you to a depraved old pirate. Happens all the time, girl. Get used to it.'

'I – did – not – love – him!' cried Amy, punctuating each word with a kick which never quite accomplished its intent. She added, through gritted teeth, 'The only boy – man - I really care about, I'll probably never see again. But I'm not kissing filthy pirates just to pass the time!'

Death roared with laughter again. 'If that's the case, Missy, I'll give up trying. But you'll have to kiss my apprentice, for he's bought you and you're *his* floozy now!'

He caught one foot as it flashed towards his crotch, raised it and gave it a tweak, sending Amy backwards to land in my lap.

'Don't let her get away, lad!' he ordered. 'Worse awaits her if she escapes!'

Obediently, I threw my arms around her and held her close, despite her struggles. I was surprised at how soft and lovely a young woman felt in my arms.

She was at a disadvantage because of her arms being tied behind her, but she still tried to elbow me in the face. I simply held her more tightly.

'I'm *not* kissing you!' she hissed.

I made what I thought were appropriate piratical noises and tightened my grip. We sat there, first watching Death and then turning our heads to the scene he was himself watching.

The green baize door was being opened from within. The large yellow-skinned man turned his head slightly, nodded, stood aside. The woman with flaming red hair stepped out.

Madame was at her side and was holding one of the lady's arms. Madame had pulled her hood forward so that her face was totally hidden: yet I thought I saw the eyes burning with a terrible light.

The other woman's face was frozen with pain or fear or both. Her eyes stared; the lines in her forehead were deep. Madame steered her forward, twitched her arm: the lady turned and said something to the doorman.

I saw his brow crease; then he nodded again. Madame strode on, with Lady C at her side moving like a sleepwalker.

Behind them I glimpsed Sandra and Vicky. They were holding clubs in their hands and seemed to be itching to use them. The doorman scowled but let them pass.

Then came the other women. Some were beautifully clothed. Some were in rags. All had faces haggard and wasted; faces that told of nightmares, not dreams. I noticed that some still had manacles and chains on an arm or a foot.

The doorman saw them, too. He stepped forward and grabbed one woman by the neck; squeezed; dropped the body; grabbed another; began shouting and pushing them back.

But it was like trying to hold back the incoming tide. The women at first did not resist; they simply kept on walking, pushing past him. He tried to dam the stream, kicking and punching and sweeping them back through the green door. But still they came, and then one turned and hit back. A moment later, they all flew at him: and what happened next was more shocking that anything I'd seen in my travels. In seconds, he was down and being torn apart by women who individually had seemed lifeless. They had become a new thing, a conglomerate body with savage power and no morals.

There was a loud groan, and I saw a flash of a knife – no, several knives, dripping redness. One pirate stood up and moved toward them as if to intervene; the nearest women flew at him, scratching his face and plucking at his eyes. The pirate's friends rose from their seats but were quickly submerged beneath a tide of shrieking women.

I pushed Amy from my knee and started for the door, my arm through her own. She resisted a moment, then looked at me, gasped in surprise, and ran with me. Madame and Lady C were a few steps behind us and Captain Death was behind them.

We hurried along the dark street that was quickly filling with people from Lady C's, pursued by her former workers – or slaves – or whatever they once were. The women were now a howling wildness that drove us along like deer chased by wolves. I suppose there were no more than thirty of them, but they seemed numberless.

We turned right, towards the ships: running now except for Madame, whom I glimpsed some ways behind us, a lantern in one hand and Lady C's arm still gripped by the other. I saw the Lady resist, then look behind her at the advancing mob and hurry forward again.

The one light at the landing was being raised and waved at us, which might have been a signal but had no effect since none of us were intending to stop or turn aside. I heard Death calling to the men at the boats.

'Prepare to launch!' he shouted. 'No one allowed on the boats except our crews and Madame Helena's girls! Pistols and cutlasses out, men!'

Red arrived now, with his own men. 'These two as well!' he shouted, pointing back to two figures being dragged through the shadows.

The next few minutes were filled with curses and confusion. I was picked up and flung into a boat, and Amy followed: she didn't feel so soft and luscious when she landed on top of me. Boats were pushed out, then called back. There was gunfire, followed by screams. I managed to push Amy to one side before being knocked flat by Vicky and Sandra, who threw themselves into the boat as it was being rowed out.

We were taken to the *Tombstone* and scrambled on deck, though three struggling figures had to be hauled up: Lady C, Tom and Pitiless Jake.

'Set sail, Buster!' shouted Death. 'Chalky, hail the *Firebird* and tell 'em to do the same! They go first; we'll follow. Snakeye, get a few men to the stern with guns and cutlasses. If anyone tries to board us, they're dead.'

Red was standing at Death's side now. 'There might be some of my old crew I'd like to take with me,' he said.

'Then go to the stern with Snakeye. You can parley with any boat that comes; but if they don't answer sweet and play fair, Snake's men will fill their guts with lead.'

At this point, a strong female arm wrapped about my waist and I was dragged away. 'Gotcha!' said Vicky. 'Madame says you're comin' down below with us, before you get trampled or shot.'

'But the galley –'

'That galley won't be needed until we're well away. C'mon, sweetie.' She hugged me, tweaked my nose and dragged me below.

Soon we were seated in a low cabin – used by some of the *Tombstone's* officers, I assume. A lantern was swaying from the ceiling above a wood table scarred and notched from many a knife or cutlass, with a bullet hole at one corner: for the furniture in this ship was as battle-marked as the crew.

The flame-haired beauty known as Lady C looked older in the pitiless lamplight. There were lines on her forehead and at the corners of her eyes, half-masked by heavy powder; a hint of a double chin; hair that was thinning and sparkled with grey roots.

'I need to relieve myself,' she said, rising from the scarred bench screwed to the floor.

Sandra, seated beside her, kicked away the Lady's feet, making her land with a bump on the bench. 'Do it here, then,' she said.

Lady C looked at Sandra with a grave sneer. 'You don't know who you're talking to, young lady!' she said in the haughty accent adopted by the rich and famous.

'I'm talkin' to a common little pimp and bully,' said Sandra. 'A slaver, to boot. I'm talkin' to the lowest of the low.'

Lady C arched her eyebrows. 'How vulgar,' she said. 'And ignorant. You know nothing of commerce. I am a businesswoman. I sit in the parliament that runs the Island. I own more houses than you've ever been to. My girls –'

'Your *slaves*. Even them as didn't have chains was slaves.'

'We have a proper business arrangement. Those in chains were bought honestly at auction. The others all signed contracts and receive a share of the takings.'

I saw Madame bristle at this. She said to Lady C: 'You cannot buy a woman "honestly". You have no right to her body, much less her soul.'

Lady C sneered at Madame: never a good idea, so I began backing away to a safe distance. 'So philosophic!' Lady C murmured. 'Tell me, are your thoughts so pure that you would deny women the right to make money using their bodies?'

Madame looked at her levelly. 'Men have ruined our lives, and we must take revenge on them. Whatever resources a woman has, she may use them to wrestle money and power and respect from men. But she must do it willingly; not be forced to it by another. She may cheat, lie, kill, break a man's heart and destroy his life: but not at someone else's command.'

'I have never –'

But I never learned what it was that Lady C had never done or permitted, for Madame raised a hand and proclaimed in a quiet voice that rang with unnerving authority: 'In some countries, there are vultures who tear the hearts from the bodies of baby girls abandoned on hillsides by their parents. You are that vulture. You will die tomorrow. I have spoken.'

And whether it was the hand, the voice or the steely eye that did it, the other woman was silenced. She turned her head away proudly; but her lip trembled.

I looked at the others. Sandra and Vicky were glaring at their former owner with sheer hatred. Amy was seated on the floor in a far corner, her legs drawn up and her forehead resting on her knees.

One of the pirate officers poked his head into the cabin. He leered at each female in turn, then addressed Lady C:

'Cap'n wants you in his cabin. For questioning. *Close* questioning, he says. And *long* questioning.' He laughed in a particularly ugly manner. When Lady C was slow in rising, he pulled her up and fairly dragged her out the door. The other women said nothing but exchanged looks that clearly meant much – except to me.

We returned to our own thoughts. Above us, there were noises of the ship getting under way: the anchor chain rattling in, ropes being hauled, sails rising, sailors chanting. Further off, to the stern I assume, were some shouts and a few explosions. Then the ship turned and I heard the water moving against our sides.

18 Pirate Justice

From my diary: *I've not been allowed to return to the Firebird, but at least they sent over some of my clothes and my diary. Amy and the other girls were very sweet to me, giving me hugs and kisses that made my heart pound fiercely for a long time after they left for their own ship. Amy whispered what a hero I was to her and how much she cared about me. Unfortunately, the pirates seem to be annoyed about all the attention I received, and I've had two piratical kicks for every soft caress.*

We sailed northwest into the star-spattered darkness, retracing our former course until it was judged that we were drawing close to the island we had half-heartedly searched for  treasure. When I was shaken awake at dawn and sent to the galley, I could see the island again off our starboard bow. Its many woods smirked at me.

Second mate Snakeye was in charge this morning. He was standing on the raised deck at the stern of the boat, talking to the man at the wheel. He scowled at me when I brought his coffee, scratched at his beard and asked what I'd thought of Scum.

'I didn't see much of it, sir. What I did see, I couldn't say I enjoyed.'

He turned his head so that his one remaining eye – the left – could bore into me like a carpenter's awl. 'But you knew Cook liked it, didn't you?' he asked sourly.

I wondered why he was asking but answered politely, 'He did say that when we first passed it, sir. About liking it, I mean.'

'So why didn't you tell anyone?' he retorted savagely.

'Tell anyone what, sir?'

A slap to the side of the head was the only reply I got. Snakeye turned back to the man at the wheel and I hurried away before he could ask any more painful questions.

One of the crew soon told me that the ex-Cook had deserted the ship at Scum. He hadn't been included in the landing party (being too slow and lazy) but had taken the smallest of the remaining boats, together with a keg of rum – the very keg I'd helped him bring up from the stores.

I worked hard for a couple of hours, cooking some porridge and setting the galley straight again. The old cook must have been searching for something before he left, for half the drawers had been yanked out and the pots were scattered on the deck.

By now, the Captains were up and calling for their coffee and bacon, followed by a message from Madame to say that bread rolls would be appreciated at lunchtime. I threw the bacon into a pan, poured some coffee from the pot that had been simmering for the past hour and began looking for the flour.

Snakeye appeared and poked me with a belaying pin. I'd just found my lump of dough with yeast working in it and was cleaning it up, for it had been thrown by the ex-Cook into a corner and nibbled by rats.

Snakeye ordered, 'Cap'n wants you. *Now.*'

I ducked another blow and hurried before him, still holding the dough in my hand.

The Captain had gathered Madame and Red in his cabin – together with Snakeye and now myself. Bones was still on the *Firebird* with Death's first mate, Jenkins.

Captain Death said gravely, 'Snake says you knew Cook was planning to desert.'

I said firmly, 'I didn't.'

Snakeye said, 'He and Cook talked about it! He said so!'

'Not about deserting,' I insisted. 'Cook just said that he

liked Scum.'

Snakeye glared at me. 'You two was plottin'. Some of the men saw you with your 'eads together. And you helped 'im carry a keg of rum up to the galley. Where'd you get that rum?'

'From the stores,' I said. 'Cook had a key and said it was Captain's orders.'

Death interposed, 'And you believed him?'

I hesitated.

''Course 'e didn't!' said Snakeye. 'Look at 'is face!'

Death seemed disappointed with me, shaking his head.

'I *did* believe him at first,' I said. 'But then he started acting oddly, and I tried to say no. But he insisted – and we were all in a hurry, so I just did what he told me.'

'You mean that *you* were in a hurry,' said Captain Death coldly. 'In a hurry to leave the ship in disobedience to orders. *My* orders.'

'No,' I said. 'No, Captain,' I corrected myself. 'You gave me no orders.'

'Ah! So you simply invented your own!'

I thought for a way around this, then gave up. 'Aye, Captain,' I said. 'I had no orders, so I decided to join the landing party secretly.'

Snakeye exclaimed, 'To help Cook escape!'

'No, to – well – to –' I couldn't bring myself to say I'd wanted to make sure Amy was safe. It sounded so pathetic.

I saw the corner of Death's lips twitch a little, as if he knew what I was thinking.

Madame suddenly intervened. 'The boy's a puppy and a fool: but he's no traitor,' she said. 'We're wasting time here, Captain.'

Death shook his head. 'Traitor or not, his disobedience has assisted a deserter. The usual punishment for that is torture, confinement and marooning. For a boy, perhaps we can reduce that to twenty lashes. There can be no abandonment of discipline, Madame. The men won't stand for it. And think: if you let off one man, the others will learn from it that they too can do as they wish.'

'What nonsense!' she flamed. 'He had no reason to disobey the Cook. He had no reason to warn you that the Cook was behaving strangely. And he has no understanding of the seriousness of this. You cannot expect a boy to think like a pirate or even a seaman.'

For the first time, I felt I liked Madame Helena. At least, I liked having her on my side for once.

Death ran his fingers through his beard, smiling to himself. I could tell he enjoyed baiting Madame. 'That's why it's only twenty lashes, not forty,' he said mildly. 'But we'll have to ask the men in any case. Floggings and maroonings are a matter for the crew to decide. In the meantime, the boy can fetch my bacon.'

'The bacon!' I exclaimed and ran off, hearing laughter behind me, not all of it kindly.

The bacon was burned but that was the least of my problems.

Just before noon there was a gathering on the foredeck. Boats had been passing between the two ships all morning, transferring people back to their proper places. The women had gone back to the *Firebird* with Red; pirate mate Jenkins had come back to the *Tombstone*; most of the remaining crew were now on their own ships.

There were exceptions. I was stuck with the pirates, and we had Tom and Pitiless Jake chained up in one of the holds below. Bones had come back to the *Tombstone*, which puzzled me: though not for long.

As the ship's bell rang out for noon, Death held up one scarred hand and the crew fell silent. He motioned to Bones, who came forward with a large leather bag tied loosely at the top. He turned it over and shook it to show that it was empty, then hung the bag on the mast in full view of the crew.

The Captain said, 'There's two mutineers down below. We have a Rule, haven't we, lads?'

There were loud murmurings of assent.

'A Rule! Anyone who violently resists capture, *is killed*. Anyone who steals a prize from us, *is killed*. Anyone who interferes with our taking of a prize, *is killed*. Anyone who mutinies against the Captain of a ship, *is killed*.'

More murmurings.

'I've had a request from our sister ship: they want to judge their own mutineers. We don't have to let 'em do that, for when those two mutinied against the *Firebird*, they mutinied against us as well. But we can pass 'em over if you like. It's up to you.'

He nodded to Bones, saying, 'Quartermaster – address the men.'

Bones held up a black wooden disk in one hand and a white disk in the other: disks used in many of the games I'd seen sailors playing on deck. His head twitched as he said, 'You men knows what to do. Come to me and take one disk, den put it in the bag on the mast. Put in one of dese big white buttons of wood if you want to send the sons of bitches back to the *Firebird*. Put in a black one if you want dem to be judged here. Choose white and we leave their fate to the *Firebird*; choose black and dey dies at our hands, maybe in dem mangrove swamps behind me.'

He waved the black disk towards the gloomy, misshapen trees I could see at the entrance to the swampy lagoon beyond him. His words and gestures stirred something in my mind, something to do with mangroves and two-toned buttons of wood which floated just out of reach of my memory. I fell to contemplating the distant swamp and was roused only by a sharp elbow to the head as Snakeye passed me to collect his disk.

I joined the line. Bones held a box of disks to me: some of dark wood, some light. I nodded and took a white one, which I carried to the bag on the mast, trying to hide it from the curious eyes of the pirates.

I thought my vote wouldn't make any difference and I was right. When Bones tipped out the bag on the deck, there was a sea of black with only sprinkles of white.

Death shouted, 'They're ours, lads!' to rowdy cheers from the crew. 'Now,' he added, 'what shall we do with 'em? Hanging? Marooning?'

Bones called back, 'Feed 'em dat mouldy pot of stew Cook left behind his trunk!' There were groans at this, and I was grateful that Bones was reminding the men how much they had gained by losing the ex-Cook.

One of the sailors called, 'Fifty lashes and dump 'em overboard far from land.'

'Drag 'em behind the ship until the sharks get 'em.'

'Eyes out, cocks off and then set 'em free.'

Death laughed at this. 'That's cruel,' he said. 'And I like the sound of it! But these men have to *die*. That's the Rule.'

Finally they decided on tying the men together and throwing them into the sea.

'But what about the lady?' asked mate Jenkins.

Death said, 'Tie her to the others. They all go together, and we do it now.'

Snakeye complained, 'I ain't had my turn with her yet!'

'We'll have none of that talk on deck!' growled Captain Death. 'There's a young lad present. And speaking of which, we have another decision to make. Snake, you may address the crew.'

Snakeye was taken aback by this; but he soon warmed to his task, describing how – as he put it - I'd plotted with Cook, loaded his boat with supplies from the galley and then tried to escape as well, by hiding in one of the boats going to Scum. Snake ended his spiteful calumny with, 'And he helped that bastard take a barrel of rum with 'im! *Our* rum, lads!'

The crew had listened quietly up to now; but at the thought of losing their rum, there were grumbles and evil looks in my direction.

Snakeye made a vile gesture at me. 'No rum! No treasure either, for this boy is a fraud. And he's a snobbing gentleman, with 'is posh ways and hoity toity accent. And you seen how he looks at us, like we's dirt? Hey?'

More grumbles; and I was both astonished and hurt. I wasn't aware of my looks, or how I talked: except that I probably looked as fearful as I felt, and was afraid to say anything that might upset the pirates.

Snakeye added, 'He treats us like we's filth, like he's some angel come down from heaven and is doin' us a favour by cookin' stew for us scum. Tie 'im to the others, I say!' He folded his arms across his chest, glaring at me. The mutters and grumbles died away and I heard the cry of a seagull, reminding me of a world of sadness.

Captain Death looked at me, then across to Bones. 'Quartermaster,' he said. 'Your turn.'

Bones looked puzzled. 'Me, Cap'n? Ah, well den... you see, it's like dis. The lad done wrong, and he knows it now. If you throw him over the side, who's gonna cook for you? Not me – I'm back to the *Firebird* once you've chosen a new quartermaster. Maybe you'll get a cook like the old one. Dey tells me Cook always washed his hands after wiping his arse... only trouble was, he washed 'em in the water he was heatin' the taters in.'

There were groans at this.

Bones laughed. 'Fancy dat, does you, Snakeye? Missin' dem extra chunky bits in your stew?' He added quietly, 'Look, dis boy is *our* boy now. We gotta teach him to be a pirate: a free man like ourselves. Besides dat, he's gonna make us rich. I promise.'

'Is he?' Death was eyeing me.

Bones pushed me forward. 'He's worked it out,' the man said confidently. 'He'll tell you in your cabin.'

'No,' said Death. 'He'll tell me now.'

Bones opened his mouth to protest, but shut it as the Captain put one hand on his pistol.

'Now,' said Death gravely.

I saw Bones trying to catch my eye, probably hoping to get me to make something up, or at least waste a little time so that Snakeye's plans could lose their momentum. But I didn't need his help.

'Mangroves,' I said.

'Mangroves, hey?' asked Death.

'Three kinds. Red, black and white. Each has its place in the swamps. As you approach from the sea, you come to the red first. Then the black. Lastly, the white.

'And what's this to me?'

'Beyond the white, there's a mangrove that's on land. Buttonwood, they call it. It has whitish wood except in its middle, which is dark. Those pieces of the Game – they came from the outer and inner parts of the buttonwood. So I expect that if we take a boat into the swamp and then head into the woods, there will be a large buttonwood tree that's been cut into. Where the light and dark wood meet, we'll find the treasure.'

I spoke more confidently than I felt, and I suspect that Death knew this. But he seemed relieved to have an excuse to keep me alive for one more meal.

'We'll suspend judgement, hey lads?' he asked, to grunts of grudging approval. 'But let's deal with the other three now. Bring 'em out, Bo'sun!'

The Bo'sun (a broad, surly man who was often at Snake's shoulder) went below with a few seamen and returned with the three convicts, their hands bound and their ankles connected by loose ropes.

The prisoners were spiritless and dirty, with bruises on their faces and rips in the Lady's dress and blouse. They stared straight in front of them as Death announced their fate. Lady C's cheek twitched a little; that was all.

They were turned back to back and a rope was passed between their bound wrists. The rope came from a reel on the winch used for lowering boats into the water. The free end of it was then passed up over one of the spars and down again to the deck for some of the crew to hold. A cannonball was secured inside a scrap of sailcloth before being tied to Pitiless Jake's ankles.

'Final words, gentlemen? Final tears, lady?'

Both men made rude gestures – or as rude as they could manage with their arms tied behind their backs. Lady C's cheeks went red; then she called back in a surprisingly steady voice:

'Shame on you, for dealing with a Lady in the same manner as these two scoundrels! Shame and waste, for you might have ransomed my life at great profit to your crew!'

The pirates looked one to the other; they hadn't thought of this. An uneasy murmuring arose.

Death held up his hand to quiet them. 'What manner of profit were you proposing?' he asked.

She said haughtily, 'I have several hundred crowns at my villa – perhaps as much as a thousand.'

'Ah… but I think there's a problem with one word of that speech,' said Death, stroking at his beard like a wise prophet disputing profits. 'What you mean is that you *had* a thousand crowns. That merciless mob we left in Scum will have ransacked your house; and anything they left, your business partners will have taken.'

The Lady said scornfully, 'My villa is two days' travel from the port of Scum and is well defended. It lies on the west side of the island. You can anchor in the small bay below the villa and an exchange can be made.'

Captain Death turned to his crew. 'What say you, men? Shall we deal? For a thousand crowns?'

There were assenting shouts, and Death turned to Lady C with a smile that promised treachery, receiving from her an equal smile.

He said, 'Pirate's honour, my Lady: your life for a thousand crowns. No less.'

She replied, '*Lady's* honour, Captain: a thousand crowns for my life, entire and undamaged.'

'We have a deal, Madame…. Bo'sun! Free the Lady!'

They cut her bonds. Then some of the crew pulled at the rope hanging from the winch, taking Jake and Tom into the air, hanging awkwardly from their tied wrists behind their backs. Another group pushed the winch about its base until the captives were suspended over the quiet water.

Captain Death called out mockingly, 'Does either of you have a thousand crowns to ransom your skins with?'

Tom made no reply. Pitiless Jake groaned out, 'Come and get it, you coward! I've hidden it up my a-'

'Rope away!' shouted Death.

The crew let go of the free end of the rope, and the two men fell into the sea. We watched as the water frothed and the ripples spread; then Tom's head appeared at the surface, mouth upwards, gulping both air and water while his feet churned below; then he was dragged down by the weight of Jake and the cannonball, and rose no more.

A ragged cheer went up from the crew.

'A fine ending,' said Death, stroking his beard again. He looked back at Lady C. 'My cabin, your Ladyship. And if we can't agree terms, you're the next one over the side!'

As the cabin door closed behind them, my only coherent thought was that for once, Madame Helena was going to be proved wrong. The Lady would live.

19 Treachery and Counter-treachery

My fellow mice: what is love, but a delusion by which we see not truly the beloved but our dreams of the beloved? And our hearts believe all dreams. (From the collected works of Bunstropple, mouse and philosopher)

By mid afternoon our ships had anchored in a quiet bay, closed by a two-thirds circle of dark rock rising nearly thirty metres above us.

We were near the western tip of Scum Island, and this bay opened to the west. At its northern side the water washed upon an arc of dark, pebbly sand; east and south there were great rocks spiking through the water.

A path zigzagged up from the northern beach, first right, then left, each pass shorter than the one below it. If there was a villa at the top, it couldn't be seen from here. Yet the path clearly led somewhere.

I didn't know what had been agreed between the Lady C and the Captain (or two Captains, for Red had been rowed across to our ship for a brief discussion), and was surprised to be called from the galley as soon as we anchored.

Snakeye had come for me once again and seemed particularly annoyed that I was being given an honour he'd wanted: to be part of the group sent up to the villa. 'You'll – just - make - a mess - of it,' he said sourly, punctuating each pause with a kick.

Death was alone in his cabin. He sent Snakeye away before lecturing me in private.

'I've got a mission for you, lad,' he said in his gruff, lifeless voice. 'And it's *you* because you're no threat to anyone. When we get to the top, that scheming tart who calls herself a Lady will give you a parchment to take to her mother, who seems to be in charge of the money up there. I've read the parchment and it gives me no trouble. But what *will* give me trouble is any false step by yourself. Understand?'

'No, sir,' I said.

He knotted a three-fingered fist in front of my face. 'You follow the Lady's instructions *exactly*,' he said. 'You say no more than is necessary. You don't catch anyone's eye, you don't give them any sass, you don't make any helpful suggestions. And if any fighting breaks out (as it might, for I don't trust the bitch further than I can kick her), then you'd better keep your head down and stay out of the way of bullets and blades. Because we won't hold fire just because your clumsy noggin is in the way. Understand *now?*'

'Aye aye, sir.'

'Let's go, then.'

We went in one boat: the Lady C, Death, myself, two large pirates armed to the teeth and one who would stay behind to guard the boat.

Our two ships had anchored along the midline of the bay, with the *Tombstone* halfway along and the *Firebird* further inside, near to the eastern rocks. We were perhaps two hundred metres from the northern beach and the boat covered this distance within a few minutes, for the water was calm and there were no obstacles to avoid.

The path up was steep in places and uneven throughout, besides being sometimes narrow enough to make you walk with one hand against the rock for reassurance. There didn't seem to be any other way up unless you were a good rock climber; in only one stretch did the gradient allow us to look across to our left and see a sloping ledge that was lower than the crest.

The sun was in the west now, and was shining upon us mercilessly. We were sweating by the time we turned left near the top and found ourselves at the edge of a circular alcove in the rock, a few metres across and clearly fashioned by heavy picks and hammers. The walls of this circle rose to perhaps three metres above our heads, and the shoulders of three men sprouted above this, with rifles levelled at us. Below the man in the middle was a gate set in the rock, built of solid wood barred with iron. In front of this gate, the rocky ground shimmered in the airless heat.

We paused to allow Lady C to take just one step into the alcove, with Captain Death behind her gripping her right arm and another pirate at her left, both with pistols held to her head.

She called to the man above the gate, 'Captain Fraser! I have a message that needs to be taken to my mother.'

The other men on the walls looked to their Captain. He pointed his rifle beyond the Lady, left and right, at the two men holding their own guns at her head.

'What are they to do with this?' he called.

'I am held for ransom,' she said. 'The letter will explain everything. It must be taken directly to my mother, who will break the seal and give you directions. This boy -'

She paused as I was pushed forward to stand between her and the rifles. She continued:

'This boy will take the letter to her and then return to us before an exchange is made.'

The man called Fraser said nothing for a long time, while the other two guards stared down their guns at us baking in the alcove. He was probably doing the same I'd done when I was told of the arrangement: trying to work out why it was being handled this way.

There was only one reason: I was the one worthless pawn in this complicated game. Captain Death wouldn't risk losing one of his men inside; Lady C didn't trust the guard to deliver the letter; neither of them trusted the other to act honestly. So I would accompany the letter and report back to the Captain and Lady that it had been received and that its terms were accepted. If anyone ratted on the agreement, I was the only one likely to be shot or imprisoned.

Finally, the man above us nodded and sent an order

down to the gate. There were muffled banging noises and the gate was pushed just far enough into the alcove for a slim boy to slip through it.

Death passed me the letter and I tucked it into my shirt.

'No one but *her*,' insisted Lady C. 'Else you're dead.'

Death added, 'And if you talk to anyone on the way – even to greet them – you're dead as well.'

I nodded. I was getting used to being 'dead' for a variety of crimes.

Death pushed me into that sun-scorched circle. I crossed it slowly, aware of guns above and behind me, and a blistering heat all about me; then I squeezed through the gate.

There was blessed shadow on the other side. The gate clanged shut again and two bars were set across it. The guard there pushed me forward through a cool passage that led upwards and out onto the top of the rocky hill. We paused within the last shreds of shadow in the passage while my guide looked up to the man called Captain Fraser, awaiting instructions.

I looked back at my guide – standing behind me and to my left - and was surprised to see that a young woman was holding my shoulder in such an iron grip.

Since her face was half turned away, I was able to look her up and down without embarrassment. She was an unusual woman on first sight, and it wasn't surprising that I'd first thought her to be a man. Her light brown hair was cropped short like a man's and her face was stern and a little boyish; and she clearly had muscles better than my own.

Her first glance towards me was cold and hard and intelligent, with no hint of womanly kindness. Yet there was something solid and peaceful about her, as if she'd gone through some long struggle and was now at rest.

Then she turned her head further towards me and I saw that her left cheek was a mass of scars – the kind of scars you get from boiling water or hot oil. She stepped around and looked directly at me, angry now: and I saw that her left ear was misshapen and that the corner of her mouth and her left eye were pinched by tight, pink skin.

'Seen enough, have you?' she growled at me. 'Move! This way!'

She tucked her pistol into her belt and pushed me towards a large house near the middle of the compound. I could see that this broad compound was protected by stone walls that were a few metres high and wide enough for someone to walk upon. The walls stretched left and right from the gateway to encircle the house together with two small, low buildings that had the look of barracks and a kitchen. The circle wasn't complete however: to our left – towards the ridge that looked across to the pathway – there was a gap, perhaps because it would be difficult for anyone to climb up that way.

I said to the woman, 'I didn't mean to stare. Sorry.'

'But you did.'

'I... Yes, I did. Sorry. I was curious –'

'Nosy.'

'Sorry. Oh – and I shouldn't be talking to you – sorry.'

She took her hand from my shoulder and walked beside me now, on my left and thus looking at me with the unscarred half of her face. By this view, she was a moderately pretty woman in her early twenties.

'If you say *sorry* once more, I'll punch you,' she said.

'Sor-' I began, but choked it off. I was relieved to see her mouth twitch. There might even have been a twinkle in her good eye.

She asked, 'Why shouldn't you talk to me?'

'In case I tell you something I shouldn't, I suppose. Which I can't do because I don't know anything useful anyway.'

'Ah,' she said. 'Or maybe you're actually the one in charge of all this – the Pirate King – and you're trying to trick me by pretending to be ignorant and useless.'

'Me?' But then I saw that she was laughing at me, and I had the humility to laugh as well.

'Who's down there?' she asked suddenly, nodding back

towards the gate.

'I – I can't tell you that.'

'*Not* ignorant, then. That leaves useless. In you go, useless Pirate Boy.'

'I'm not a pirate.'

'So you say. Inside.'

We had come to the front door of the big house – the *villa* I suppose I should call it.

'Wait,' I said.

She paused and turned back to look at me. And either because I was desperate to make amends for staring at her scars, or because I sensed something special in her, or because I simply felt pity for her, I said:

'I do know something useful, I think. Last night, in Scum itself….'

I told her of the death of the huge doorman, the capture of Lady C and the wildness of the freed women. Her eyes held mine during my story, looking deep into them, seeking something: the truth perhaps.

She breathed, 'So Sula is dead? You're sure?'

'The doorman? I saw him fall, and the women stabbing at his body. There was blood everywhere. He must be dead.'

She touched my face with her hand, gently. 'Don't tell this to the Countess,' she asked. 'Please?'

I nodded.

Another woman was standing at the door of the villa, older than my guide but also damaged: in her case, a missing hand - and a nose that had been broken long ago and set badly. She too had a gun in her belt.

'What's up, Maria?' she asked my guide.

'Not sure yet,' said Maria. 'But –'

She bent and whispered a few sentences in the other woman's ear and they exchanged a long glance before the older one nodded and set off across the compound.

We entered the villa and I was led through high, prettily decorated rooms and then down a long, winding corridor hung with beautiful tapestries. At the end of this was a solid-looking door barred with iron; Maria knocked and received a response that was too quiet for me to make out. She turned the knob and told me to follow her inside.

A slender woman with white hair was sitting across the room from us, writing in what looked like an old-fashioned accounting ledger. She put down her pen and beckoned us forward, frowning at me and then (when I came in range) skewering me with her sharp green eyes.

She turned those eyes on Maria; they glittered with annoyance. 'What's this about?' she asked sharply.

Maria curtseyed and said, 'Beg pardon, your Grace, but this boy has a message from Lady C. Her ladyship is outside the gate, with at least two pirates holding guns to her head.'

The green eyes fixed on me once more as I took the parchment from my shirt and offered it to her. She received it between a thumb and forefinger held as far as possible from my own dirty hand.

She studied the seal and poked at it, as if to check that no one had opened the document already. Then she took a silver paper knife from the table and pried the seal free. She read the parchment twice, then put it down. Her fingers tapped the table and her eyes were distant.

'Boy,' she said finally. 'How many of your men are outside the gate?'

'Whatever it says in there,' I replied, nodding at the parchment.

'Ten?' she asked, rather sneakily I thought.

'If that's what it says,' I shrugged.

'Answer me honestly, or you're dead!' she promised.

Suddenly, I lost all self-constraint. 'Why does everyone keep telling me I'm dead?' I complained. 'Do I have a tattoo on my forehead that says it? Madame, I can't tell you anything. Either you agree to the terms written there, or you don't. That's the only message I can take back.'

'You will call me Countess or Your Grace!' she flamed.

'Only if you call me Pirate King or Lover Boy,' I said.

She stared at me, horrified. Out of the corner of my eye, I could see Maria fighting a smile.

The woman rose and slapped me across the face. I said nothing. I was getting used to this sort of treatment.

'I will write a reply for Lady C and instructions for the guard,' she said to Maria. Taking out two small sheets of parchment, she quickly wrote two notes, folded them and sealed them shut with wax from a candle on her desk.

Then she took a key from a ring hanging on her belt and opened a large safe in the wall behind her: so large that it was more like a long bread oven. I could see in it various bags, a pile of documents and a few pistols.

She checked inside four heavy bags and weighed them on some scales beside the desk. Then she ordered Maria to put them in a knee-high chest sitting by the wall, first removing some silks from it.

She waved us away. As we left the room, carrying the heavy chest between us, I sneaked a look behind me: she was staring at her ledgers again, her face cold as stone.

Maria closed the door behind us and took a few steps up the corridor. Then we set the chest on the floor and she quietly broke open the two notes entrusted to her. While she was puzzling over them, there were footsteps further along the corridor: and we were soon joined by the woman from the door and a broad, tall, simple-looking girl.

They whispered for a few minutes, pausing occasionally to look at me or the doorway to the Countess's room.

Finally, Maria pointed at me. 'You stay here,' she said. I nodded, then watched them push the door open and go inside. The door was pulled to behind them.

I heard an angry exclamation and some murmurings. I hesitated, then hurried to the door and listened at the keyhole. The words were indistinct, but they went something like this:

Old lady: 'How dare you! When Sula comes –'

Maria: 'He's not coming back. He's dead. But I expect you

already knew that.'

Lady: 'Go to your rooms! And pray God to spare you from the punishment you deserve!'

Maria: 'God has a punishment in store for *you*, and we're here to deliver it. You've beaten us and burned us and had us tortured and abused for the last time.'

Lady: 'Oh, so you're high and mighty now –'

Maria: 'Some of the girls wanted to make this slow for you, and painful too, just as we've had it from yourself and Sula and the Lady and all the other perverts and beasts you employ. But I said no: we'll show mercy where we've received none. You'll die quick, and go straight to the hell that awaits you.'

Lady: 'Guards! Gua –'

There was a single shot.

I knew I should creep back to the chest now; but I lingered, hearing little except whispers until Maria's clear voice was raised:

'We're not doing it that way, Shannon. It'd be wrong.'

The other woman replied, 'But it's safer that way.'

'We have to treat him fair. We mustn't become like them outside – or like her on the floor.'

Shannon persisted, 'The boy's nothing to us.'

Maria said firmly, 'He's a person like you and me. He deserves his chance. Besides, he *is* something to me, because he told me about Sula and didn't look at me like I was dirt.'

I heard them walking back and retreated. When the door opened, I was standing by the chest again as if I'd been there all that time. The three women came up to me and Maria pushed a bundle of papers into my hands.

'Tell us what this says,' she ordered. 'I can make out some of it, but we need to be sure.'

I took the first paper, from the Countess to Lady C. 'This says the terms will be met exactly as proposed.'

'What terms?'

I picked out the parchment I'd brought to the Countess.

'The box of money is to be set down in the middle of that area outside the gate. I take the letter to the pirates. The pirates bring Lady C to the box. The guards open the gate. The pirates take the box, while Lady C goes through the gate at the same time.'

Maria said, 'All pointing their guns at each other from start to end, I suppose. Makes sense. Fraser won't fire because Lady C could be killed. The pirates won't fire because they're totally exposed in that alcove. What are the old witch's instructions to the Captain at the gate?'

I looked through the last paper, frowned, then read it again. 'It says the guards should lure as many pirates as possible into the space next to the gate and shoot them all. Including Lady C if necessary.'

'Evil bitch,' said Shannon, the women from the door. 'Her own daughter!'

I added, 'Then it says something about picking off the others as they come in sight of the lower ridge.'

Maria looked at the other women, saying, 'That's what I thought it said. We can't pass those instructions to Fraser.'

'We can, but now we'll have to scrag *him* first,' said the woman from the door, pulling out her gun and pointing it at me. 'This is a good way to get rid of the pirates and the witch's daughter. Then we take care of the guards.'

'We're not doing it that way!' insisted Maria. 'Pirate Boy has treated us fair, so he deserves a break, just like the break we wanted and never got. We'll have to find a way to keep him out of it.'

'Scrag him!' said the large third woman suddenly, smiling at me in a thoroughly ghoulish manner.

'No, Ruthie. He's a friend. *Friend*.' Maria patted me on the shoulder.

Ruthie's brow furrowed. Then she smiled again. 'Friend. Scrag him!'

Maria sighed and turned to the other woman. 'Shannon, we've got the guns from the safe now. We have six guns and plenty of women able to use them. There's seven guards, but they aren't expecting this. We can take them if we get them to split up. What if –'.

She set out a plan that was simple and cunning - and thoroughly ruthless. She looked at me after describing it.

'Pirate Boy here *could* ruin it all,' she admitted. 'Without the witch's instructions to Fraser, it's going be our word against his. So if the boy tips off the guard or Lady C, we'll cop it and he'll become a hero. Can we trust you, Pirate Boy? Or do we have to –'

'Scrag him!' exclaimed Ruthie with gusto.

'I have a suggestion,' I said (not at all wanting to be scragged, whatever that was). 'Why don't I write a new note to Captain Fraser? Not a long one, because it would be harder to make that look like the old lady's handwriting. Just something brief, with her signature and a seal.'

'You could do that?'

'I think so. I'm good at copying.'

They hurried me back into the room and sat me at the old lady's desk. I tried not to look at the body crumpled on the floor, blood seeping from somewhere. Paper and pen were pushed in front of me.

I studied the original instructions, then practised scribbling on some scrap paper. I took a fresh sheet and began writing, saying each phrase out loud first and waiting for a nod of approval:

Captain, I require you to follow the instructions which Maria will give –

'Not *give*. She'd use a fancier word.'

- which Maria will provide.

In haste,

'That's good. He'll think that's why she hasn't written down the instructions.'

I pondered over the signature and copied it a few times on my piece of scrap. Then I wrote it quickly. It looked good enough, though the final 's' of *Countess* wasn't right.

Maria blotted the paper, folded it, dripped wax on it and sealed it with the old lady's stamp. She re-sealed the note written by the Countess to Lady C and her captors, then pushed everyone out the door and along the corridor.

Ruthie took one handle of the chest and I followed, trying to hold up my end and keep pace with her long stride. A thousand coins weighed more than I'd expected.

As we crossed the compound, I turned back and saw the other woman – Shannon - scurrying off towards one of the smaller buildings.

We came to the wall, where the three men stood with rifles still pointed down into that sun-baked alcove. The captain saw us coming and descended a short flight of stone steps to speak with us.

'You took your time.'

Maria said, 'Took a while to get the money sorted out.' She nodded at the chest, and I gratefully set down my end of it. She held out one of the papers to the captain of the guard. 'The other one is for Lady C,' she said. 'It tells her that we'll do what the pirates ask.'

The captain snapped off the seal and read the message I'd written to him. He looked at Maria, frowning.

'What's going on?' he asked. 'I'm not taking orders from you.'

Maria shrugged. 'If you want to argue about it with Her Grace, be my guest. She's been on the toilet most of the morning, but if you shout through the keyhole I expect she'll give you her orders direct.'

For reply, the man punched Maria in the face. She staggered, then placed her left hand over her cheek.

He hissed, 'You don't speak to me like that, you dog-faced slut! Tell me Her Grace's commands, and I'll have none of your crap with it!'

Maria wiped away a streak of blood, then pointed at me. 'Go stand in the passage that leads down to the gate,' she said. 'Ruthie, go with him. Take the chest.'

As we withdrew five or so paces to stand in the shadow, Maria ran through the instructions: first, the exchange of money exactly as proposed. Then the careful plan she had hatched. I couldn't hear everything she said, but I knew it went something like this:

'She says call back one of the two men from the front gate now, and I'll send Shannon to take his place. Get the other two from the barracks as well, with their guns. Once you've swapped the chest for Lady C, you'll take all the men except one and hurry down to the ridge. Set up ready to ambush the lot of them. Her Grace says when they're halfway along that longer stretch that comes back across towards this side, you'll be able to pick them off easy enough. They'll be carrying the chest, which will slow them down.'

He said angrily, 'You don't have to tell me that. I know how to organise an ambush!'

'I'm just passing on what *she* said to tell you. Or do you want me to leave bits out?'

'Get on with it.'

That leaves one man at this gate, right? I'll stay here with him. So we've got two armed at this gate, two at the front, and you with four others on the ridge. And Her Grace suggests maybe I can send a few women to help reload the guns at the ridge. She didn't know if you'd want that.'

'Send two women,' the captain said; and I heard this clearly because he was walking towards us now, talking to Maria over his shoulder. 'Go!' he commanded her.

As the captain turned to address Ruthie, I saw Maria looking at me from behind him. Her cheek was bloody and her eyes were asking a question. I nodded quickly and she nodded back before turning to go.

The exchange went smoothly. The captain gave me the second paper and let Ruthie and me out through the gate, carrying the heavy chest. We dropped it in the middle of the alcove and Ruthie patted me on the head.

'Scrag you!' she chuckled, then waddled back inside.

I walked around the corner of the alcove and handed the

paper to Captain Death, who glared at me fiercely, though not as fiercely as Lady C.

'Why so long?' he snarled.

I shrugged. He ripped open the paper and read it, then passed it to Lady C.

'How many at the gate?' he asked.

'Three men with rifles; one big girl with big hands waiting to scrag me,' I said. I was feeling rather light-headed.

'That's all?'

'Another two men on the way, I think.'

'But no more? Did you see men moving about, going to another part of their compound, maybe? Or was there talk of them trying to attack us?'

'Nothing I could see,' I said.

'You mean you weren't looking. Fat lot of use you are!'

I said, 'I was taken straight to the villa by a woman, then back again. I didn't see any men except those at the gate.'

Death nodded. 'Okay. Lady C: your arm, please.'

He led her out, a gun to her head. Two pirates eased their heads around the curve of the path and fixed their own guns upon the guards on the wall.

Lady C opened the chest and took out the bags one at a time, untied them, opened them for Death to look into, then replaced them. The chest was closed again.

The gate opened and the captain of the guard came out slowly, a pistol pointing towards Death. He beckoned to Lady C, who walked quietly towards him while Death dragged the chest out, his own gun still pointing at Lady C.

Finally we were heading down the path again – a path we had ascended less than an hour ago, though to me this seemed to have happened in the distant past.

I hurried forward to Captain Death who was stepping out quickly, wanting I suppose to put some distance between us and the gate in case the guards decided to chase after us.

'There's something you ought to know,' I said. 'An ambush.'

He swung round and snatched me by the throat. 'Didn't I ask you?' he cried. 'And didn't you say nothing?'

'I couldn't. Not with her there. Listen...'

I told him the bare bones of the ambush plans, adding: 'The women are planning to shoot the guards. The five on the ridge will be hardest for them to finish off, but if we keep the guards busy, that gives the women more of a chance.'

'Ah,' said Death, again stroking his beard in the way that I now connected with his deepest plottings. 'And it helps *us* if they fight one another to the death. Only five men there, and the other two being shot up above? But I expect the ladies will let the guards open fire on us before those witches pull their triggers. Your scheming friend will be counting on that. Ah....Yes... *Got it!*'

He laughed – an evil cackle of a laugh – and consulted with his men. He then told me what I had to do, and I refused.

He said, 'No? Then we'll have to create a diversion in a different way, boy. We'll throw you off the cliff, with your body bouncing down those rocks all the way to the bottom. That would work. *Or* you could just do what you're damn well told to do! At least that way you'll have a small chance of survival.'

A few minutes later, I was alone as I turned the corner to my right and began the long traverse exposed to the five rifles on the ridge. I was walking slowly, keeping my eyes fixed on the path; I knew that if I looked up to see where the guards were, they would realise something was going on. I stopped twice and looked back along the path, as if waiting for the pirates to catch up. When I was a few steps from where I thought I would disappear from the guard's view, I stopped yet again, turned back and shaded my eyes with one hand.

This was the signal for two pirates to come around the corner, carrying the chest. They were stooped over as if with the weight of it, but really in order to show as little of themselves as possible to the rifles.

They crept along, then stopped as if setting down the chest to get a better grip on it. Their bodies dipped low.

Then there was a shot – not from the guards, but from the path above us. I now bolted down the path until I found a place hidden from the ridge.

The shot had come from Captain Death's pistol, and it hit its target. I peeked around a lump of rock and saw a guard sliding down the slope above and to my left; his body came to a steeper section and disappeared from my sight.

There was a lot of shooting going on now, from different directions: the two pirates crouched by the chest; Captain Death from some rocks he had climbed into further up the path; the remaining four men on the ridge (as open to our view as we were to theirs); and then I heard shots from the top of the hill as Maria and Shannon – once the sounds of our battle caused a distraction – each calmly put a bullet into a guard's head from point blank range.

Another man on the slope fell; then two at once, from fire behind them. The final man – the captain – stood and turned his gun towards this new threat and I saw him stagger back from one blast, then fall from another and bounce away down the slope.

We hurried downwards now, Death at the rear with his pistol ready but nothing to shoot at. Finally we came to the beach and loaded the chest onto the boat. The men pulled at the oars; we were away.

'Look!'

Death was pointing back up the sloping rock. On the ridge where the guards had gathered, other figures had appeared. The large one must be Ruthie, and she seemed to be pushing someone towards the edge. Then Ruthie withdrew and we saw Lady C standing with her back to us, one arm towards some other women, as if pleading – or more likely, lecturing.

There was a command, then several shots cracked the air

at once. Lady C collapsed backwards and her body fell, hitting the slope three times and then dropping like a limp doll into the sea.

So Madame's prediction had been right, after all.

As the men bent to their oars again, Captain Death was still staring up the slope.

'There's only women up there,' he said. 'We could take 'em easy, don't you think, Lads?'

There were guffaws of laughter at this.

Death continued, 'The moon drops around midnight. We'll creep up – fifty of us, say – climb the walls, and then we'll have ourselves a bit of fun and a bit of fancy and bit of treasure. For to be sure there's more to be had.' He patted the chest with one hand.

'What?' I cried out, horrified. 'But they gave us the treasure – they helped us escape – they spared my life.'

The others laughed at me.

'We'll save one for you,' promised one man. 'Maybe that big one we saw on the cliff. Is she enough woman for you?'

'But –'

'One ain't enough - he wants two!' chortled another.

I said, 'But we promised them. We made a deal… Pirate's honour and all that. Surely that counts for something?'

Captain Death shook his head, laughing. 'Ha ha! I neglected to tell the Lady what the Pirate's Code says about women. There's only one class of person that can't be a pirate – the ladies. They have no standing; they're lower than the ship's cat. You can make them any promise you like and not be bound by it. A pirate's word to a man is a solid thing; made to a lady, it's all mist and moonshine. Ha!'

I closed my mouth on the protests about to spill out. I could see that all I would get was a beating.

'It's like this, boy,' said one of the pirate crew. 'We has freedom like no others. No man tells us what to do.'

'No woman neither,' said another, pulling at an oar.

'Especially that,' said the first pirate.

Captain Death said, 'Women are a trap and a slavery. At the start, you draw together with a woman because of the pleasure; but she won't let you rest there. Once she's had her pleasure, she must have your heart as well; and then she wants your money and your time and your attention to her incessant talk, talk, talk. She'll tie you down to a house, to squawling brats, to her ugly mother and vile cousins.'

'Too right!' said the man at the oar.

'With men, we have a Code,' said Death. 'If they come between us and our prize or our pleasure, we kill them without mercy. Yet if they stand aside and let us live free, taking what we want, we leave 'em alone. That's the Code. But we have a different way with women – ah, remember that women are put here for our pleasure and comfort. It's in the holy writings, hey? At least, the way *we* read 'em!'

'But –' I began, then held my tongue once more.

He said with terrible calmness, 'The ladies are here for our pleasure and comfort. So those women up there on the hill: we'll have our fun with 'em tonight, and then we'll bring those that are still breathing back to the ship, for to do a little washing and cleaning and warming our beds until they start to nag at us, when they'll become food for the sharks.'

'Which'll take about a week,' said a pirate.

'Last time it was only three days,' said another.

Captain Death leaned across and put a hand on my shoulder, saying confidentially, 'The world is cold and heartless, lad: should we not be the same? We must take our lead from Nature and act without mercy. If we are to survive and prosper, we have to be bloody in tooth and claw like Nature itself. That's written in a scientific book somewhere: for a pirate may read books like any other man. We're just being true to our natures. We're wolves, aye – wolves that think. You and me and all men.'

I said nothing. I was thinking of the question on Maria's face before she turned away for the last time, and my nod of reply, promising to honour her trust in me.

20 Before Midnight

From my diary, at night: *It's just as Jupiter said: I've come to the point where, like my own father, I have to choose between my honour and my safety. But it's very hard, much harder than I thought it could be. I don't know whether anything I do will make any difference. So why take the risk?*

The sun was nearing the horizon as they winched the chest of money on board the *Tombstone*. I headed for the galley, still fuming. I stoked the fire and threw some fish and potatoes into a stew pot, not caring that some of the fish heads hadn't been cut off. I watched the stew seethe, and seethed myself.

As the pot came to a boil, I decided I had to do something about the women: but I didn't know what. However, I knew who to ask. So I set the food to one side and went aft to find Captain Death. He was at the port railing near to his cabin, talking through his plans with a few officers.

'Captain, sir,' I said, 'Can I go across to the *Firebird* and collect a few provisions?'

He looked over the rail at the boats already busy between the two ships, or being got ready for the raid. He looked back to the horizon, where the sun was finally surrendering itself to the blood-red sea. Then he shook his head at me. 'We don't need anything just now.'

'I thought –' I struggled to think of something he might approve of. 'I thought I'd get a cask of rum. Bones promised to send one over to replace the cask that Cook stole. We've only half a cask left in the store.'

This was a lie, but I was counting on no one in earshot knowing that.

One of the officers said, 'Aye, the men will want their grog before they head out tonight.'

Then Snakeye did me a favour, though that wasn't his intention. 'A cask of rum, aye, that's only fair: the boy owes us that! But he's got to buy it out of his share of the booty.'

Captain Death was amused by this. 'That's right!' he exclaimed. 'Boy, go fetch the rum and I'll put it on your account. There's a boat heading across in a few minutes.'

Snakeye added in a sneering tone: 'And see if you can persuade your friend Bones to come out with us tonight. Appears he's afraid of the dark.'

'Yes,' said Death thoughtfully. 'Tell him about the fine ladies. You might have to lie a little though, for the ones I saw weren't easy on the eye! And tell the big black man – Jupiter, ay? – tell him about the big girl waiting for him, the one we saw on the hill. Snake here couldn't get those two to volunteer, but Snake doesn't have a way with words like you, lad.'

'Aye, sir,' I said through clenched teeth.

'And I'll send across with you that chest of money we took today. That'll be the *Firebird's* share; I'll gamble on tonight's takings being double that or more. Plus our takings in pleasure and comfort, hey lad?'

On the boat across to the *Firebird*, I was thinking about Bones and how – surely – he would find a way to stop the planned attack. And the more I thought about it, the odder it seemed to me that this queer little man – with his tattoo and his performing cat and his exquisite cooking – could so easily become a focus for ideas and even leadership. Not that he really was "little"; he was of average height, but he had this trick of appearing small and unimportant. And as for *queer*: well, beyond all his antics and jokes he was surely the most sensible man aboard.

I hurried across the *Firebird's* deck in the darkening

gloom, seeking Bones and finding him at last in a cabin used by some junior officers. I saw them through the small window; they were sitting at a table, talking earnestly about something. There was a light in Bones' eye as he leaned across the table, sketching in the air with his pipe.

And then I knew.

They looked up as I knocked and entered quickly, and I saw a couple of faces tighten with alarm and then relax.

I said quickly, 'I need to speak with you, Bones – sir. It's urgent. Very urgent.'

Bones smiled at the group in the disarming way he had. 'We can continue dis after supper, maybe?' he asked. 'I got to get the food out now, anyway.'

They let us go, and I saw the men turn back to talk urgently as I shut the door.

'The galley's as private as anywhere,' said Bones, leading me there and starting to move pots about. His meals were already cooked and keeping warm on the stove. 'What's up, Jack?' he asked.

I poured out my tale of the ladies on the hill, laying it on a bit thick about how they'd been tortured and imprisoned, for I knew now that this would secure his sympathy.

'We can't let the pirates attack them,' I said. 'This is the ladies' only chance of freedom. They deserve to be helped. And I owe it to them.'

'Aye,' said Bones, putting a lid on a pot. 'But what can I do about it?'

'I don't know,' I said. 'But you'll think of something. You always do. And – and I know you care about them. You sometimes pretend not to care about people, but you're an honourable man at heart. I've always known that, Captain.'

Bones turned towards me. His head gave its usual twitch before he spoke. 'Captain?' he queried.

'I know who you are,' I said. 'And I know you'll help.'

He pulled the galley stool from its locker and sat upon it.

He gave me a long look. 'When did you guess, Jack?' he asked softly.

I said, 'Only a few minutes ago, when I saw you at the table and those officers all looking at you with such respect. I remembered what you once said, that you had this instinct for the sea and the ability to command.'

'Ah. Perhaps I shouldn't have told you that.'

'And of course all the other things make sense now – you inking in that tattoo; rarely lighting that pipe and never smoking it; always knowing so much more than a jobbing cook should; your theatrical way of talking to the ladies.'

'I did wonder if you'd suspect me for that.'

I thought a moment. 'I didn't see beyond the walk, the shaven head, the accent. Wait a moment: the scar – the faint scar on your hand where the pirates on that first ship branded you long ago. Did you cover that up somehow?'

Bones – or perhaps I should say Captain Jones now - looked down at his left hand, a little smile on his face. 'It's still there, Jack,' he said. 'I've just been careful. I try not to turn that side of my hand towards you. Did you never wonder why I would sometimes pick up a plate in an odd way, or use the wrong hand for moving a pot?'

I shook my head.

Captain Jones clapped me on the shoulder, then spoke very quietly. 'Well done, lad. Jupiter knows, of course; no one else, unless Madame is even deeper and more devious than I believe. And now you must forget that *you* know, at least for a few hours.'

'You're planning to take the ship,' I whispered.

'Tonight,' he said. 'Which is why your sudden transformation into a gallant rescuer might give us a problem.'

'But we *have* to –!'

'Shhh! I've thought of a plan now. But it will involve you in some danger. Are you willing to risk your life?'

I hesitated, struggling with the sudden sharpness of a decision that might kill me. Then I remembered the quiet, pained face of Maria, and her trust in me. I nodded.

'Right, then,' he said. 'Where have you got to with cooking supper for the *Tombstone*?'

'Just threw some fish and potatoes on to stew, but took them off again after half an hour. And I promised to take back a keg of rum. That was my excuse for coming across.'

'Rum? It's looking better and better, lad. I think we can do this.' He shooed Tiddles off a shelf and felt into a deep cubbyhole there. He pulled out some boxes until he found the one he wanted; opened it; poked the white powder with one finger; nodded.

'More than enough, lad. Let's see. A keg of rum... no, half a keg, with the same of hot water and some sugar and spices; then I'll add three tablespoons of this. The pirates will feel light-headed and excited as they go up the hill, but before morning they'll be as sick as dogs.'

He explained his plan to me as we set out food for the men of the *Firebird*, alternating between whispers to myself and Bones-style ejaculations for the benefit of the crew.

'Hurry along dere!' he cried to the men who dawdled in the lines to collect their food. 'Me and Jack's gotta feed another crew after you lazy parasites.'

He left me passing out the food while he hurried off to arrange a boat for us. Within half an hour – with the darkness complete except for the moon's glow behind high clouds – Jupiter untied the boat and rowed us out into the cove, a keg of rum at our feet.

We turned the wrong way as soon as we were away from the side of the *Firebird*, heading not for the *Tombstone* but for the rocks along the east side of the bay.

'This is the best we can do, Jack,' said Captain Jones after we'd spent several minutes weaving between the rocks. We were still twenty metres from the shore, but the water was calm even though it was cold and deep.

I tied my shoes around my neck and put on the dark woollen gloves the Captain offered me. A black cap was already pulled down over my forehead and I'd rubbed soot on my face.

'Let's have a look,' Captain Jones said. He spread the soot a little more, then patted me on the shoulder. 'Brave lad,' he said warmly.

'Thank you, sir.' I reached across to the low rock we were hovering next to and pulled myself up onto it. I'd left my socks on; that gave a better grip on slippery rock.

'How will you know which rock to return to?' he asked next: as always, he was a step ahead of me.

I looked about. 'I'll go the shortest way to the beach,' I said. I'll make a mark there – somehow – and when I return, I'll just head out direct from the same place.'

'That's right. And here – put these in your pocket.' He handed me two white handkerchiefs that were surprisingly white in the darkness.

He added, 'Soaked in phosphorus salts, lad. Always have a little in the cupboard, just in case. Good for theatrical performances, see. Leave one handkerchief on the beach where you'll see it – head high and secure – and take one in your pocket. You can wave them when you're back out here on the rocks, to attract our attention. And if you get into real trouble on the hillside, wave and keep on waving. We'll see it eventually and come for you.'

'Thank you, sir.'

I turned and began clambering over rocks, heading as straight as I could. Twice I had to swim; once I slipped and grazed my knee. But I gained the beach in ten minutes and – after putting my shoes on - tied one handkerchief around a tangle of weeds sprouting from the steep hillside.

It took as long again to scramble around to the start of the path, bent over and peering at the uneven rocky ground, cursing the lack of light but knowing that the darkness was my security. I knew that if the pirates saw me and guessed what I was up to, they would be up the hillside in a flash - and then they would finish me as well as the ladies.

I had to climb most of the path on all fours, fearing both a sudden gleam of moonlight and a false step off the edge.

This part of my journey seemed to go on forever, as in a dream endlessly repeated, though I suppose it took only half an hour. This was exhausting; when finally I came to the turning into the alcove, I lay flat for several minutes until my heart stopped pounding and my breathing was easy.

At last I put my head around the turning and called softly into the darkness:

'Maria! I need to speak with Maria!'

I repeated this only once before an answering voice boomed, 'Who's there?'

I imagined every head in the *Tombstone* turning in murderous synchrony towards that voice.

'Shhhh!' I called back. 'We must be quiet. It's the boy – Jack – the one who came to the house - the villa. I need to speak to Maria.'

'Step out where we can see you!' The voice was only slightly less booming this time, and I saw a hundred pirate hands reaching for their cutlasses.

'All right. But keep *quiet!*'

I stood and walked into the alcove, hands spread to show I had no weapons, though in this darkness they probably couldn't see that anyway.

'Scrag him!' came a second voice – one I recognised immediately – and a gun went off.

I fell to the ground and lay senseless for a moment.

'Ruthie!' shouted the first voice, and something clattered on the wall. I began to feel about my body for blood.

After a minute, the voice called down to me again: 'Are you all right?'

I sat up. 'I think so,' I said, a bit ashamed now. 'The bullet must have missed. But not by much,' I added quickly.

'I've sent Ruthie to fetch Maria. Stay there.'

A few minutes later, the door was unlocked and opened a crack. Dim light spilled out, throwing new shadows into the shadows hanging about me.

'Are you alone?' asked Maria from beyond the door.

'Yes,' I said.

'Come inside, then.'

I crossed to the door and squeezed through it. Maria shut it quickly and put the bar across. There was a shaded lamp set on the floor, whose light spilled upwards and made her scars stand out. At the end of the passage lurked other figures. She beckoned to one of them.

'I don't have much time,' I said anxiously. 'I need to get back before they know I've come.'

'This won't take a moment. Ruthie!' she called back over her shoulder. 'Quickly!'

The big girl shambled over and stopped before me, her head down.

'What have you got to say?' Maria asked her.

'Sorry,' said Ruthie. She wiped away what might have been a tear.

'That's all right,' I said. 'You missed me.'

Ruthie smiled suddenly, took a step forward and lifted me from the floor, squeezing me so hard that my ribs creaked. 'Friend,' she murmured in my ear.

'Put him down,' ordered Maria. 'Down, Ruthie. I said *down!*'

Ruthie let me go, patted me on the head, then waddled away back up the passage.

'Thanks,' said Maria. 'She was very upset. When she gets like that, she's likely to harm herself. Now what the hell are you doing here, pirate boy?'

I told her as quickly as I could get it out, making it sound as serious as possible. Even so, I could sense her hesitation.

'We can put armed women all along these walls,' she said. 'We can pick off the pirates one by one.'

'You won't see them,' I argued. 'And don't forget that these are sailors: they spend their days climbing the rigging. They'll be up the cliff and over your walls, right and left of you. And there'll be fifty of them. You might shoot ten; after that they'll take you – and then they'll – they'll do everything horrible that's ever been done to you before, and worse. Then they'll kill you.'

She gazed into my eyes for a long time, and I realised that she was trying to decide whether she could trust me.

She asked quietly, 'So why did you come tell us this? What's it to you, young pirate?'

I was pleased to note that I was no longer the "pirate boy". I said, 'I'm not a pirate. We were captured by them a short while ago.'

'So why are you putting your life at risk? Was it my great beauty drove you to it? Or are you wanting payment for this – did you spy a little more gold in that safe?'

'I don't want anything,' I said sharply. 'Nothing except the knowledge that you're safe. You and the others. Promise me you'll go - and go soon. Maybe the pirates won't wait until midnight; they could be here in less than an hour. And when they do come, you need to be long gone so they can't catch you if they chase after you.'

Maria reached across and touched my face gently. 'You're a good man,' she said. 'I haven't met many of those in my life. Thank you.'

I felt my face going hot. 'Look,' I said, the final advice spilling out as fast as my heart was beating. 'Captain Jones – he's not a pirate, he's the one who helped me get away to warn you – he says you should make it look as if you left hours ago. Put out all the fires now. Put out the lamps, too. Take any horses or ponies with you and load them with only the things you need. Lock all doors and gates, anything to slow the pirates. And take your weapons, because there's always a chance that the pirates will try to land a party further around the coast, to cut you off. And he says to lock the safe and leave one lamp burning there, with a body in front of the safe, so they'll see it and waste time trying to get the safe open.'

'We've got plenty of bodies to choose from,' she said grimly. 'And the rest we can do as well.'

Then she looked at me oddly. 'Come with me,' she said.

I stared back blankly. 'I – Maria - I don't think –'

'Don't try to explain,' she said, with a bitter edge to her words. 'I saw the horror in your eyes.'

'No! It wasn't that. I think – I *know* I'd like to come. But there's a boat waiting for me to return. And there's a chance that the pirates will notice I've gone, so I need to get back before they suspect what I'm doing. And – besides – I don't think I would be any use to you. I'm not even much use on a ship.'

'You're brave and kind – and handsome enough for me. Goodbye, pirate boy. Kiss me.'

She put her arms about me and kissed me full upon the lips, a kiss that lasted a dozen heartbeats. I didn't know what to do; but as she sighed and pulled away, I took her face in my hands and kissed her forehead and then the smooth cheek and then the one that was scarred. She sighed deeply again and put her head upon my shoulder; we stood like that a while.

'We'll meet again,' she said. 'Keep safe till then.'

I found myself on the other side of the door. The bars thumped down into place. The darkness was complete.

Descending the path was much harder than the climb, partly because my head was whirling but mostly because there's no easy way to go down a slope forwards on all fours. Halfway down, the moon left the clouds and lighted my way, illuminating me as a black, crawling crab.

Finally I was on the beach and hurrying across the rock and shingle; I found the handkerchief easily enough and shoved it into a pocket before removing my shoes and working my way out from the shore.

After what must have been at least ten minutes, I concluded that I'd strayed too far to the right and began swimming and crawling in the opposite direction. Then I noticed that the wind had picked up, and the water between the rocks had turned choppy; then I noticed that I'd left the rocks behind and was caught in a current sweeping me back to the right, towards the *Tombstone*. I began to swim in earnest, against the current this time.

After a few minutes of this, I could see that I hadn't made any progress at all; if anything, I was closer to the pirate's ship and further from our own. I was also suddenly tired, and very cold. The choices seemed to be evenly balanced between continuing my struggle and drowning here, or letting the current take me to my death on the *Tombstone*.

A wave came at the wrong time and I swallowed a lot of water. When I opened my eyes again, I was facing the wrong way – towards the shore now – and had a sudden flash of common sense. I swam back to the rocks: not against the current, but across it. I managed to fasten onto a rock and then climb upon it. I lay there groaning, then thought to pull out my handkerchief and wave it weakly.

'You can put that away, boy,' came a deep voice nearby, with a chuckle behind it. 'I been sitting here watching you for the past five minutes.'

I crawled to the further edge of the rock. Jupiter grinned at me from the boat, his teeth bright in the moonlight.

I asked reproachfully, 'Why didn't you come get me?'

He shrugged. 'Reckoned you'd work it out soon enough. Climb in. We gotta get back soon. Unless you want to swim some more?'

On the *Firebird*, men were moving about purposefully. Conversations were being held in whispers and there was an air of impatience, like a family poised to go on a holiday but unable to start until someone finds the map.

I hurried off to wash and find dry clothes while Jupiter rowed across to the *Tombstone* once more. While I was spooning hot soup between my chattering teeth, the boat returned.

Captain Jones came into the galley: except that he was all Chief Cook Bones now. 'How's the soup, boy?' he asked cheerily. 'Pull dat other pot onto the flames; we got a few men goin' across to the *Tombstone* soon. Dey's wanting to join the raiding party and Cap'n Red says hot food and grog first.'

'Aye aye, sir – Bones, I mean. Soup and grog.'

'Never mind the grog. Dere's a barrel of it hot waitin' in the *Tombstone* for Cap'n Death to share round. But go find some biscuit to go wid the soup.' He winked at me, then turned to call out to Red (who I now realised had been lurking nearby):

'Cap'n, soup's up in ten minutes. Shall I bring yours to the afterdeck?'

Red looked in at us, frowning. I concentrated on stirring the pots, while Bones knuckled his forehead and grinned at the Captain.

Bones said to him, 'You'll bring a young lady back for the lad perhaps, Cap'n? Not dat he'd know what to do wid her! Ha hee!'

Red scowled and strode off. 'Bring soup for me and Jenkins when it's ready,' he called back over his shoulder.

I looked at Bones and opened my mouth to ask what was going to happen, but he forestalled me.

'No questions, lad,' he said brightly. 'We both got t'ings to do.'

Well, *I* had the soup to heat through and the biscuit to set out; all Bones seemed interested in was getting Tiddles to dance for scraps of meat, which he did just below the captain's deck, under an oil lamp hung from a spar. Several men gathered to watch, laughing and clapping. Red himself came to the railing of his deck and watched closely, then shook his head and walked away.

Five men came for this hasty meal: probably the five hardest and meanest persons on the ship, if you didn't count Madame. They finished their soup and disappeared over the side with Red, talking in low, excited voices about what they were planning to do to the women.

'You don't want to listen to dat talk,' said Bones quietly in my ear. 'Your thoughts show on your face. And dat ain't all dat's showing. You got a patch of soot by your left ear.

And I swear you got a bit of red paint about your lips, like what the ladies wear. Go wash it off afore someone sees.'

I was surprised to see that Red and the five hard men were being rowed to the *Tombstone* by Jupiter and the kind-ly Stephens, as if those two were joining the raid. But I said nothing about it, knowing by now that there were surpris-ing depths in the plans of Bones – and Jones.

A strained period of waiting followed. I washed the pans, fed Tiddles and then started tidying the galley, just trying to keep busy.

Midnight passed, and the world was now as black as my fears. I polished the brasswork around the galley stove and was so deep in my own thoughts that I didn't notice the approach of soft footsteps, and jumped a mile when some-one tapped me on the shoulder.

'Oh, your face!' exclaimed Amy. 'You went white as a sheet – or Bunstropple's ghost!'

She was holding me by the shoulder and laughing at me. Then she threw her arms about me. 'I've been so worried about you,' she whispered in my ear.

'What are you doing here?' I whispered back while hold-ing her tight. 'Madame will be furious!' Madame Helena had strict rules about the girls being out after supper.

'I hadn't seen you for so long. And I didn't see you when you came tonight – where did you go to after supper?'

'I had something to do. I'll tell you another time.'

I pulled back and looked at her. She smiled at me. I knew she was expecting me to kiss her. But I had no desire for that now; it would have seemed a betrayal.

'You'd better get back to the cabin.' I tried to lead her away but she resisted, pouting.

She said reproachfully, 'I thought we were friends.' I smiled to hear my own words echoed, but with our posi-tions sweetly reversed.

'We are,' I promised, though I had my doubts, wondering whether I would be ignored again if a suitable officer appeared. I also couldn't help wondering whether she'd learned that I might be richer than she'd once thought.

I pulled her along the deck, but stopped. We could hear a boat approaching – no, into the light of the ship came a string of boats roped together, the first rowed by Jupiter and the foretopman Stephens, the others empty. There was no light in the boats, which would have come across the bay like shadows on the water.

'Those must be the boats that took the pirates to the beach,' I whispered to Amy. 'That's why Jupiter and Stephens agreed to row them across. I understand now....'

'But why were the pirates going to the beach?' she asked.

'I'll tell you that later as well.'

We watched as the two men tied the boats to the rear of the ship and came aboard, where they were met by Bones and a few officers.

A swell of noise followed Bones along the ship, all the way to the rear deck. I followed, pulling Amy by the hand.

There was a group of twenty men by now, all with pistols. Bones was at their front and the others stopped to let him climb up and approach the acting captain: the tall, bearded first mate Jenkins who had been in charge of the boat that had captured us. He was standing near the steps, talking to a second officer also from the Tombstone. They wore cutlasses and had pistols tucked into their belts.

'It's like dis,' said Bones in a quiet voice that yet carried clearly to the men. 'We has plenty of guns, and dese men has made me Captain. You can join us, or you can take a boat back across to your own ship.'

I saw Jenkins stare at Bones, then turn to look at the twenty guns pointing towards him. His right hand strayed towards his belt; stopped.

'Why the choice?' he asked. 'Why?'

'Because all men deserve one chance to change,' said Bones. 'Dis is yours.'

I swear I saw on Jenkins' face a struggle between the two choices; not so the man at his side, who laughed and spat.

'If you're fool enough to let us go, we're off,' he said.

Jenkins frowned, but nodded in agreement. 'Nothing like a pirate's life,' he said in a hollow voice. 'Nothing.'

Bones took their guns and had them tied to the railings, from where they watched dumbly as the boats were hauled up and lashed onto the deck. Then they were escorted to the side of the ship, where the smallest boat was waiting, a lantern in it. A group of us leaned over the side to watch them clamber down into the boat.

'You'll row straight out from the ship a few strokes and wait dere while we get under way,' commanded Bones. 'If you try to row away before we go, you'll be shot. If you interfere wid the ship, you'll be shot. If you try to hail the *Tombstone*, you'll be shot. Now be off wid you.'

The men pushed off from the ship and shipped oars, bobbing gently on the water. There were some calm, quiet commands by Bones and then I saw old Misty take the wheel as the men began setting the sails and hauling up the anchors.

There was a gentle wind from the north; enough for us to angle across the bay towards its mouth to the west.

'Lamps out!' came the command and we disappeared into the darkness.

'Six fathoms and sandy,' called a man softly from the chains. 'Six and a half.... Six again... Seven now... Eight and shoaling...'

The *Tombstone's* ghostly lines grew before us, then slipped past on our starboard side. There were some startled shouts from its deck and we could see men scrambling to the rails. We were past them; we were approaching the mouth of bay; there was one hopeful gunshot that sent a bullet whistling overhead; then we were out into the sea, and the crew all cheered.

The Captain's voice was all Jones now: 'Light the lamps. Due west, Misty. And let's have more sail, lads. There's open water for the next four hours and I'd like to be far, far away before the pirates think of giving chase.'

Jupiter's bass voice added, 'Which won't be until the party on the hill finds there's no girls and no gold –'

'– because Jack went up and warned 'em off –'

'– and they'll come down and find there's no boats –'

'– because me and Jupiter took 'em –'

'– and they'll have to be taken across to the ship a few at a time in that small jolly boat –'

'– and by then they'll have the gripes from the special grog Bones gave 'em!'

There were roars of laughter at each line, and several men were dancing a jig to this exchange between the main plotters of the scheme.

When the lanterns were lit, I found that Amy and I had been joined at the rail by the other women. Vicky and Sandra were laughing; Amy was squeezing my hand and asking what I'd had to do with all this; Madame was looking up at the Captain's deck, where Bones was being congratulated by an excited group of officers and men.

She called across to him: 'Captain!'

He left the men and came across to us, leaning on the railings at the corner of the rear deck and looking down at our group. 'Here's to a safe and profitable voyage, gentle ladies and brave lad,' he said, with a little bow.

'Your hat, Captain,' said Madame. She stepped across and held up a large, dark felt hat that looked familiar, though I couldn't recall why.

She said quietly, 'Emma – the boy's aunt – thought you might be wanting this. Congratulations, Captain. Come, girls: some of you are wearing far too few clothes to be out on deck.'

She led her group away, while Bones looked at the hat in his hand, smiled, winked at me and put it on his head. It was a hat I'd sometimes seen him wearing when he visited Aunt Emma's house, in those ancient days before my world had been turned upside down.

21 The End of the Game

The game ends when one player has landed at two ports in every continent and returned to the port he started at, having lost no more than 80 men at that point.

We sped away into the west, pausing only once in three days when the night sky was blackened with cloud. Then we commenced a broad zigzagging journey north, stopping at three places mentioned in the parchment and one that wasn't.

Within the first week, the ship's crew were transformed. They were hardworking and disciplined as never before, arriving on time for their shifts and answering commands with a crisp "Yes, sir!"; and oddly enough, they were happy as I'd never seen them. The ship itself was cleaner and tidier, with ropes coiled neatly and the storage areas organised so that I didn't have to spend hours below deck looking for salt beef or biscuit.

Red's tough regime had seemed at the time to be brutally effective; but I saw how much better the ship could be run by Jones' quiet and good-humoured insistence. Men like Barber, Taylor and Stephens, who had been timidly obedient to the orders shouted at them, were now full lieutenants who worked their socks off and commanded respect and willingness from the crew. The senior men dined every evening with the Captain, sometimes with Madame Helena in attendance; and the room rang with easy laughter.

I was now officially the Ship's Cook. This responsibility was made easier by the appointment of an assistant cook – Matthew, the remaining twin who was apparently still useless as a deckhand. I was teaching him all that Bones had taught me: and it was good to be busy with this and many other tasks, for it took my mind off other things until I climbed into my hammock each night.

'Are we going back to get the treasure near Scum Island?' I asked one morning, after bringing Captain Jones his morning coffee in his cabin.

'No, Jack,' he said. 'We'll abandon that small casket of jewels. It isn't worth a lot, and it's tucked into a bees' nest five metres up a tree. I was stung eight times while hiding it, and I expect its recovery would be equally painful.'

'Oh. Are we going anywhere near that area?'

He smiled at me, knowing what was in my mind. 'She'll have left the island long ago, lad,' he said. 'That game's finished now. If you ever meet her again, it'll be the start of another game, another history. Maybe that will happen; but almost certainly not. Let it go.'

I nodded. 'Spin the wheel and roll the dice, sir. It's the next voyage that matters, hey?' I spoke lightly, but he wasn't fooled.

He looked at me steadily, saying, 'You don't believe she's gone forever, do you?'

'No, sir.'

'Nor should you. Every man should live with hope in his heart; without it, he might as well be dead. I had a hope, Jack: a hope of escape. And you made it happen. I'll always be grateful for your bravery and your loyalty.'

I felt my face go red. To cover my embarrassment I asked, 'What happened to you after that?'

'I can't tell you that, Jack. The less you know, the safer for us both.'

'What about the Inquisitor? You made something happen to him. Jupiter wouldn't say what it was. But I think it must have had something to do with the Inquisitor's brother as well. Is that right?'

He laughed then and clapped me on the shoulder. 'Sit down, Jack. Let me tell you a tale, for I think you deserve to hear it. The Inquisitor's younger brother –'

'Your friend Arthur.'

'That's him. Imagine him sitting on the cold stone floor of a dungeon cell in a small but solid prison, his hair gone grey and grown long and matted, a bruise on one cheek and scars about his wrists and ankles because of the chains. A woman comes in – his wife – having bribed the guards to allow her to visit. She washes her husband's wounds while she tells him how their young child is growing into a sturdy toddler; cuts and cleans his hair as she chatters; holds his hand a while and whispers her love to him - all this being observed by the guard. She leaves him.'

I closed my eye and tried to picture the man watching his wife walk away, stopping himself from calling her name, knowing he mustn't make it worse for her.

The Captain continued, 'After the wife has gone, Arthur starts telling the guard that he's really King Arinaeus, and this is his palace. Then he decides he must be the Grand High Priest. Finally he proclaims that he's the Inquisitor, and starts shouting that he'll have them all tortured. The guard calls other soldiers to help; they shorten Arthur's chains and laugh all evening at his ravings.'

'In the middle of the night, two men from the King's Guard come to the dungeon with a couple of bottles of wine to share with the one night guard on duty. They have a fine old time of it, and the dungeon guard falls asleep because the wine is drugged. When he wakes, his friends are gone. He panics and does a quick tour of the cells, but it's all right: all five prisoners are still in their places.'

'The next morning, the old man in cell number three is still raving that he's really the Inquisitor. But that is clearly nonsense: he's chained hand and foot, he has the same scratches and bruises he had the day before, he wears the same dirty, stinking clothes he's worn for the past month and he even has the same haircut his wife gave him.'

'Meanwhile, Arthur's wife and child are on a ship crossing to a country not far from Albion, but distant enough for them to disappear from the eyes of the King's court. And with them is a stooped grey-haired man who hourly is growing in strength, and who in a year's time – perhaps less – will be strong enough to overthrow King Arinaeus himself.'

I couldn't stop myself: I clapped at this point, and Captain Jones removed his hat and took a bow.

'Did you plan all that while you were in prison?' I asked.

'Let's just say it was a story I told myself over and over again until I had it word perfect: like many another story, Jack. Prison is a lonely place and sometimes your thoughts are your only companions.'

'And did –'

'Not another word. Back to the galley, Cook.'

'Aye aye, Cap'n sir.'

During this period of treasure seeking, Madame appeared on deck more often, usually standing with Captain Jones and talking with him for hours. She gave up wearing her veil and once or twice wore a dress that was almost womanly.

Sandra and Vicky became sailors and proved themselves to be as good as the men at any task. They were even allowed to eat with the crew, and the sea shanties around the table sounded much better with their strong, high voices harmonising alongside the basses and baritones and tenors.

Amy was now the special pet of Misty the sailing master and received daily lessons from him about navigation. She was soon plotting courses, reckoning positions and calculating the effects of wind and tide with a speed and accuracy that brought a tear to the old man's bleary, drunken eye.

Except that he rarely drank these days. Amy didn't approve of it, and he seemed to like being bossed about by her. On the few occasions when he made free with a bottle, you could see his heart wasn't really in it.

Tiddles had filled out and was now a fierce destroyer of rats. He still performed the occasional trick for Bones – I mean Jones – but for most purposes he was now my cat and bossed me about the galley just as Amy bossed the ship's master Misty.

We ran out of treasure to ransack and there was talk

among the crew that we would soon be setting a course for home. However, the ship turned east and travelled across a sea that was new to most of the sailors, meeting boats that had odd triangular sails and crewed galleys, with a dozen oars working each side as if they were the legs of some gigantic insect creeping upon the glassy surface.

One Thursday, land was sighted; the day after, we drew near to the shore. The water was blue-green and clear, and the port was surrounded by woods that climbed rounded green hills, beyond which rose the snowy peaks of distant mountains. We anchored outside the bay and basked in gentle sunlight.

I was clearing away the breakfast pans when Jupiter came for me.

'Captain would like a word,' he said. 'And he says to tell you one thing before you go: *the guard stand together.*'

I nodded, wondering what this portended.

In Jones' cabin, Madame was already seated at the old wooden table, her hands folded in her lap. Tiddles was patting at the hem of her long black dress, but at a look from those stern eyes he slunk away and hid behind a chest.

Captain Jones was studying a map spread out on the table, marking off distances with a brass instrument. He looked up and waved me to a seat.

As he rolled up the map, he began: 'You'll have noticed, Jack, that we've gone a little out of our way.'

'More than a little,' said Madame Helena, her eyes fixed on his face, reminding me of a snake trying to mesmerise a bird.

'Aye. This is the nearest port to the Kingdom of Curchan.'

I blinked; Madame did not.

The Captain looked at me, then at Madame. 'I have some business to complete here,' he said. 'You may have guessed what it is.'

'Of course,' she replied. 'Do you think I would have contrived a voyage in this manner, and in this ship, solely for the purpose of recovering a few jewels and gold pieces? I can have those in Magus by clicking my fingers. We are both of us here to recover the Ruby; it was always about the Ruby.'

'You do not believe the Ruby to be lost, then?' asked Captain Jones quietly.

She replied, 'The King's men believed you had taken the Ruby. When they didn't find it in your possession or on the *Firebird*, they tortured you to discover where it was. You claimed you did not know. The Inquisitor was at first convinced that you were hiding it somewhere; then when torture brought no confession, he decided that your mind had become deranged and you had thrown the Ruby into the sea. I believe there is another, simpler explanation.'

'Which is?'

'You do not know what happened to the Ruby, because you never had it.'

Captain Jones inclined his head. He said, rather hesitantly, 'Curchan is like no other place on earth. I once told Jack that the people are simple and unsuspecting; and indeed, they are kind and generous and rather childlike. But I was wrong to call them simple.'

He paused, thinking before he spoke again. 'My time there was in some ways like walking through a dream. Many things in Curchan are not what they appear to be. The people are not dishonest, but their intentions are often hidden and their smiles conceal great cunning. Perhaps only thus have they survived the attempts of many adventurers to steal their treasures, of which the Ruby is only one.'

Madame said, 'You never had the Ruby. They simply made you *think* you had it.'

He inclined his head again. 'That's the most likely conclusion, Madame. But if I didn't have the stone then, I know how to possess it now. I intend to return to Curchan and complete my task.'

Madame's eyes had not left the Captain's face. She asked

softly, 'And if you were deceived before, Captain, how will you succeed this time?'

He met her eyes. 'Have you ever been to a magic show and watched a conjuror? At first the magic is impenetrable. But once you've worked out how it's done, you can't be tricked again.'

She murmured the final clue on the parchment, her eyes still fixed on those of the Captain: '*Hail the sun for seven days at full six, then pass on foot beyond the high pass. The lost one bides in the highest window of the highest tower.*'

I was shaking my head and tried to speak; Madame tore her eyes from the Captain and gave me such a stare that it took my breath away.

'What?' she demanded.

I said, 'Nothing. Except – if the Curchans have this Ruby, it should be left with them. Everything I've heard about it is bad. People cheat and lie and kill for it. Best to leave it where it causes least harm.'

Madame's face went pink: one of the few instances of uncontrolled emotion I'd seen in her. 'Leave it?' she asked sternly. 'Leave one of the four jewels of power in the hands of a people who will squirrel it away, hiding its light, throttling its life and potency? A people who will use it for petty acts of kindness, maybe healing the sore paws of kittens or inventing lullabies for babies? This is a jewel of *power*; it is a waste – a shameful waste – for it to be left in their hands.'

'You would do better?' I asked; and was suddenly afraid as her eyes dug deep into my own. I felt something pulling at my thoughts – no, ripping at them. I closed my eyes; but the claws were still deep within my head.

'I can use that stone like no other,' she said. 'I know the commands and have the power to bend it to my will. It is mine by right, and woe to the man who stands between me and my destiny.'

She turned to look at the Captain again; I felt the heat of her gaze leave me, and opened my eyes a crack to see her reach across and touch his arm, saying, 'And what will happen to the man who brings me the Ruby? He will sit at my right hand; he will have every good thing at his command, for I will command it for him.'

Captain Jones laughed drily. 'I believe you, Madame,' he said. 'But between you and the Ruby lies a whole kingdom under an odd protection: a people who cannot be swayed by your craft and who would doubtless burn you alive or – even worse – simply laugh at you. Which is why you must bargain with me.'

'Bargain?' she asked archly.

'I go to Curchan with Jack and Jupiter. You stay with the ship. We'll have two days' trek up to the plateau, and then (assuming we can obtain transport there from the passing traders) another two days' ride to Curchan. At the least, it will take two weeks for us to get there, recover the Ruby and return; at the most, a month. You'll wait a month, then if we haven't come back, the *Firebird* sails away. You'll divide the treasure as agreed and keep our three shares for our eventual return, if ever we do make it back to Magus.'

She said, 'I could lie and say that I agree to this, knowing that you cannot stop me if I change my mind.'

'That is true, Madame Helena. But although you are deep and dark and devious, I know that you are a woman of your word. In any case, I will make you swear by that which will bind you.'

'Then I will not agree.'

'In that case, kiss the Ruby goodbye.'

Their eyes were locked now. I looked from one to the other, scarcely breathing.

'One thing,' she said. 'We can agree for the ship to sail. But I will not agree to be on it.'

'I accept that,' he said. 'Yet you must swear that no one will be forced to leave the ship with you – not by trick or power or womanly wiles or any attempt of yours to persuade them.'

'I accept that,' she said, 'so long as you swear to me that if you recover the Ruby, you will return directly to the ship.'

'I swear that I will return directly to the ship, whether I've recovered the Ruby or not,' said Captain Jones. 'It's a long walk home otherwise.'

They both nodded and held out a right hand each, then clasped hands palm to palm, eyes still locked.

'By that which may not be named, I swear it,' said Madame Helena.

'By that which I am not afraid to name, I swear it,' said Captain Jones.

They released hands, but their eyes were still locked, as if daring the other to blink first.

'Wait a moment!' I complained. 'I haven't said I'll go with you. Why should I? I don't want to take the Ruby from those people. I think it's a terrible thing to do.'

'Don't come then, Jack,' said the Captain lightly, his eyes still fixed on Madame's face; but I could see that he was hurt, in a way I'd not thought he *could* be hurt.

I remembered Jupiter's words: too late, perhaps.

'All right,' I said. 'I've trusted you before, Captain. I'll do it one more time.'

'And I've trusted you, Jack,' he said softly, turning to look at me. 'More than you know. You've never let me down, and I'll not let you down either.'

Madame stood up suddenly. 'When?' she asked.

'Tomorrow at dawn,' said Captain Jones. 'I'll give orders to the crew this evening. You'll be Commodore of the ship, Madame. Taylor – one of my lieutenants – can be acting Captain. He's a man you can trust. We'll call a meeting of officers to discuss all this.'

Later that day, the *Firebird* moved into the harbour of Klingchat and dropped anchor. Provisions were bartered for (Amy doing the negotiations with the help of Misty – who knew the language – and myself who knew what we needed for the voyage home). We took on water, pork, mutton, exotic fruits (half of which I didn't know the names of), nuts and a dozen chickens.

I packed a canvas bag with clothes and eating utensils, adding a knife and pistol as directed by Jupiter and the Game of Pirate as requested by Captain Jones. 'For we'll be sitting about for hours at a time, lad: we may as well have something to do.'

Amy came to the galley as I was tidying it for the last time – and the phrase "last time" kept going round in my head, for I was convinced that we wouldn't return. She pulled out the galley stool and sat on it watching me, her hands fidgeting with something.

Finally I wiped my hands and put away my cloths. The galley was clean and ready for my successor Matthew. It seemed an age ago that Matthew's brother had been lost to the mermaids, and a further age back to the time when both twins had been threatened with ejection over the side of the ship; now it was I who would be leaving.

'I'll miss you,' Amy said. 'More than anything in the world. You know that?'

I felt guilty. I'd been avoiding Amy – at least, avoiding situations where we might be alone together. Not because I didn't care: oh, I cared about her all right. In my unreliable fantasies, she was back to being the Amy I loved: kind and good and clever and pretty. More pretty now than when we'd set out on this journey, for the sun and wind and exercise had brought colour to her rather pale face and firmness to her body. She wasn't buxom and vivacious like Sandra and Vicky or stylishly alluring like Minerva; but she had a simple beauty and a hard-won dignity.

I cared about her. But if I closed my eyes to think of her, another face took her place, the scarred, lovely face that troubled my dreams: a face disfigured and wearied and yet – to me – strangely beautiful and noble.

'I'll miss you too,' I said, which was true. 'I'll be back,' I added – which I wasn't sure about at all.

'This is for you, Jack,' she said, passing me the object she'd been holding. It was a chain with a locket. I stifled a groan; I couldn't believe she was going to make me wear a picture of her around my neck.

'Open it,' she suggested.

I put on a false smile and pressed the catch. Then I really did smile. Inside was a tiny drawing of our imaginary client, the mouse trader and philosopher Omar Vlstg. He wore a pirate hat and was waving a short sword in the air.

'That's brilliant!' I said, giving her a hug which she quickly turned into a kiss: a kiss which was as lovely and sweet as she was herself. I tried not to think of Maria.

At dawn, a boat rowed us from the *Firebird* to the landing, where I clambered out first and secured the ropes. Captain Jones stepped out and gave a hand to Jupiter. We unloaded our few bags, then stood a while on the landing, watching the boat row back to the ship.

'End of one adventure,' said the Captain. 'Start of another. Got your bag, Jack? With the Game in it?'

'Aye aye, sir.'

Jupiter said to me, grinning, 'Nice locket you got on. From a young lady, is it?'

I tucked the chain into my shirt and tried to look mature and mysterious.

Klingchat was a busy, dirty port full of boats from many lands. Its multicoloured and variously attired humanity offered us carpets, food, caged birds, cheap jewellery and a hundred other items at every step along the main street. It was tiring just to have to repeat 'No!' and 'I said no!' and 'Go *away!*' as we walked on.

We followed a dusty road out of Klingchat and were soon swallowed by a sleepy forest that covered the gently sloping hillside. The road narrowed at every curve and by midday it was little more than a path for the sheep that – so Captain Jones told us – were driven up to pasture on the plateau above us in spring and brought back to the town as winter loomed.

We lunched in a quiet grassy corner where the trees parted to allow a stream to pass through. We had bread, fragrant sheep's cheese and wine – though it was the water that was most deliciously intoxicating for its clean taste and its music.

'Can I have a look at the Game, Jack?' asked Captain Jones as we were packing away the remnants of lunch.

He placed the box on his lap, his hands resting on the beautifully carved and decorated wood. 'There's something you two need to know,' he said. 'Just in case I don't make it to Curchan – or back.'

He opened the box and pushed the pieces about with one finger. 'Aren't they special?' he asked. 'The ships, the spinning compass, this carved rat. Made in Curchan itself. Did I ever tell you that, Jack?'

'No, sir. Why would Curchan make something like this? It doesn't have a sea coast.'

'I took an old wooden Game of Pirate with me when I visited the country. I showed the King's court how to play it and they were enthralled, for they love all games and this was totally new to them. I gave them my old Game, the day before I left the country. They astonished me the next morning by presenting me with this beautiful replica. Replica, did I say? No, this is far superior to what I'd given them. And the generosity of their gift almost broke my heart, lads: for I knew that I was about to steal their greatest treasure, their Ruby.'

I said, 'The Ruby – wait a minute. But you didn't steal the Ruby. You said so, yesterday.'

Captain Jones shook his head. 'Madame Helena said that. I allowed her to think it was true. I stole that Ruby, Jack.'

Jupiter asked, 'Then where is it, boss?'

Captain Jones said, 'Where I put it, the very day I took it: right here.'

He took from the box the twelve-sided Runes of Destiny and weighed it in his hand before rolling it upon the grass.

'*Fair sailing*,' he said, looking at the marking on its upper face. 'Let's pray it proves to be true.'

He picked up the Runes of Destiny and held it out to us

on his palm. It was a beautiful white stone, about the size of a large horse chestnut, cut into a perfect dodecahedron. On each of its twelve faces there was a delicate black symbol, which you could interpret by looking at a table set out in the rules.

The Game of Pirate was a common pastime for many at sea and many more who had never been near a boat. Its rules and objects were well known to children in the playground and old men sitting outside the local inn.

'Look again.'

The stone seemed to shiver; then its white faces disappeared and the runes faded. It was now a jewel of such deep, deep redness that it made me think of a living heart.

'Look upon the Ruby of Curchan.'

Jupiter and I stared, our mouths open. A full minute we stared, before the stone trembled again and was once more a carved white stone marked with black symbols.

'So you had it after all,' said Jupiter.

'Aye,' said Captain Jones. 'And then I entrusted it to Jack; and I entrusted Jack to you, Jupiter; and I entrusted myself to you both. We stand together. Do we still stand?'

Jupiter nodded. 'That we do, boss.'

'We do,' I said.

'Thank you, lads. And now we must be going. We need to return this stone to Curchan, where it belongs. That's the only place where the Ruby will be safe from evil men – aye, and devious women, too. Are you with me?'

We nodded solemnly, clasped hands and swore that the last man alive would do this deed.

Then we set out through the forest, towards the distant Kingdom of Curchan.

Lightning Source UK Ltd.
Milton Keynes UK
UKHW02f2343250218
318474UK00005B/131/P